SATAN'S PREP

SATAN'S PREP

Gabe Guarente

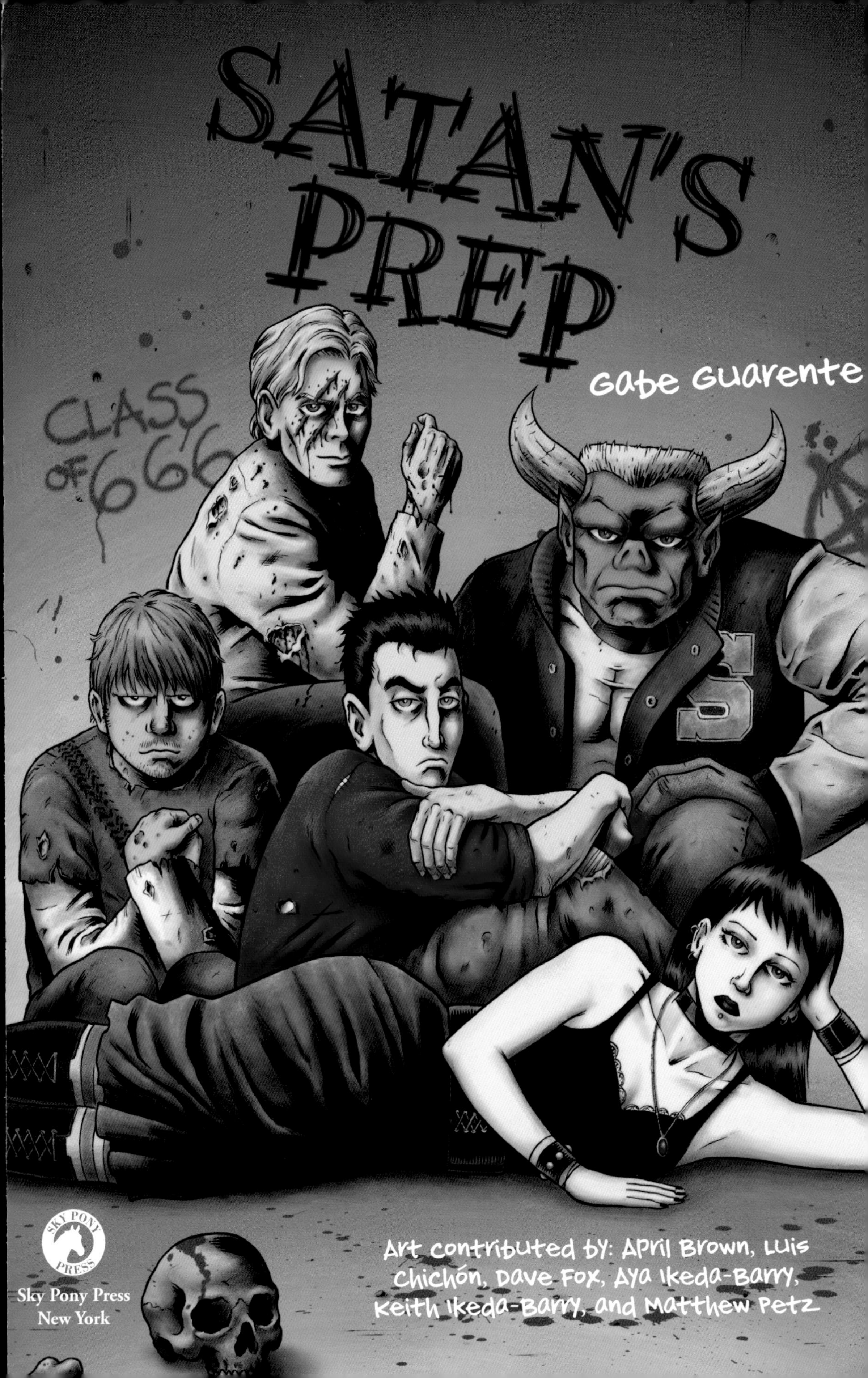
CLASS OF 666

Art contributed by: April Brown, Luis Chichón, Dave Fox, Aya Ikeda-Barry, Keith Ikeda-Barry, and Matthew Petz

Sky Pony Press
New York

Sky Pony Press books may be purchased in bulk at special discounts for sales promotion, corporate gifts, fund-raising, or educational purposes. Special editions can also be created to specifications. For details, contact the Special Sales Department, Sky Pony Press, 307 West 36th Street, 11th Floor, New York, NY 10018 or info@skyhorsepublishing.com.

Sky Pony® is a registered trademark of Skyhorse Publishing, Inc.®, a Delaware corporation.

Visit our website at www.skyponypress.com.

10 9 8 7 6 5 4 3 2 1

Manufactured in China, April 2014
This product conforms to CPSIA 2008

Library of Congress Cataloging-in-Publication Data is available on file.

Cover design by Danielle Ceccolini
Illustration credit Dave Fox

ISBN: 978-1-62873-592-5
Ebook ISBN 978-1-62873-961-9

For my Aunt MaryAnn

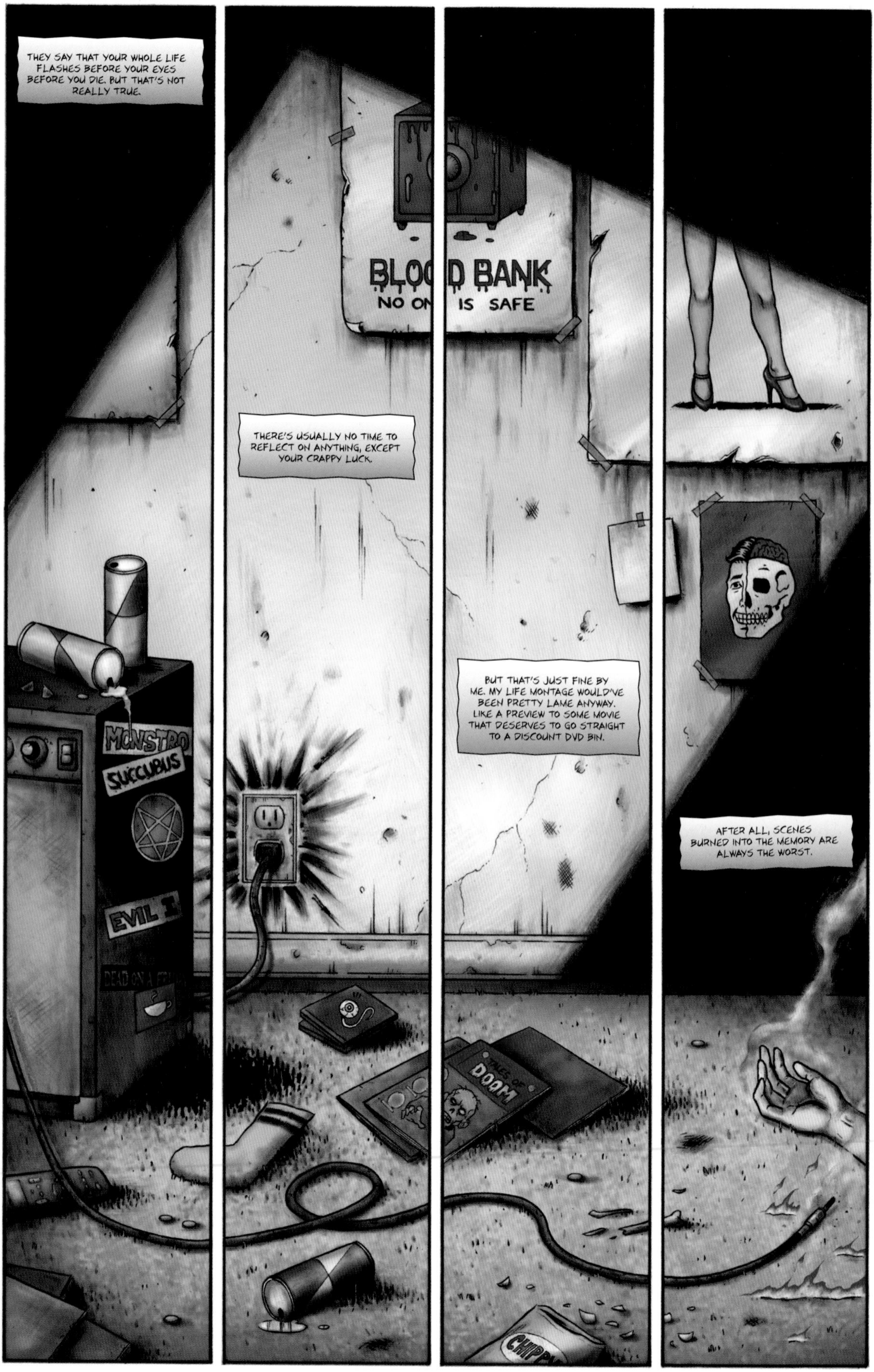

THEY SAY THAT YOUR WHOLE LIFE FLASHES BEFORE YOUR EYES BEFORE YOU DIE. BUT THAT'S NOT REALLY TRUE.
BLOOD BANK
NO ONE IS SAFE
THERE'S USUALLY NO TIME TO REFLECT ON ANYTHING, EXCEPT YOUR CRAPPY LUCK.
MONSTRO
SUCCUBUS
EVIL I
BUT THAT'S JUST FINE BY ME. MY LIFE MONTAGE WOULD'VE BEEN PRETTY LAME ANYWAY. LIKE A PREVIEW TO SOME MOVIE THAT DESERVES TO GO STRAIGHT TO A DISCOUNT DVD BIN.
AFTER ALL, SCENES BURNED INTO THE MEMORY ARE ALWAYS THE WORST.
TALES OF DOOM

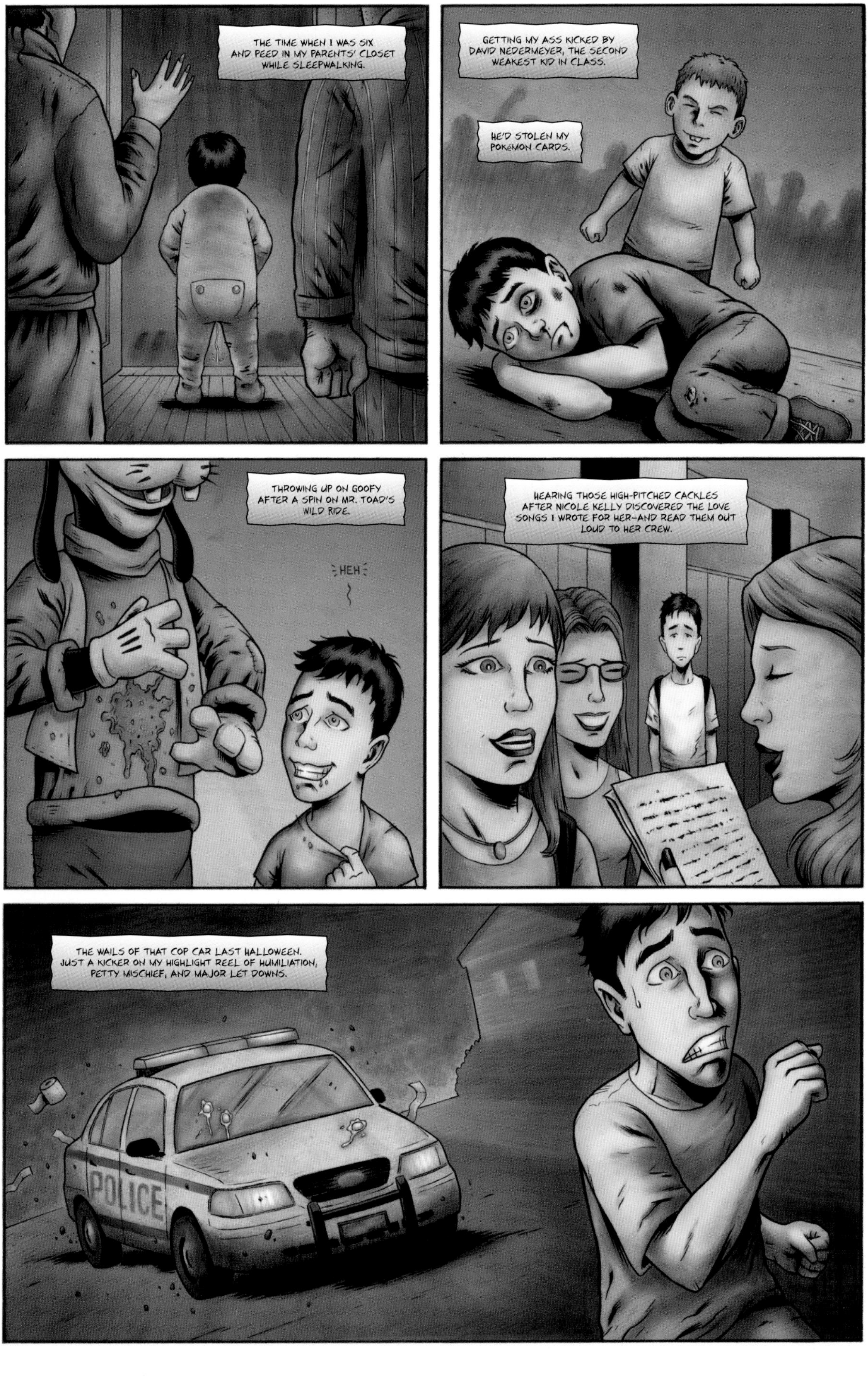
THE TIME WHEN I WAS SIX AND PEED IN MY PARENTS' CLOSET WHILE SLEEPWALKING.
GETTING MY ASS KICKED BY DAVID NEDERMEYER, THE SECOND WEAKEST KID IN CLASS.
HE'D STOLEN MY POKéMON CARDS.
THROWING UP ON GOOFY AFTER A SPIN ON MR. TOAD'S WILD RIDE.
HEH
HEARING THOSE HIGH-PITCHED CACKLES AFTER NICOLE KELLY DISCOVERED THE LOVE SONGS I WROTE FOR HER—AND READ THEM OUT LOUD TO HER CREW.
THE WAILS OF THAT COP CAR LAST HALLOWEEN. JUST A KICKER ON MY HIGHLIGHT REEL OF HUMILIATION, PETTY MISCHIEF, AND MAJOR LET DOWNS.
POLICE

THE EXPLODING BRAINS

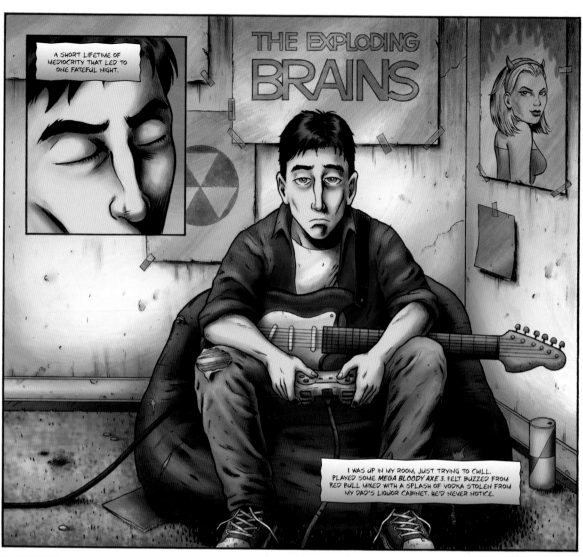

A SHORT LIFETIME OF MEDIOCRITY THAT LED TO ONE FATEFUL NIGHT.

I WAS UP IN MY ROOM, JUST TRYING TO CHILL. PLAYED SOME *MEGA BLOODY AXE 3*. FELT BUZZED FROM RED BULL MIXED WITH A SPLASH OF VODKA STOLEN FROM MY DAD'S LIQUOR CABINET. HE'D NEVER NOTICE.

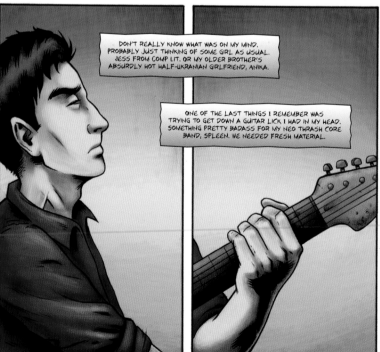

DON'T REALLY KNOW WHAT WAS ON MY MIND. PROBABLY JUST THINKING OF SOME GIRL AS USUAL. JESS FROM COMP LIT. OR MY OLDER BROTHER'S ABSURDLY HOT HALF-UKRANIAN GIRLFRIEND, ANIKA.

ONE OF THE LAST THINGS I REMEMBER WAS TRYING TO GET DOWN A GUITAR LICK I HAD IN MY HEAD. SOMETHING PRETTY BADASS FOR MY NEO THRASH CORE BAND, SPLEEN. WE NEEDED FRESH MATERIAL.

BUT THAT CHEAPO AMP I GOT FROM MY BUDDY NICK WAS ACTING ALL WEIRD. IT CRACKLED AND HISSED AND MOANED LIKE SOME POSSESSED LITTLE DEMON.

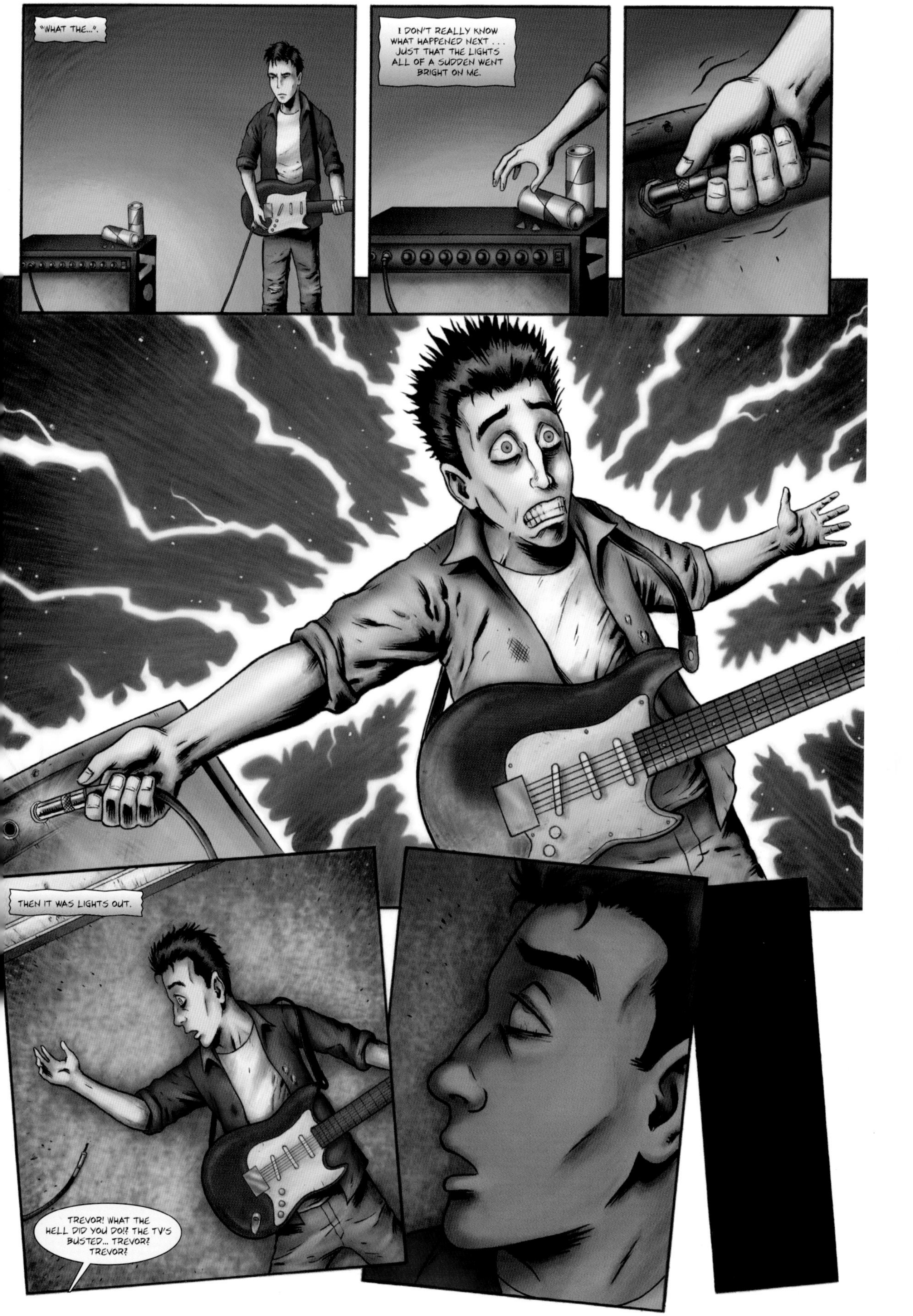
"WHAT THE...".
I DON'T REALLY KNOW WHAT HAPPENED NEXT . . . JUST THAT THE LIGHTS ALL OF A SUDDEN WENT BRIGHT ON ME.
THEN IT WAS LIGHTS OUT.
TREVOR! WHAT THE HELL DID YOU DO!? THE TV'S BUSTED... TREVOR? TREVOR?

PART I

Pencils/Inks/Graytone:
Dave Fox

Colors:
Aya Ikeda-Barry

Lettering:
April Brown

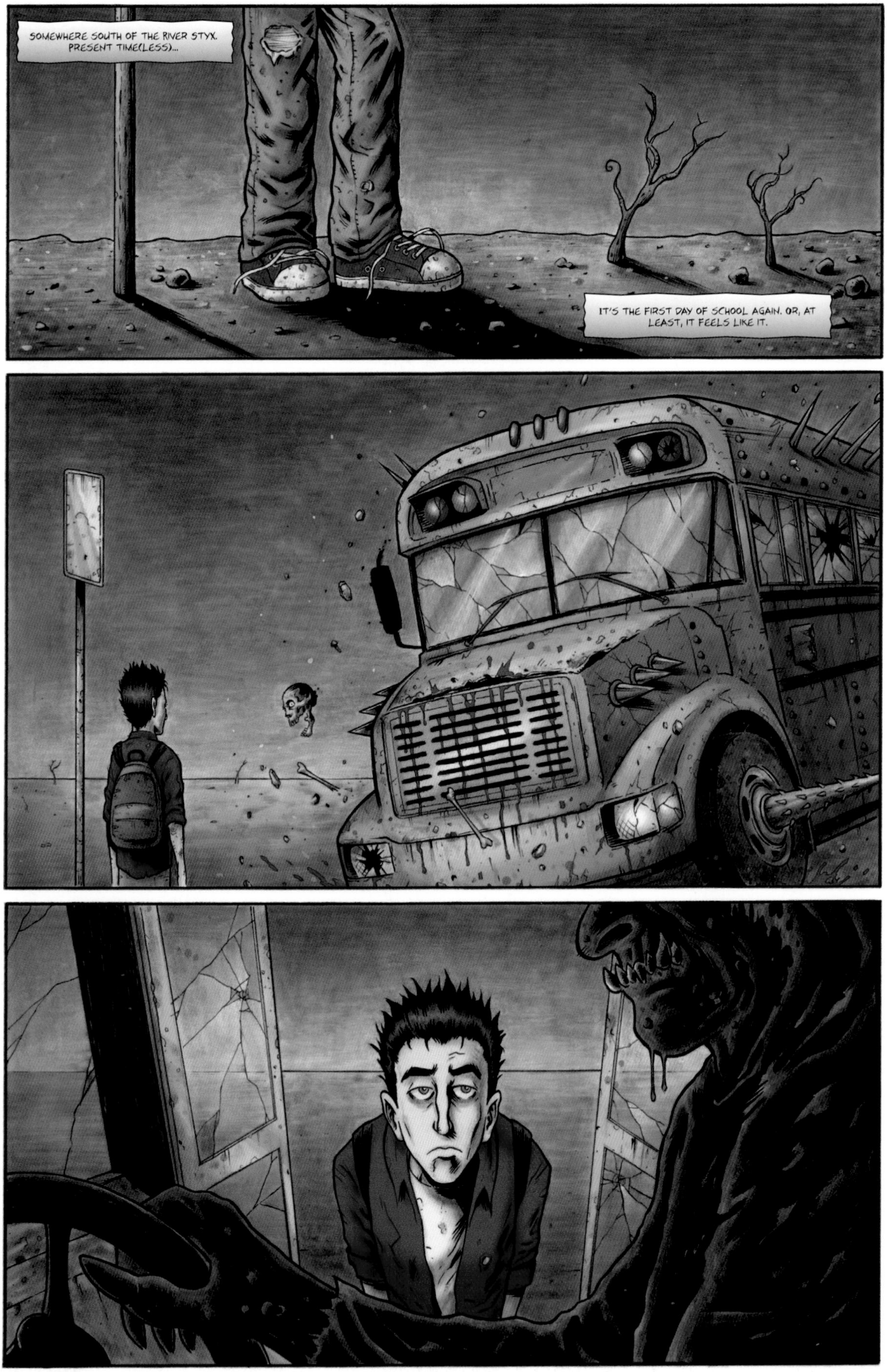
SOMEWHERE SOUTH OF THE RIVER STYX. PRESENT TIME(LESS)...
IT'S THE FIRST DAY OF SCHOOL AGAIN. OR, AT LEAST, IT FEELS LIKE IT.

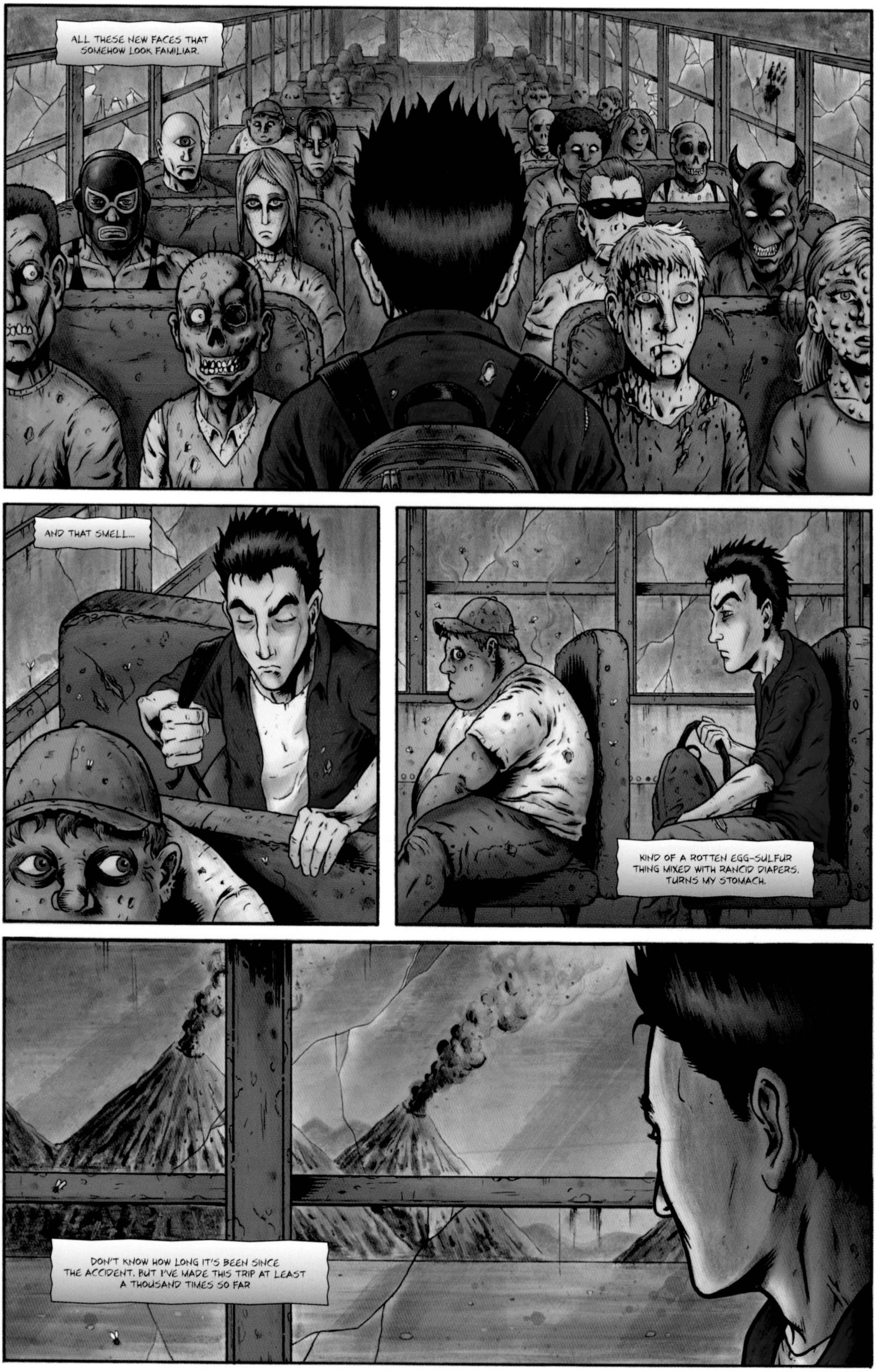
ALL THESE NEW FACES THAT SOMEHOW LOOK FAMILIAR.
AND THAT SMELL...
KIND OF A ROTTEN EGG-SULFUR THING MIXED WITH RANCID DIAPERS. TURNS MY STOMACH.
DON'T KNOW HOW LONG IT'S BEEN SINCE THE ACCIDENT. BUT I'VE MADE THIS TRIP AT LEAST A THOUSAND TIMES SO FAR

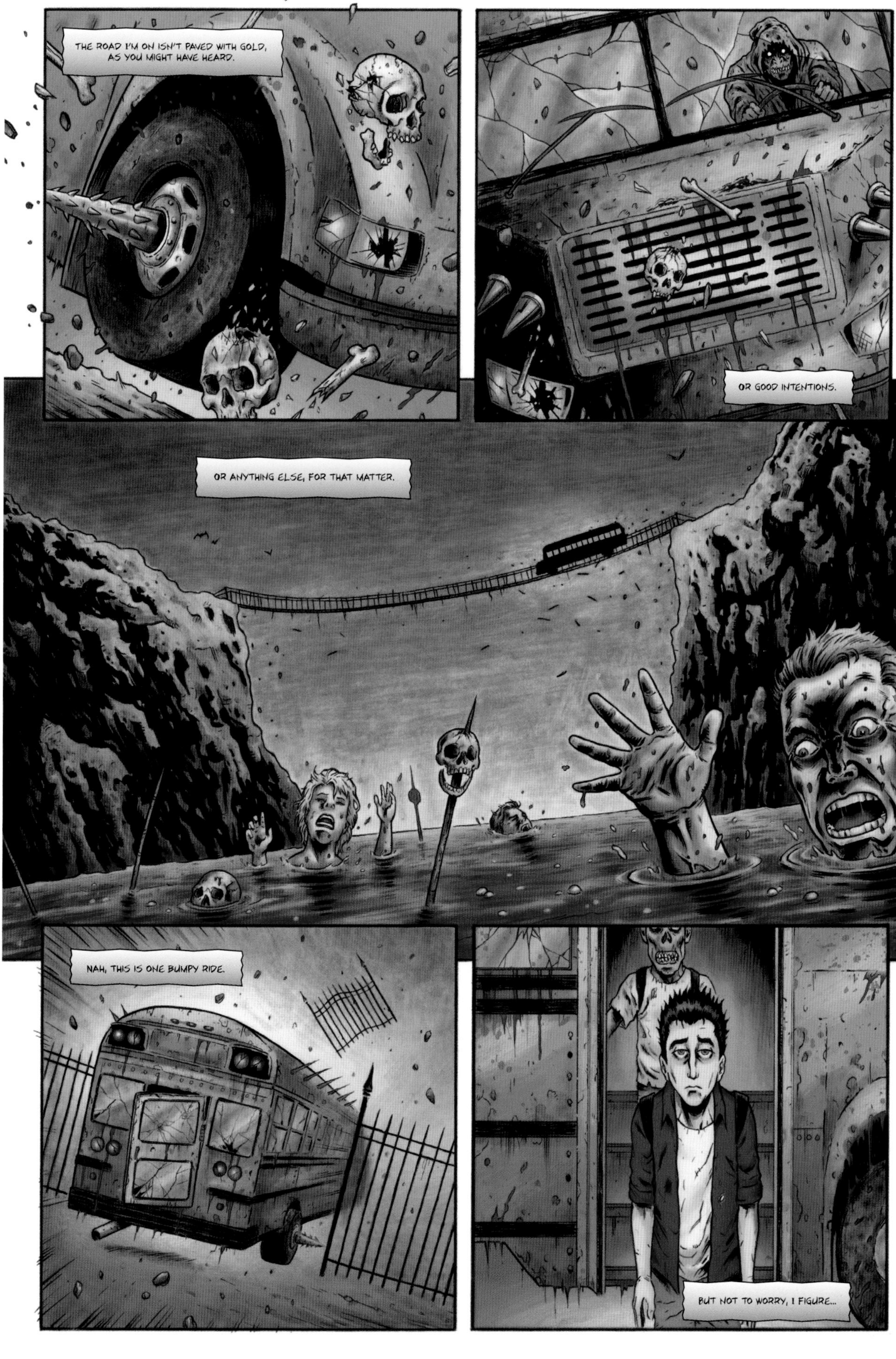
THE ROAD I'M ON ISN'T PAVED WITH GOLD, AS YOU MIGHT HAVE HEARD.
OR GOOD INTENTIONS.
OR ANYTHING ELSE, FOR THAT MATTER.
NAH, THIS IS ONE BUMPY RIDE.
BUT NOT TO WORRY, I FIGURE...

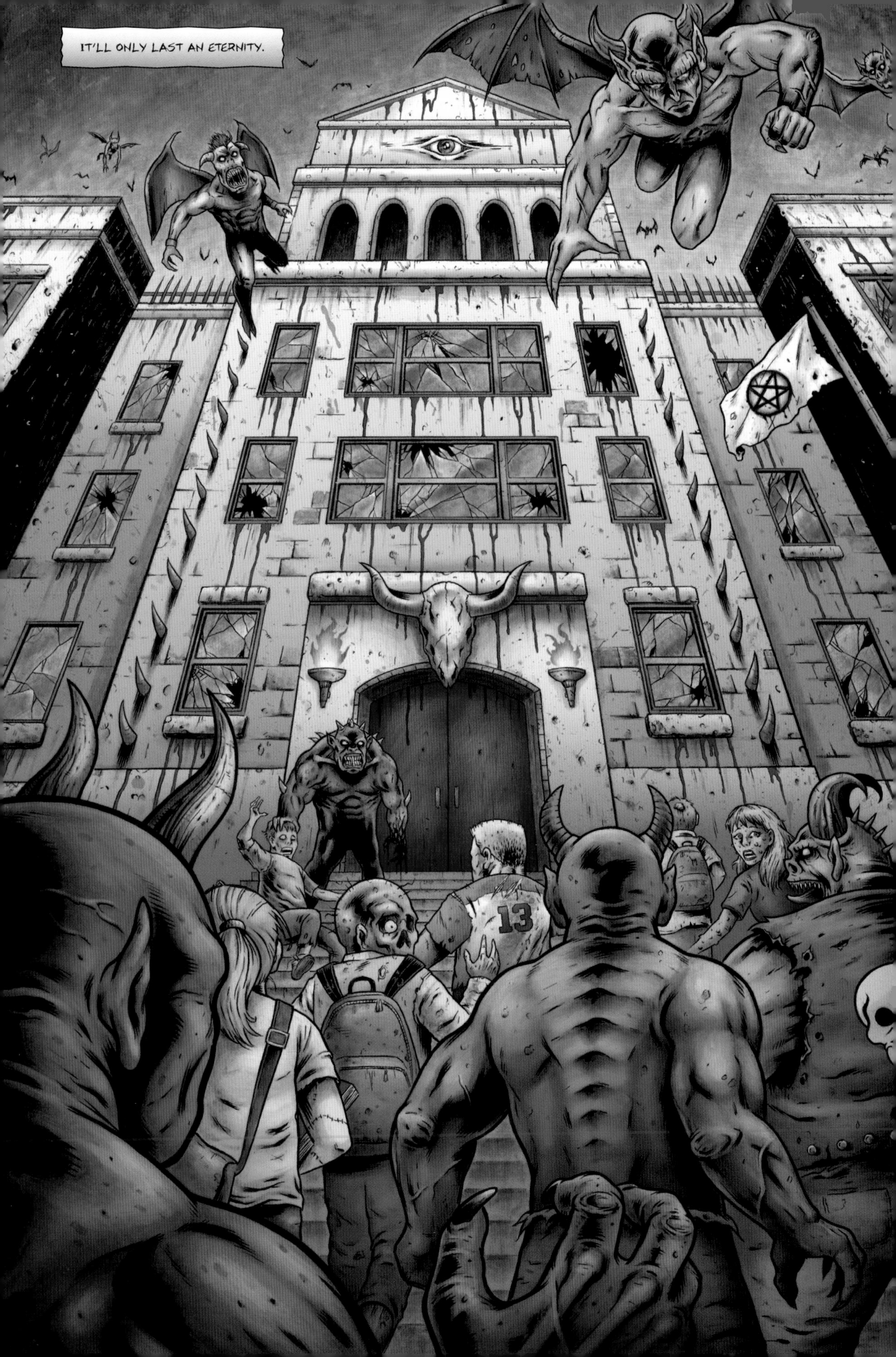
IT'LL ONLY LAST AN ETERNITY.
13

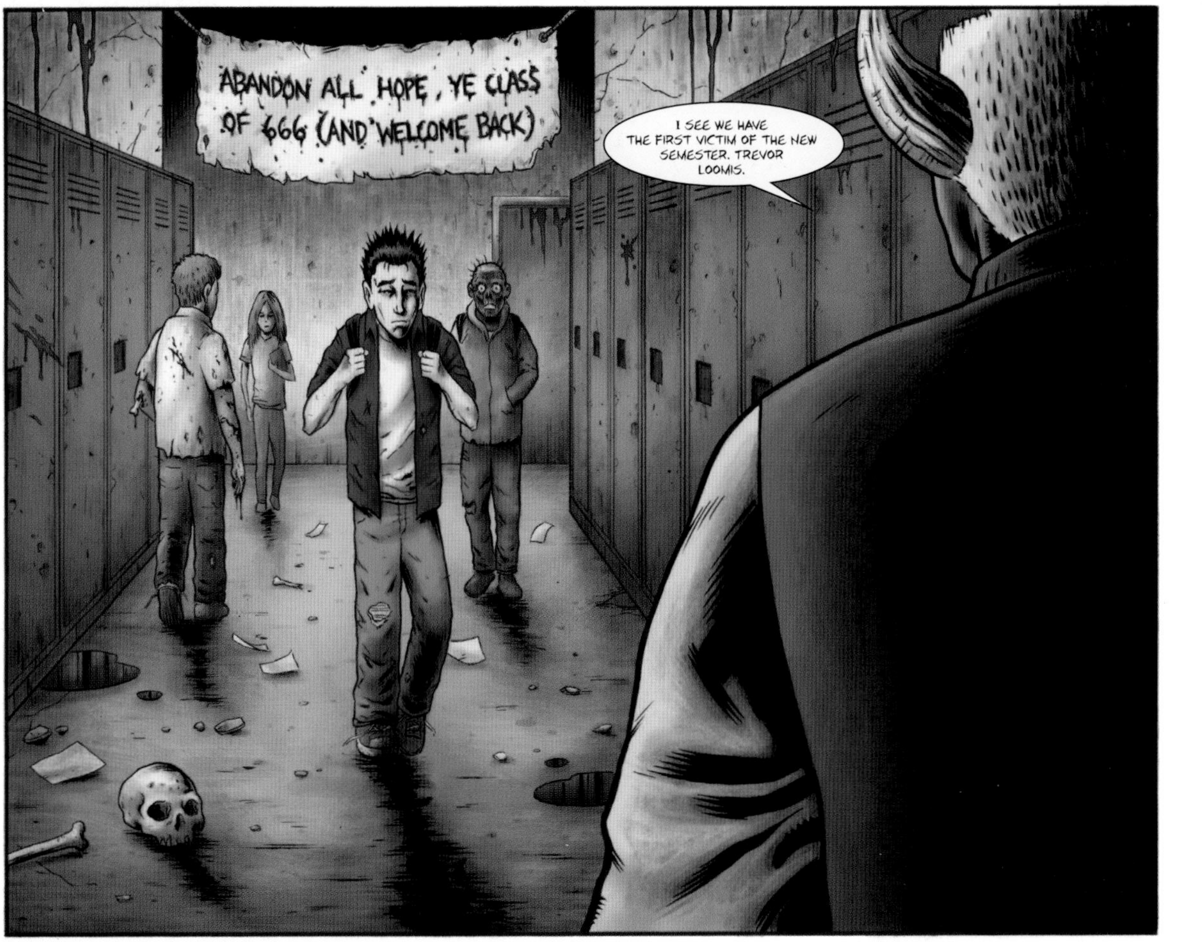
ABANDON ALL HOPE, YE CLASS OF 666 (AND WELCOME BACK)
I SEE WE HAVE THE FIRST VICTIM OF THE NEW SEMESTER. TREVOR LOOMIS.

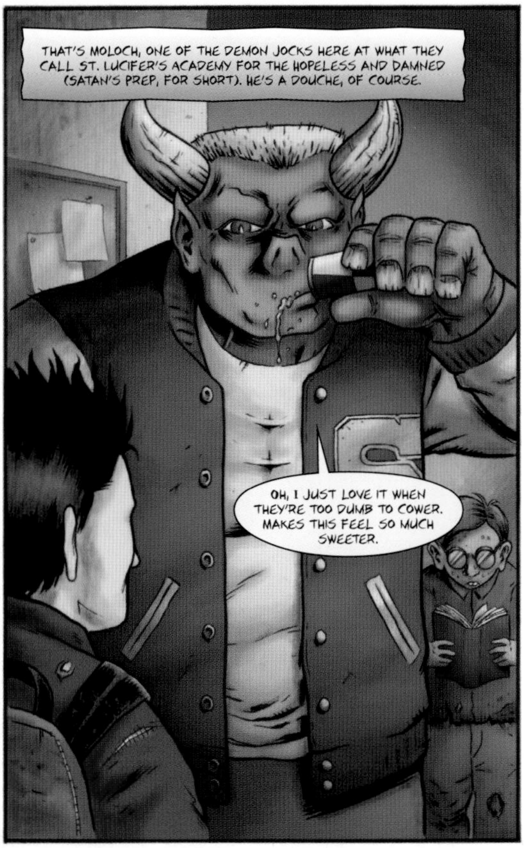
THAT'S MOLOCH, ONE OF THE DEMON JOCKS HERE AT WHAT THEY CALL ST. LUCIFER'S ACADEMY FOR THE HOPELESS AND DAMNED (SATAN'S PREP, FOR SHORT). HE'S A DOUCHE, OF COURSE.
OH, I JUST LOVE IT WHEN THEY'RE TOO DUMB TO COWER. MAKES THIS FEEL SO MUCH SWEETER.

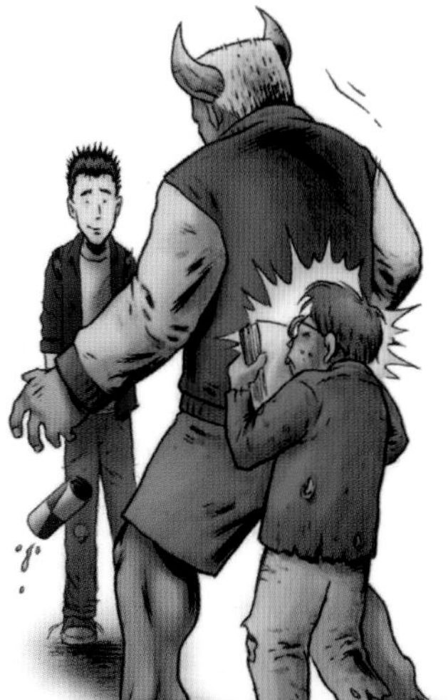

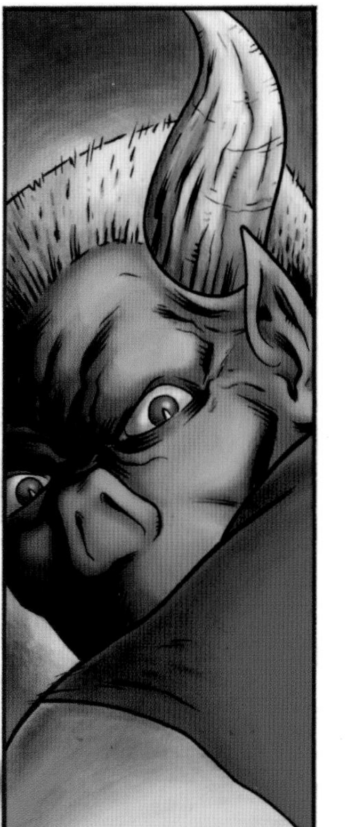

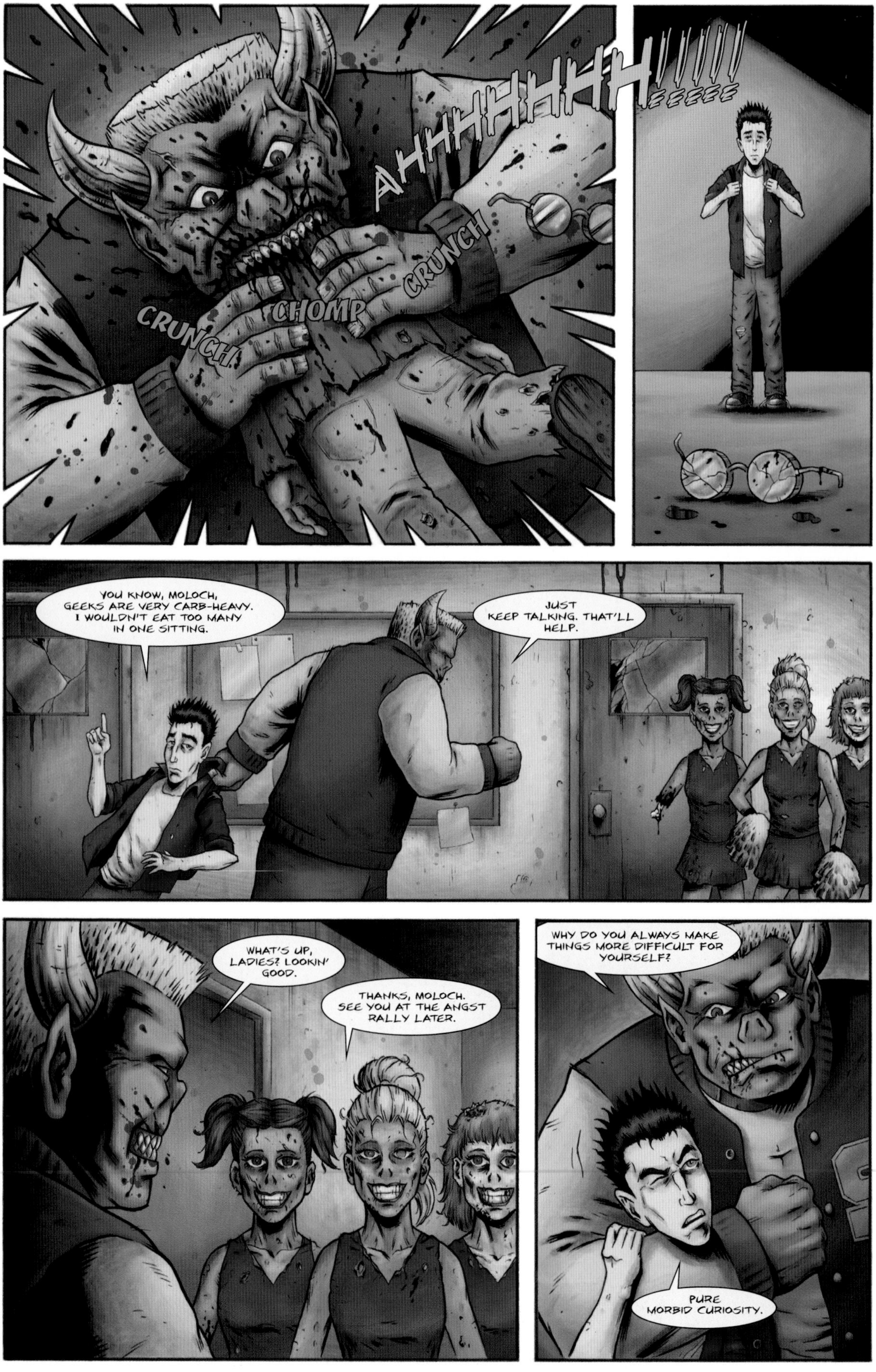
AHHHHHHHH!!!!!!!eeeee
CRUNCH
CHOMP
CRUNCH
CRUNCH
YOU KNOW, MOLOCH, GEEKS ARE VERY CARB-HEAVY. I WOULDN'T EAT TOO MANY IN ONE SITTING.
JUST KEEP TALKING. THAT'LL HELP.
WHAT'S UP, LADIES? LOOKIN' GOOD.
THANKS, MOLOCH. SEE YOU AT THE ANGST RALLY LATER.
WHY DO YOU ALWAYS MAKE THINGS MORE DIFFICULT FOR YOURSELF?
PURE MORBID CURIOSITY.

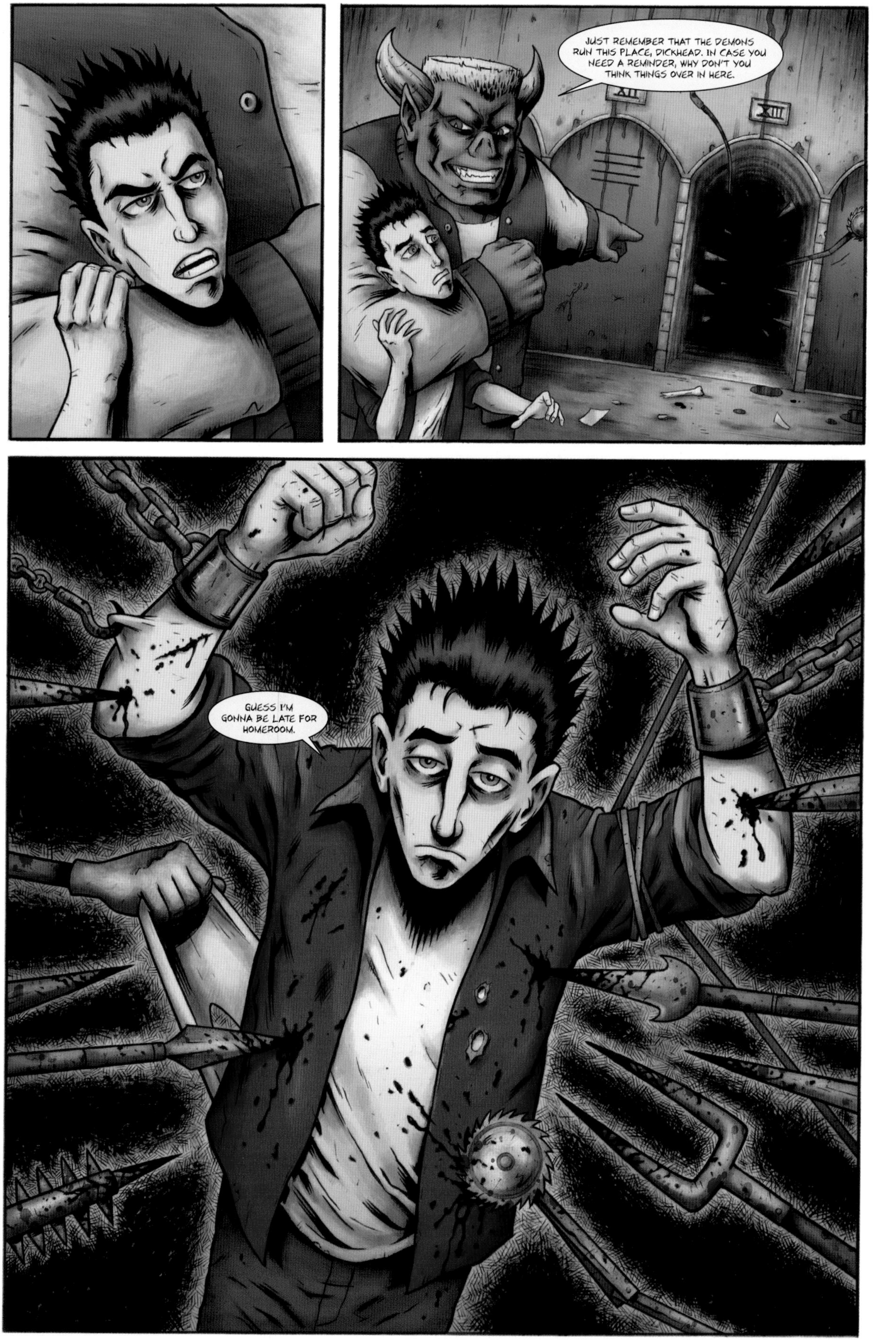
JUST REMEMBER THAT THE DEMONS RUN THIS PLACE, DICKHEAD. IN CASE YOU NEED A REMINDER, WHY DON'T YOU THINK THINGS OVER IN HERE.
GUESS I'M GONNA BE LATE FOR HOMEROOM.

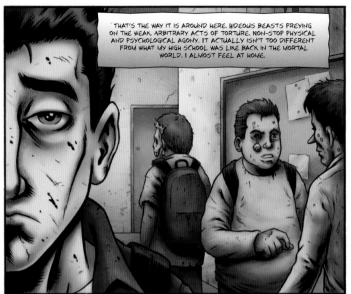

THAT'S THE WAY IT IS AROUND HERE. HIDEOUS BEASTS PREYING ON THE WEAK. ARBITRARY ACTS OF TORTURE. NON-STOP PHYSICAL AND PSYCHOLOGICAL AGONY. IT ACTUALLY ISN'T TOO DIFFERENT FROM WHAT MY HIGH SCHOOL WAS LIKE BACK IN THE MORTAL WORLD. I ALMOST FEEL AT HOME.

TREVOR LOOMIS. PLEASE REPORT TO VICE PRINCIPAL CERBERUS'S OFFICE. IMMEDIATELY.

GREAT.

THEY NEVER DID TELL ME WHY I ENDED UP IN THIS PLACE. TRUST ME, I ASKED. BUT IT TAKES A WHILE TO GET THROUGH THE RED TAPE.

CERBERUS WILL SEE YOU NOW.

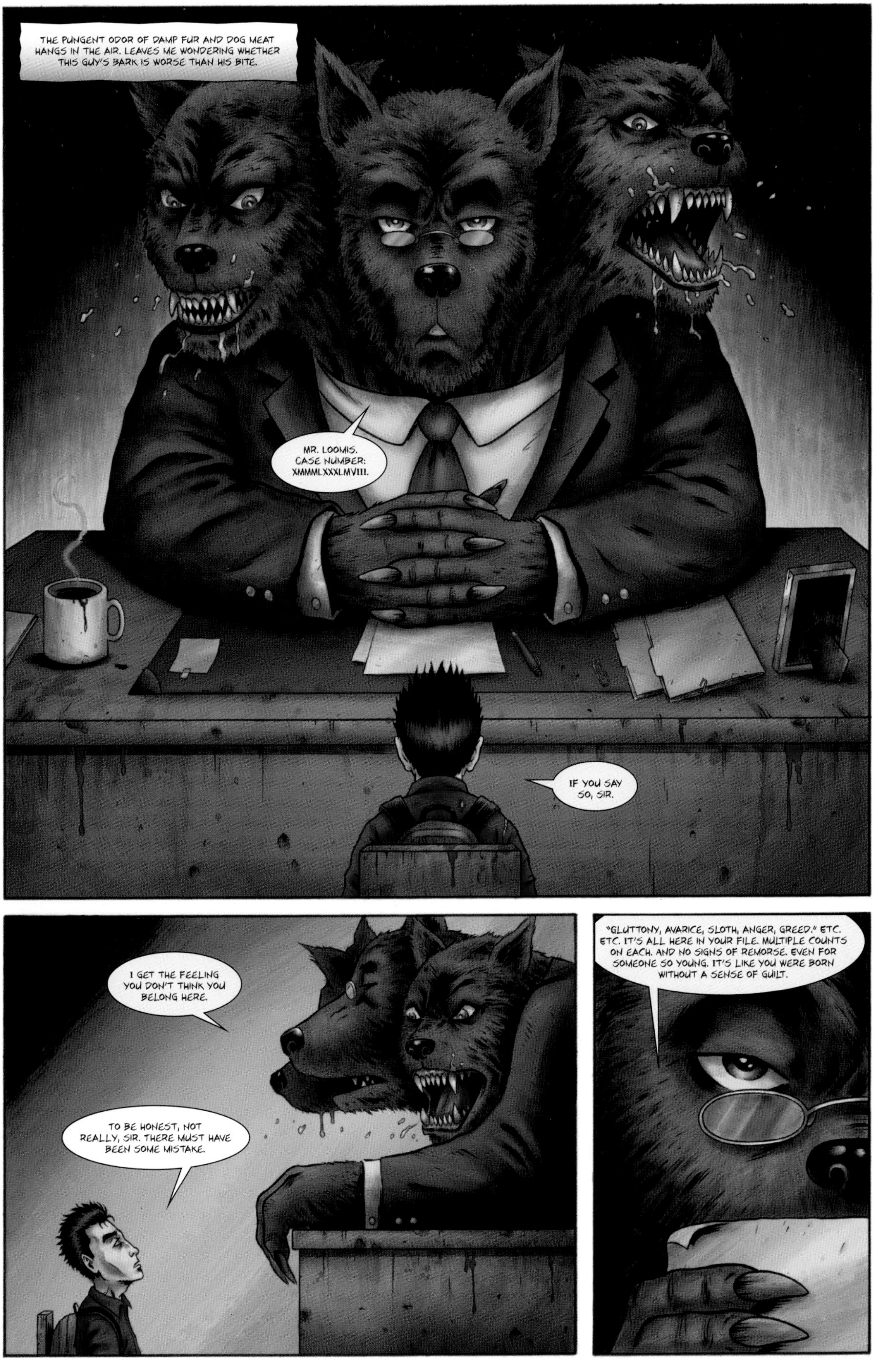
THE PUNGENT ODOR OF DAMP FUR AND DOG MEAT HANGS IN THE AIR. LEAVES ME WONDERING WHETHER THIS GUY'S BARK IS WORSE THAN HIS BITE.
MR. LOOMIS. CASE NUMBER: XMMMLXXXLMVIII.
IF YOU SAY SO, SIR.
I GET THE FEELING YOU DON'T THINK YOU BELONG HERE.
TO BE HONEST, NOT REALLY, SIR. THERE MUST HAVE BEEN SOME MISTAKE.
"GLUTTONY, AVARICE, SLOTH, ANGER, GREED." ETC. ETC. IT'S ALL HERE IN YOUR FILE. MULTIPLE COUNTS ON EACH. AND NO SIGNS OF REMORSE. EVEN FOR SOMEONE SO YOUNG. IT'S LIKE YOU WERE BORN WITHOUT A SENSE OF GUILT.

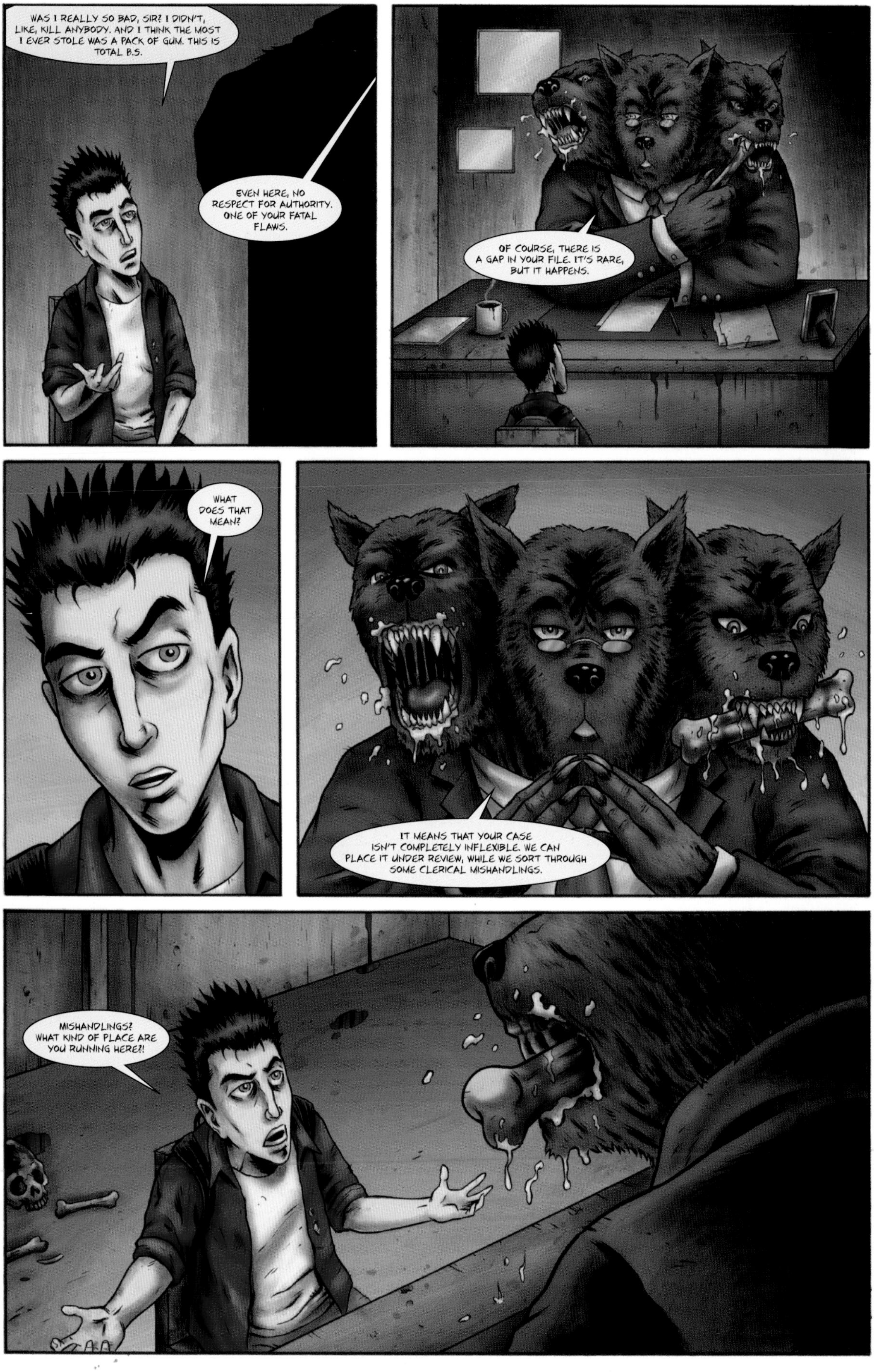
WAS I REALLY SO BAD, SIR? I DIDN'T, LIKE, KILL ANYBODY. AND I THINK THE MOST I EVER STOLE WAS A PACK OF GUM. THIS IS TOTAL B.S.
EVEN HERE, NO RESPECT FOR AUTHORITY. ONE OF YOUR FATAL FLAWS.
OF COURSE, THERE IS A GAP IN YOUR FILE. IT'S RARE, BUT IT HAPPENS.
WHAT DOES THAT MEAN?
IT MEANS THAT YOUR CASE ISN'T COMPLETELY INFLEXIBLE. WE CAN PLACE IT UNDER REVIEW, WHILE WE SORT THROUGH SOME CLERICAL MISHANDLINGS.
MISHANDLINGS? WHAT KIND OF PLACE ARE YOU RUNNING HERE?!

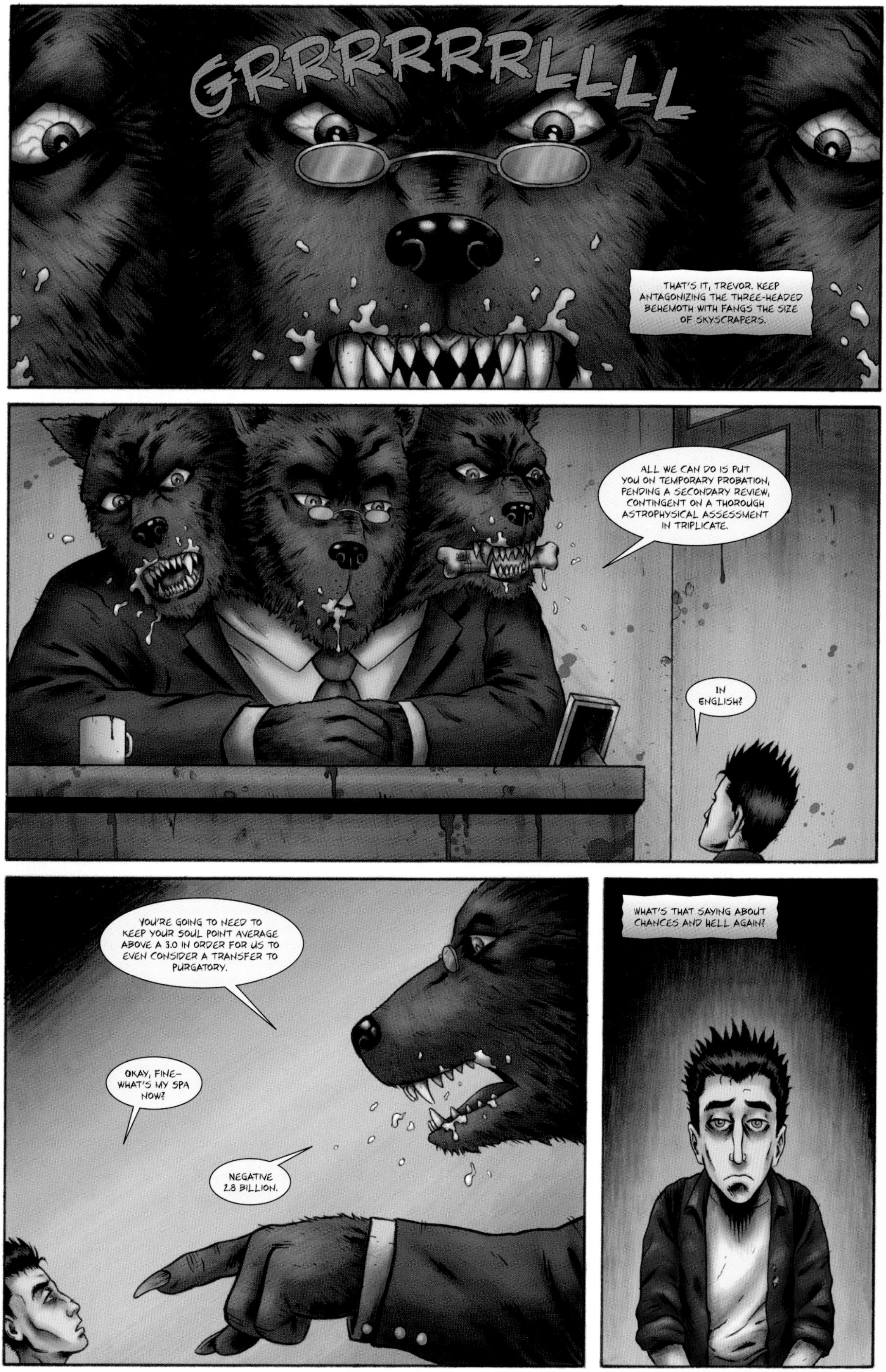
GRRRRRRLLLL
THAT'S IT, TREVOR. KEEP ANTAGONIZING THE THREE-HEADED BEHEMOTH WITH FANGS THE SIZE OF SKYSCRAPERS.
ALL WE CAN DO IS PUT YOU ON TEMPORARY PROBATION, PENDING A SECONDARY REVIEW, CONTINGENT ON A THOROUGH ASTROPHYSICAL ASSESSMENT IN TRIPLICATE.
IN ENGLISH?
YOU'RE GOING TO NEED TO KEEP YOUR SOUL POINT AVERAGE ABOVE A 3.0 IN ORDER FOR US TO EVEN CONSIDER A TRANSFER TO PURGATORY.
OKAY, FINE— WHAT'S MY SPA NOW?
NEGATIVE 2.8 BILLION.
WHAT'S THAT SAYING ABOUT CHANCES AND HELL AGAIN?

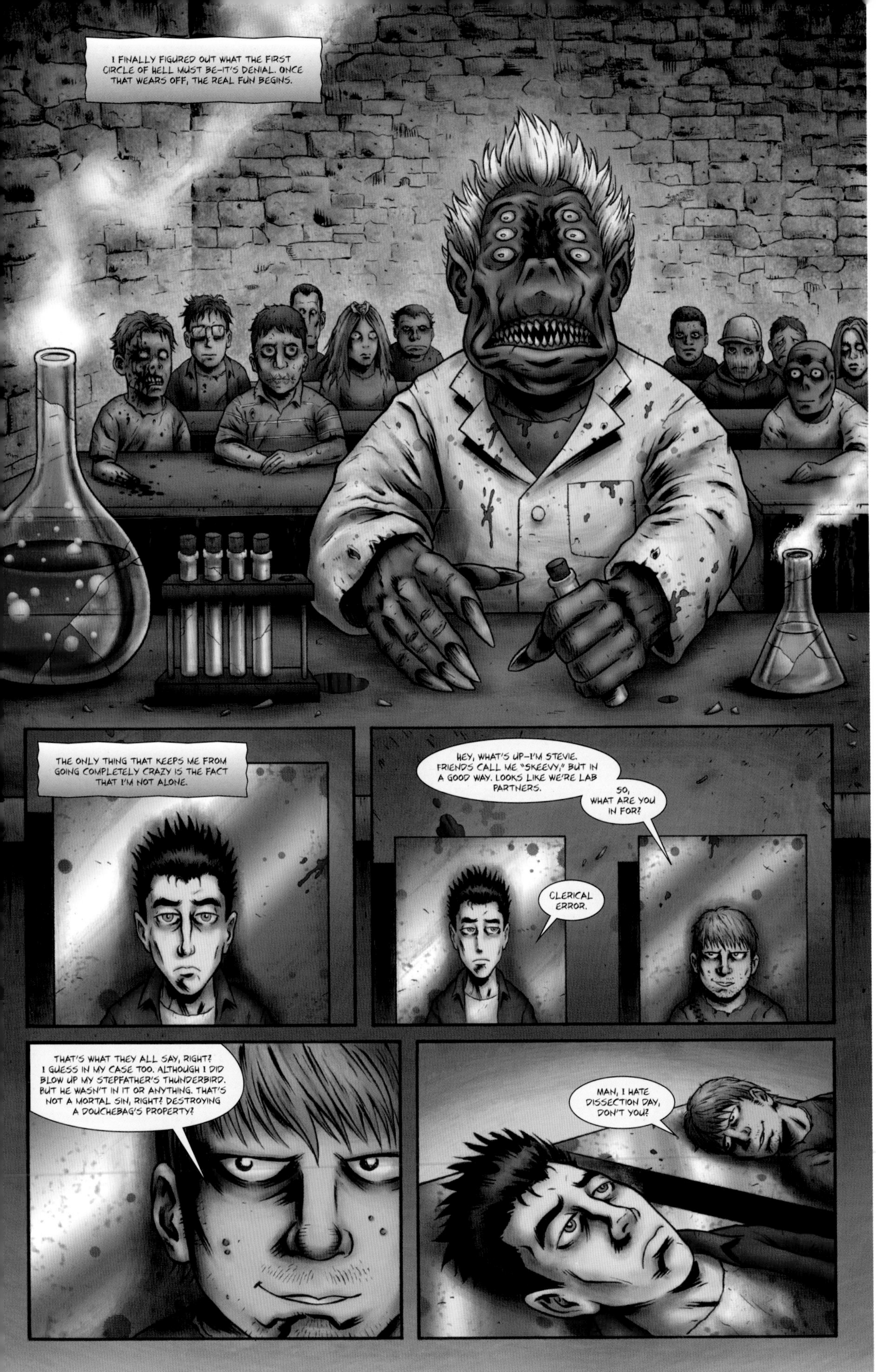
I FINALLY FIGURED OUT WHAT THE FIRST CIRCLE OF HELL MUST BE—IT'S DENIAL. ONCE THAT WEARS OFF, THE REAL FUN BEGINS.
THE ONLY THING THAT KEEPS ME FROM GOING COMPLETELY CRAZY IS THE FACT THAT I'M NOT ALONE.
HEY, WHAT'S UP—I'M STEVIE. FRIENDS CALL ME "SKEEVY," BUT IN A GOOD WAY. LOOKS LIKE WE'RE LAB PARTNERS.
SO, WHAT ARE YOU IN FOR?
CLERICAL ERROR.
THAT'S WHAT THEY ALL SAY, RIGHT? I GUESS IN MY CASE TOO. ALTHOUGH I DID BLOW UP MY STEPFATHER'S THUNDERBIRD. BUT HE WASN'T IN IT OR ANYTHING. THAT'S NOT A MORTAL SIN, RIGHT? DESTROYING A DOUCHEBAG'S PROPERTY?
MAN, I HATE DISSECTION DAY, DON'T YOU?

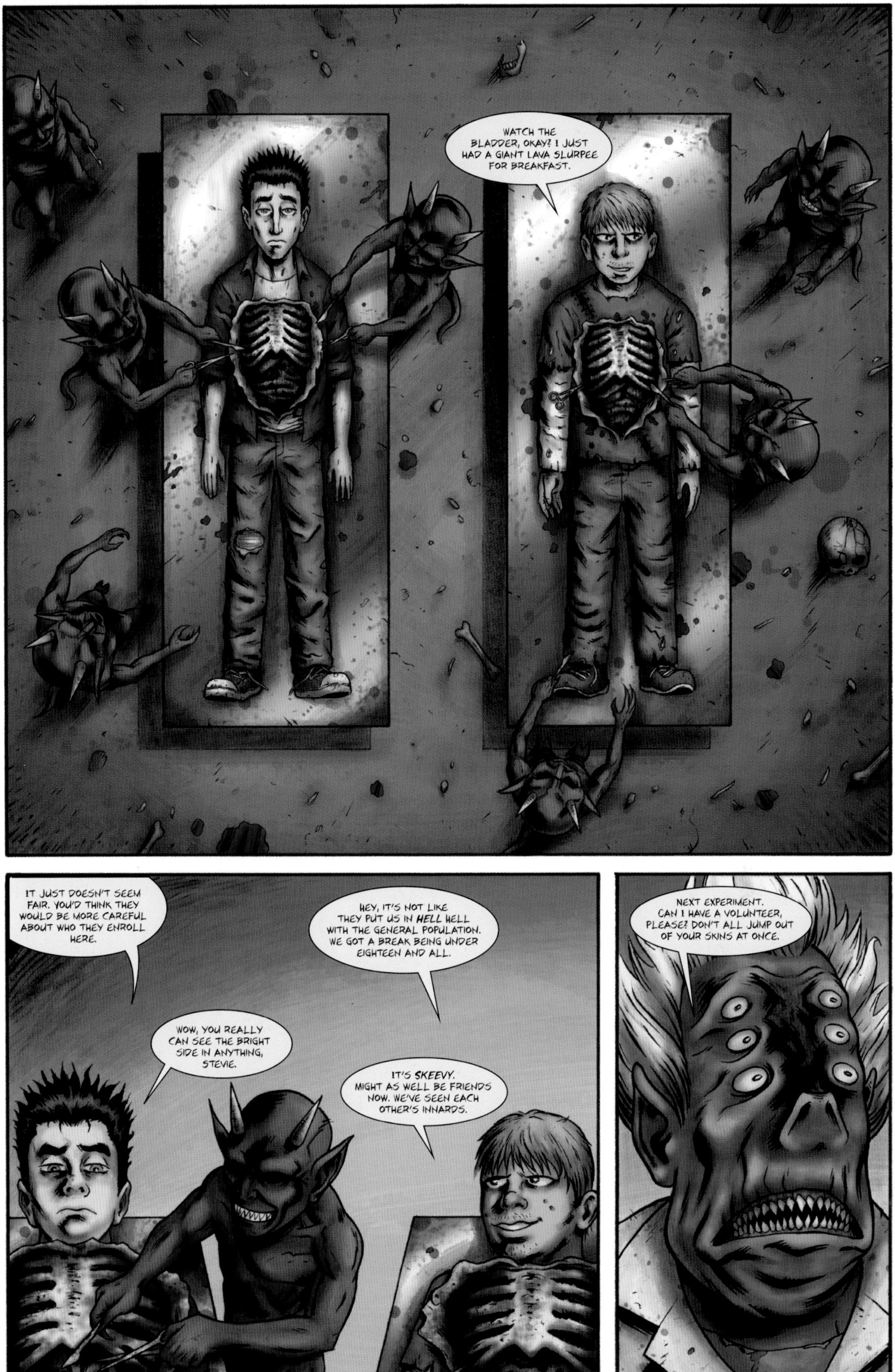
WATCH THE BLADDER, OKAY? I JUST HAD A GIANT LAVA SLURPEE FOR BREAKFAST.
IT JUST DOESN'T SEEM FAIR. YOU'D THINK THEY WOULD BE MORE CAREFUL ABOUT WHO THEY ENROLL HERE.
HEY, IT'S NOT LIKE THEY PUT US IN HELL HELL WITH THE GENERAL POPULATION. WE GOT A BREAK BEING UNDER EIGHTEEN AND ALL.
WOW, YOU REALLY CAN SEE THE BRIGHT SIDE IN ANYTHING, STEVIE.
IT'S SKEEVY. MIGHT AS WELL BE FRIENDS NOW. WE'VE SEEN EACH OTHER'S INNARDS.
NEXT EXPERIMENT. CAN I HAVE A VOLUNTEER, PLEASE? DON'T ALL JUMP OUT OF YOUR SKINS AT ONCE.

MILES STRATHAVEN. CLASS KISS ASS.

OH, OH, OH, PICK ME. PICK ME!

I KNEW HIM IN MY OTHER LIFE, ACTUALLY. HE WAS A RICH KID WHO LIVED A FEW TOWNS AWAY AND HOSTED LEGENDARY SKI TRIPS—ESPECIALLY THE ONE WHERE HE BIT IT ON SOME DIAMOND SLOPE WHILE CHUGGING A BOTTLE OF JACK DANIELS. THERE WAS A BIG MEMORIAL SERVICE DAYS LATER. I DIDN'T GO.

WE'VE JUST DEVELOPED THIS NEW FORMULA AND IT'S A MARVEL, IF I DO SAY SO MYSELF.

IGNOMINIOUS HYDROCHLOROX 873. ALTERS THE SOUL'S CHEMISTRY IN SUCH A WAY THAT EVERYTHING YOU HATE ABOUT YOURSELF COMES RISING TO THE SURFACE.

HEY, MAN—WHY DON'T YOU TRY IT FIRST?

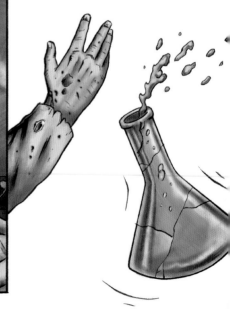

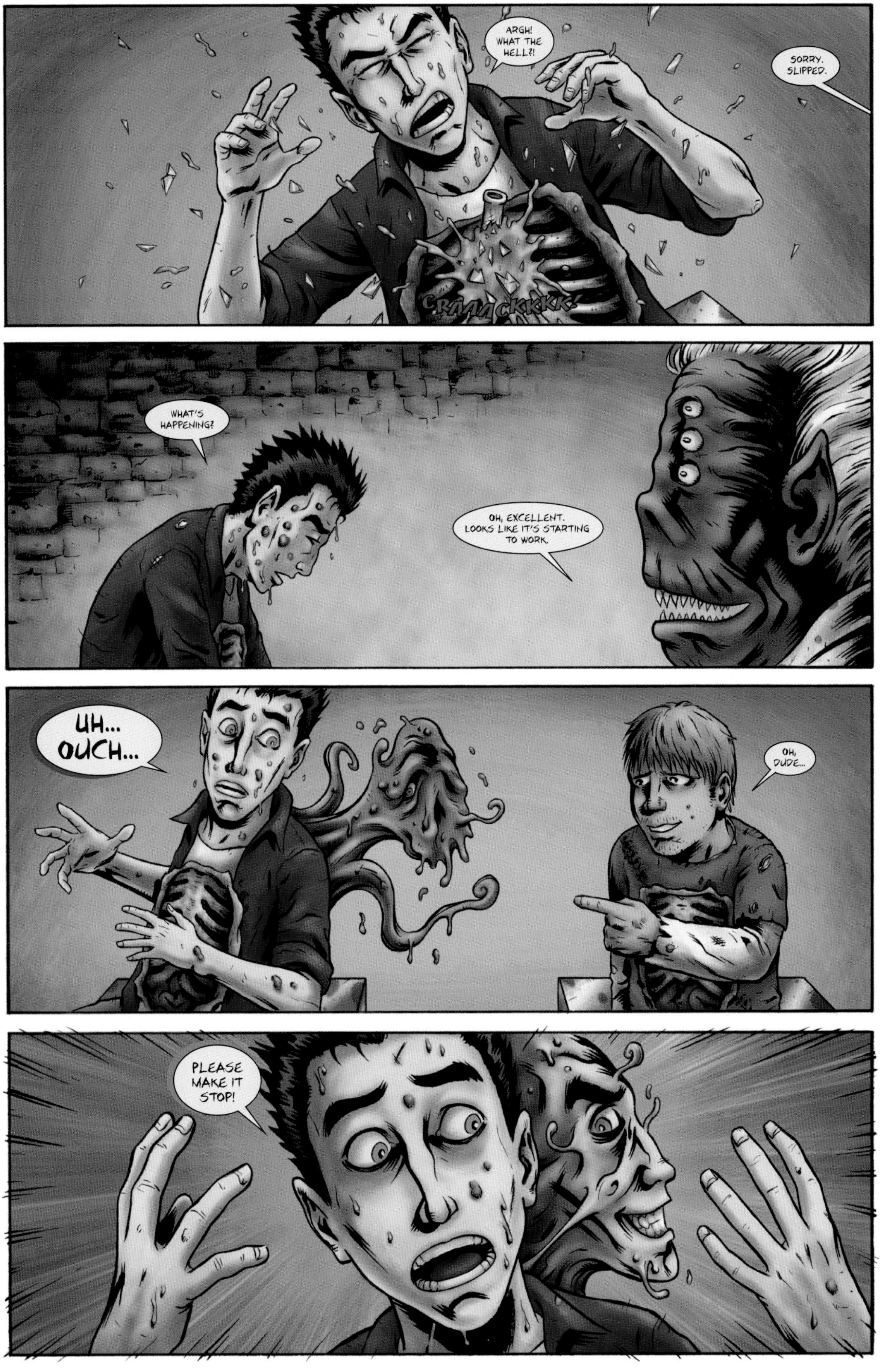
ARGH! WHAT THE HELL?!
SORRY. SLIPPED.
CRAAACKKKK!
WHAT'S HAPPENING?
OH, EXCELLENT. LOOKS LIKE IT'S STARTING TO WORK.
UH... OUCH...
OH, DUDE...
PLEASE MAKE IT STOP!

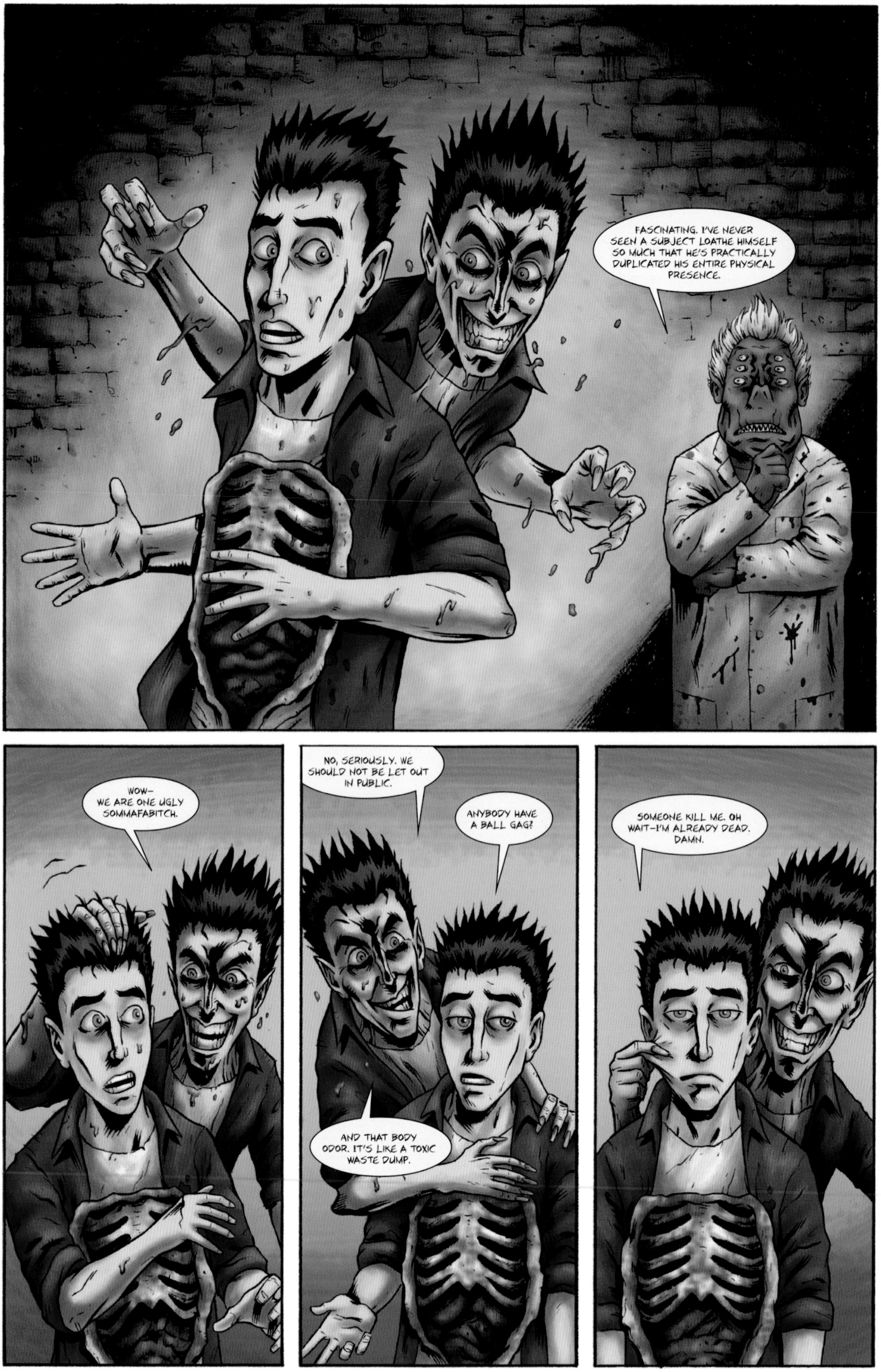
FASCINATING. I'VE NEVER SEEN A SUBJECT LOATHE HIMSELF SO MUCH THAT HE'S PRACTICALLY DUPLICATED HIS ENTIRE PHYSICAL PRESENCE.
WOW– WE ARE ONE UGLY SOMMAFABITCH.
NO, SERIOUSLY. WE SHOULD NOT BE LET OUT IN PUBLIC.
ANYBODY HAVE A BALL GAG?
AND THAT BODY ODOR. IT'S LIKE A TOXIC WASTE DUMP.
SOMEONE KILL ME. OH WAIT–I'M ALREADY DEAD. DAMN.

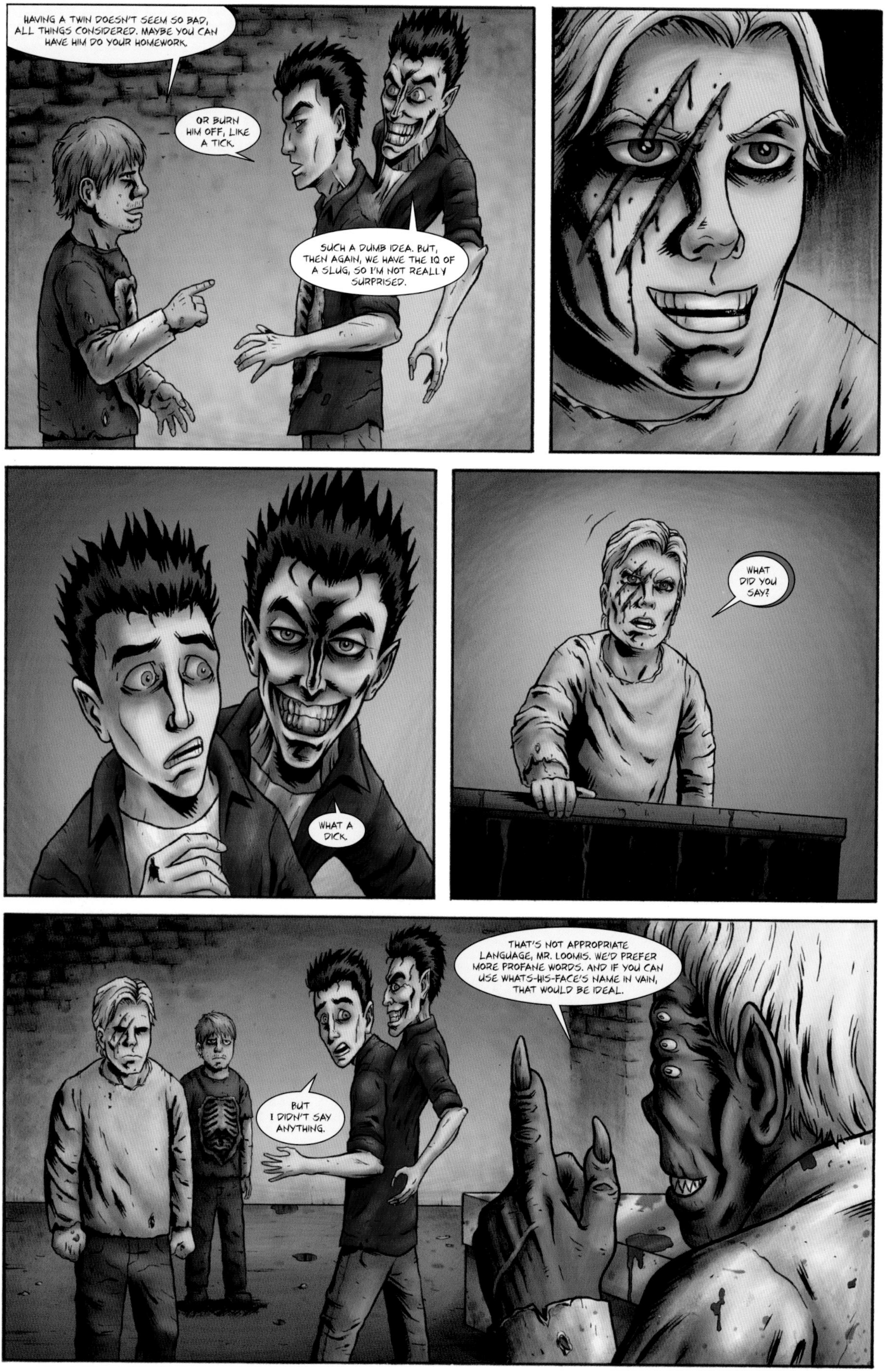
HAVING A TWIN DOESN'T SEEM SO BAD, ALL THINGS CONSIDERED. MAYBE YOU CAN HAVE HIM DO YOUR HOMEWORK.
OR BURN HIM OFF, LIKE A TICK.
SUCH A DUMB IDEA. BUT, THEN AGAIN, WE HAVE THE IQ OF A SLUG, SO I'M NOT REALLY SURPRISED.
WHAT A DICK.
WHAT DID YOU SAY?
BUT I DIDN'T SAY ANYTHING.
THAT'S NOT APPROPRIATE LANGUAGE, MR. LOOMIS. WE'D PREFER MORE PROFANE WORDS. AND IF YOU CAN USE WHATS-HIS-FACE'S NAME IN VAIN, THAT WOULD BE IDEAL.

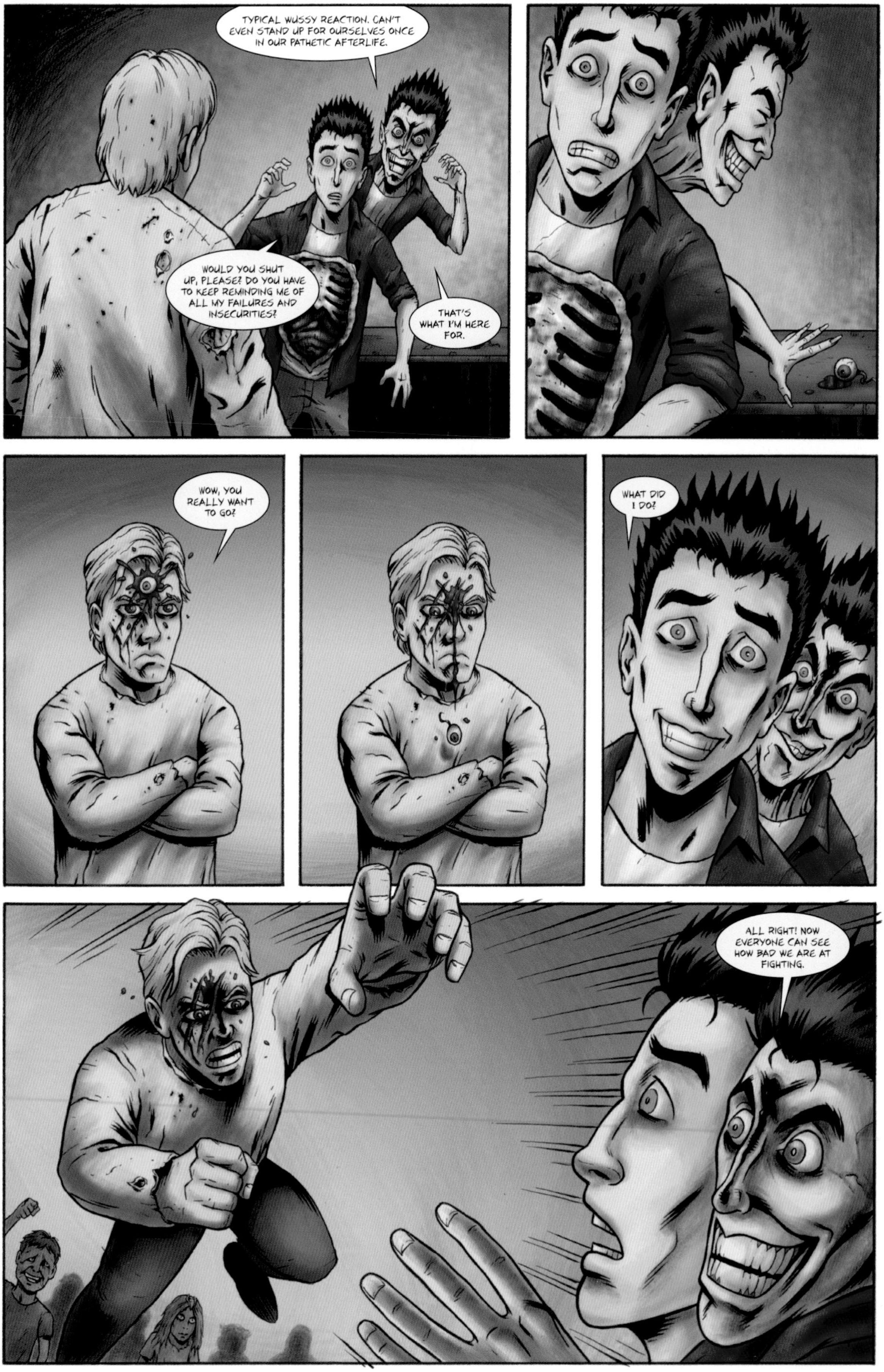
TYPICAL WUSSY REACTION. CAN'T EVEN STAND UP FOR OURSELVES ONCE IN OUR PATHETIC AFTERLIFE.
WOULD YOU SHUT UP, PLEASE? DO YOU HAVE TO KEEP REMINDING ME OF ALL MY FAILURES AND INSECURITIES?
THAT'S WHAT I'M HERE FOR.
WOW, YOU REALLY WANT TO GO?
WHAT DID I DO?
ALL RIGHT! NOW EVERYONE CAN SEE HOW BAD WE ARE AT FIGHTING.

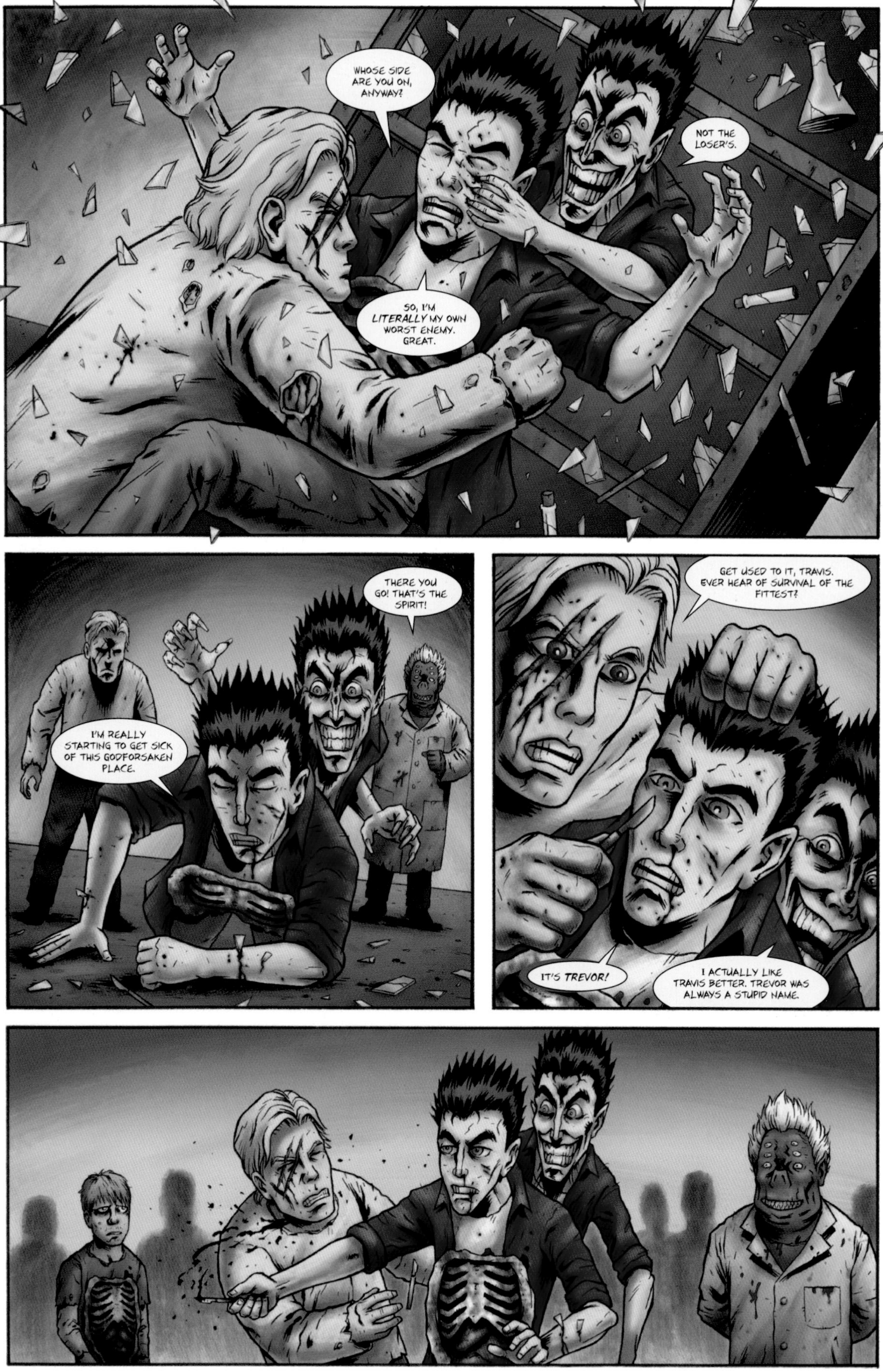
WHOSE SIDE ARE YOU ON, ANYWAY?
NOT THE LOSER'S.
SO, I'M *LITERALLY* MY OWN WORST ENEMY. GREAT.
THERE YOU GO! THAT'S THE SPIRIT!
I'M REALLY STARTING TO GET SICK OF THIS GODFORSAKEN PLACE.
GET USED TO IT, TRAVIS. EVER HEAR OF SURVIVAL OF THE FITTEST?
IT'S *TREVOR!*
I ACTUALLY LIKE TRAVIS BETTER. TREVOR WAS ALWAYS A STUPID NAME.

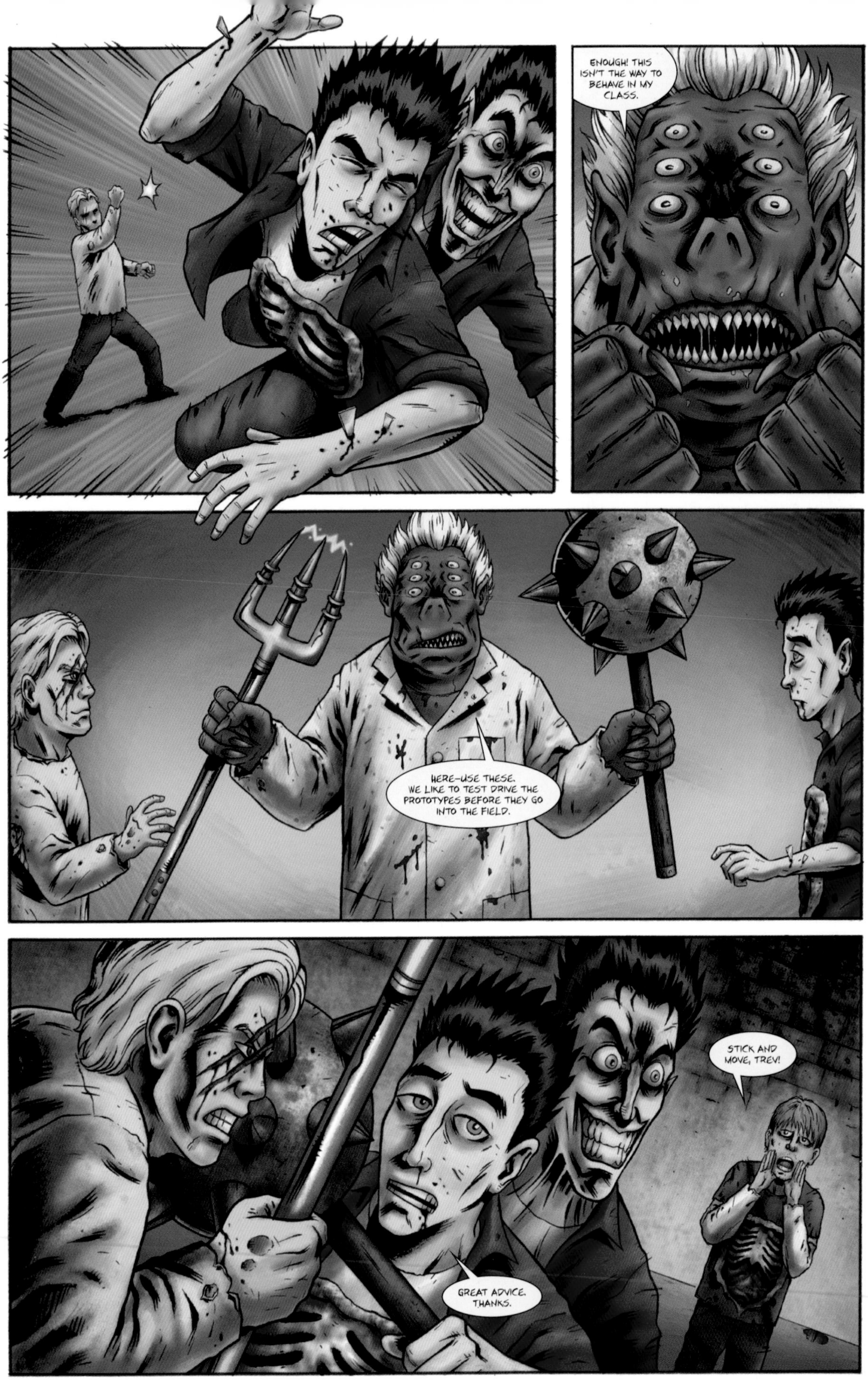
ENOUGH! THIS ISN'T THE WAY TO BEHAVE IN MY CLASS.
HERE–USE THESE. WE LIKE TO TEST DRIVE THE PROTOTYPES BEFORE THEY GO INTO THE FIELD.
STICK AND MOVE, TREV!
GREAT ADVICE. THANKS.

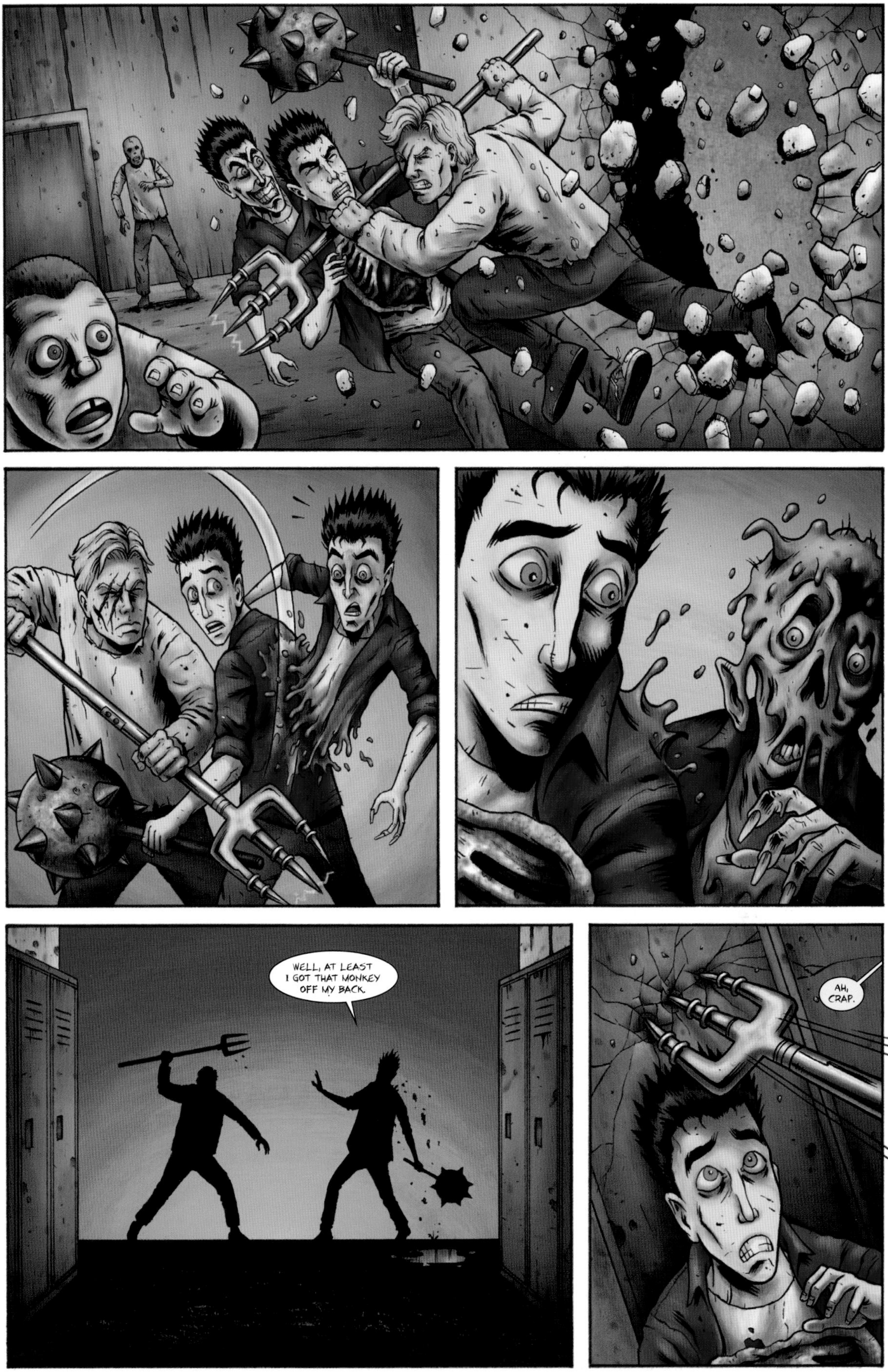
WELL, AT LEAST I GOT THAT MONKEY OFF MY BACK.
AH, CRAP.

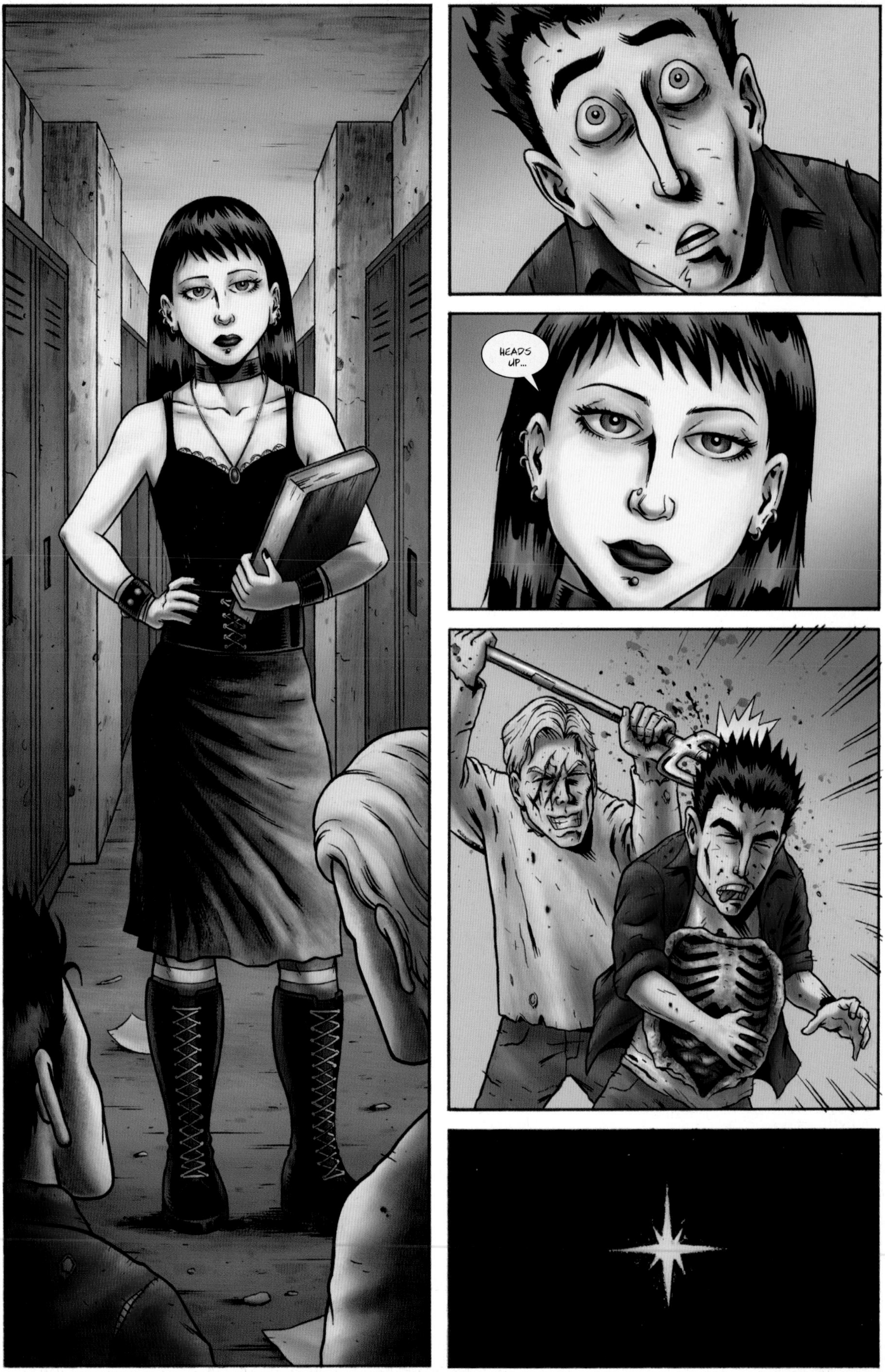
HEADS UP...

PART II

Pencils/Inks/Graytone:
Dave Fox

Colors:
Aya Ikeda-Barry

Lettering:
April Brown

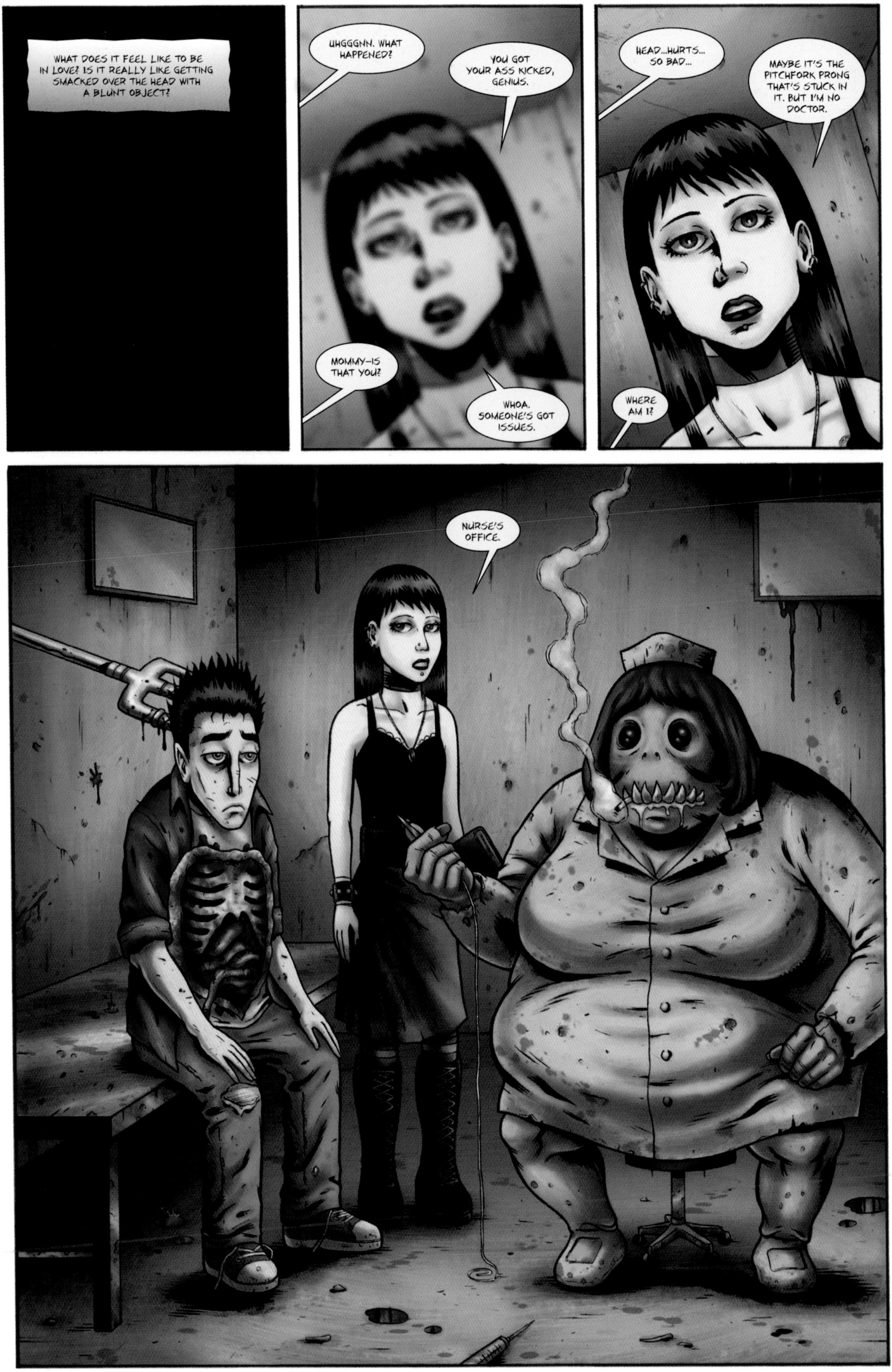
WHAT DOES IT FEEL LIKE TO BE IN LOVE? IS IT REALLY LIKE GETTING SMACKED OVER THE HEAD WITH A BLUNT OBJECT?
UHGGGNN. WHAT HAPPENED?
YOU GOT YOUR ASS KICKED, GENIUS.
MOMMY—IS THAT YOU?
WHOA. SOMEONE'S GOT ISSUES.
HEAD...HURTS... SO BAD...
MAYBE IT'S THE PITCHFORK PRONG THAT'S STUCK IN IT. BUT I'M NO DOCTOR.
WHERE AM I?
NURSE'S OFFICE.

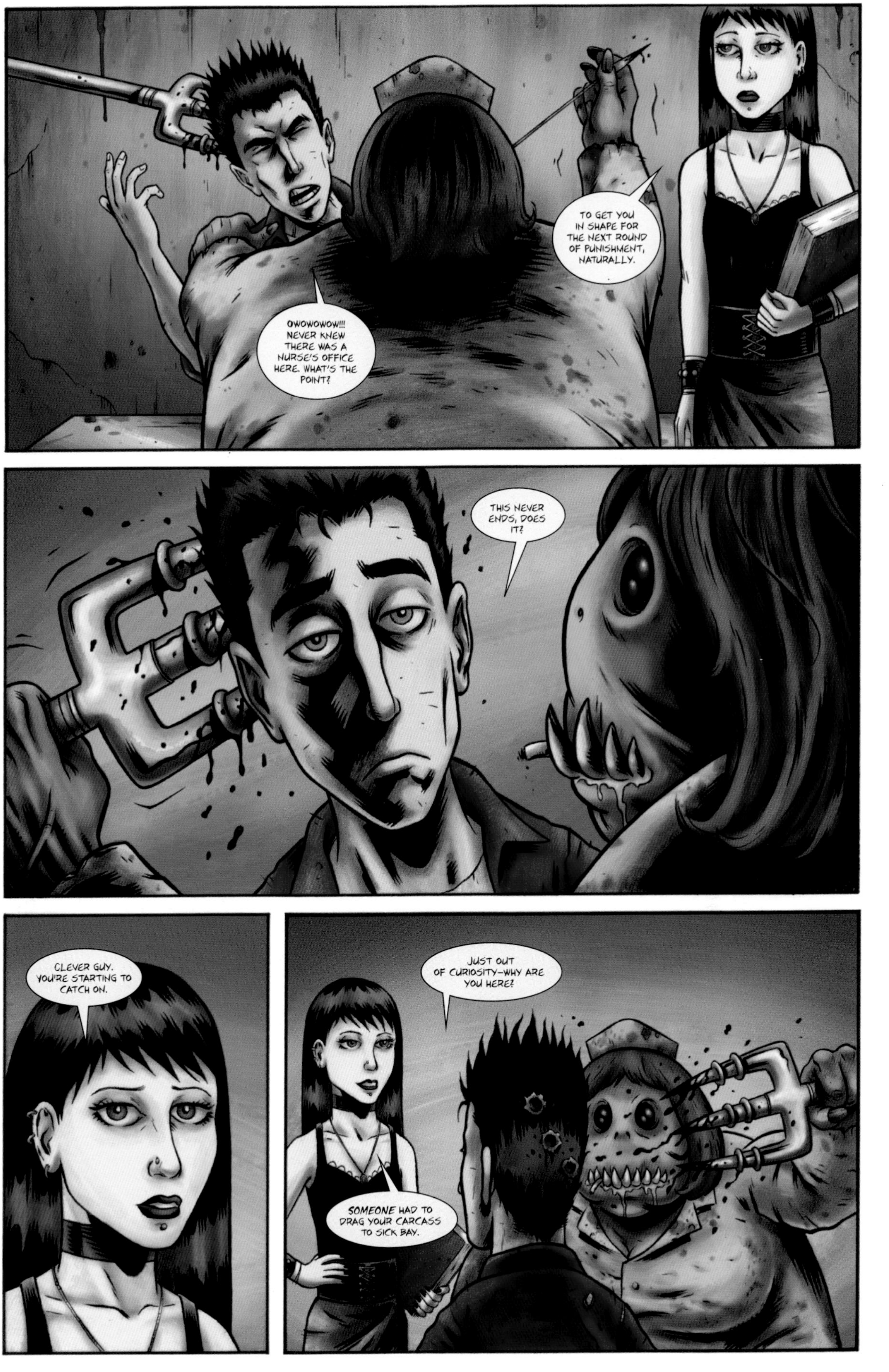
OWOWOWOW!!! NEVER KNEW THERE WAS A NURSE'S OFFICE HERE. WHAT'S THE POINT?
TO GET YOU IN SHAPE FOR THE NEXT ROUND OF PUNISHMENT, NATURALLY.
THIS NEVER ENDS, DOES IT?
CLEVER GUY. YOU'RE STARTING TO CATCH ON.
JUST OUT OF CURIOSITY—WHY ARE YOU HERE?
SOMEONE HAD TO DRAG YOUR CARCASS TO SICK BAY.

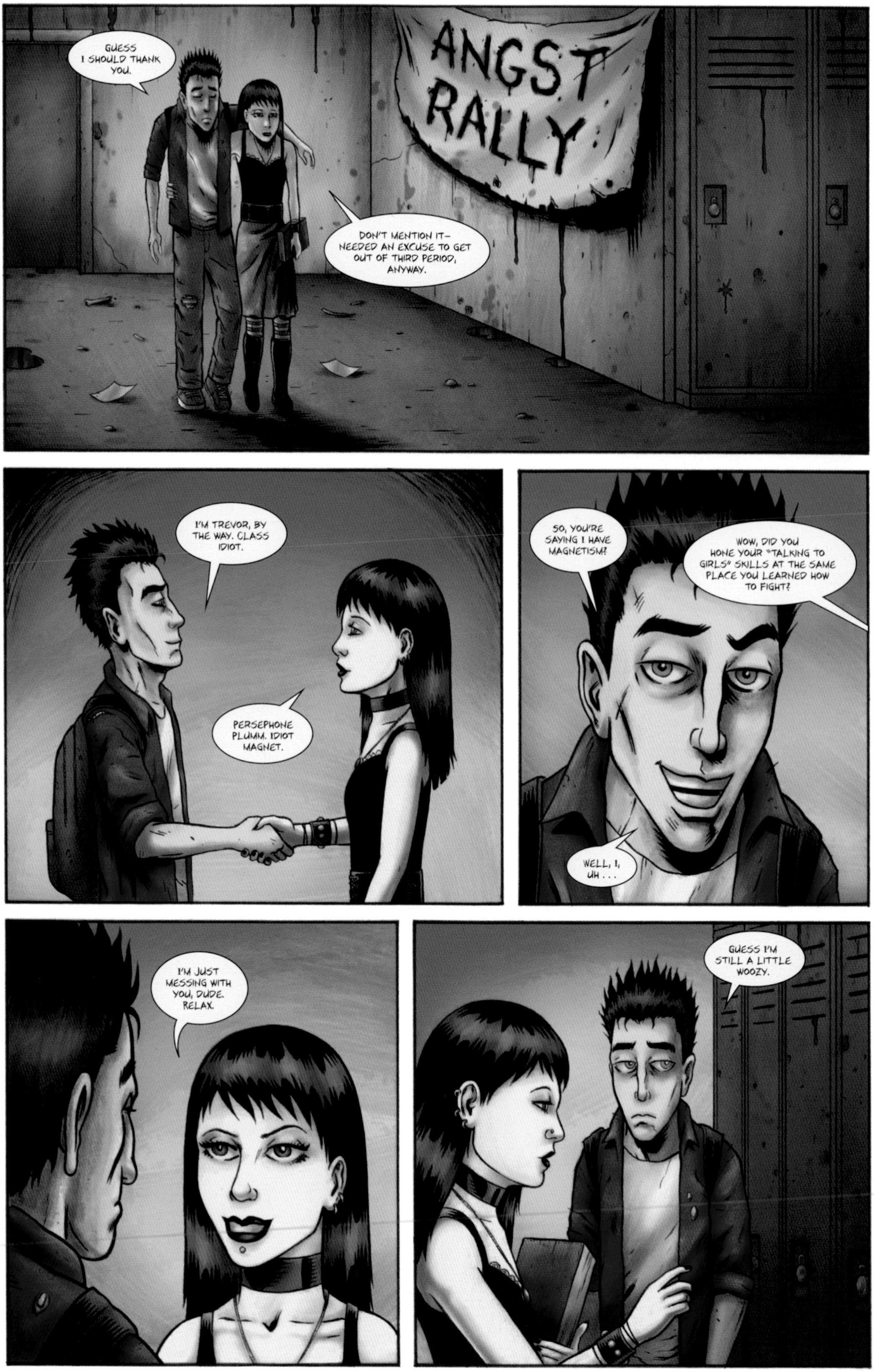
ANGST RALLY
GUESS I SHOULD THANK YOU.
DON'T MENTION IT— NEEDED AN EXCUSE TO GET OUT OF THIRD PERIOD, ANYWAY.
I'M TREVOR, BY THE WAY. CLASS IDIOT.
PERSEPHONE PLUMM. IDIOT MAGNET.
SO, YOU'RE SAYING I HAVE MAGNETISM?
WOW, DID YOU HONE YOUR "TALKING TO GIRLS" SKILLS AT THE SAME PLACE YOU LEARNED HOW TO FIGHT?
WELL, I, UH . . .
I'M JUST MESSING WITH YOU, DUDE. RELAX.
GUESS I'M STILL A LITTLE WOOZY.

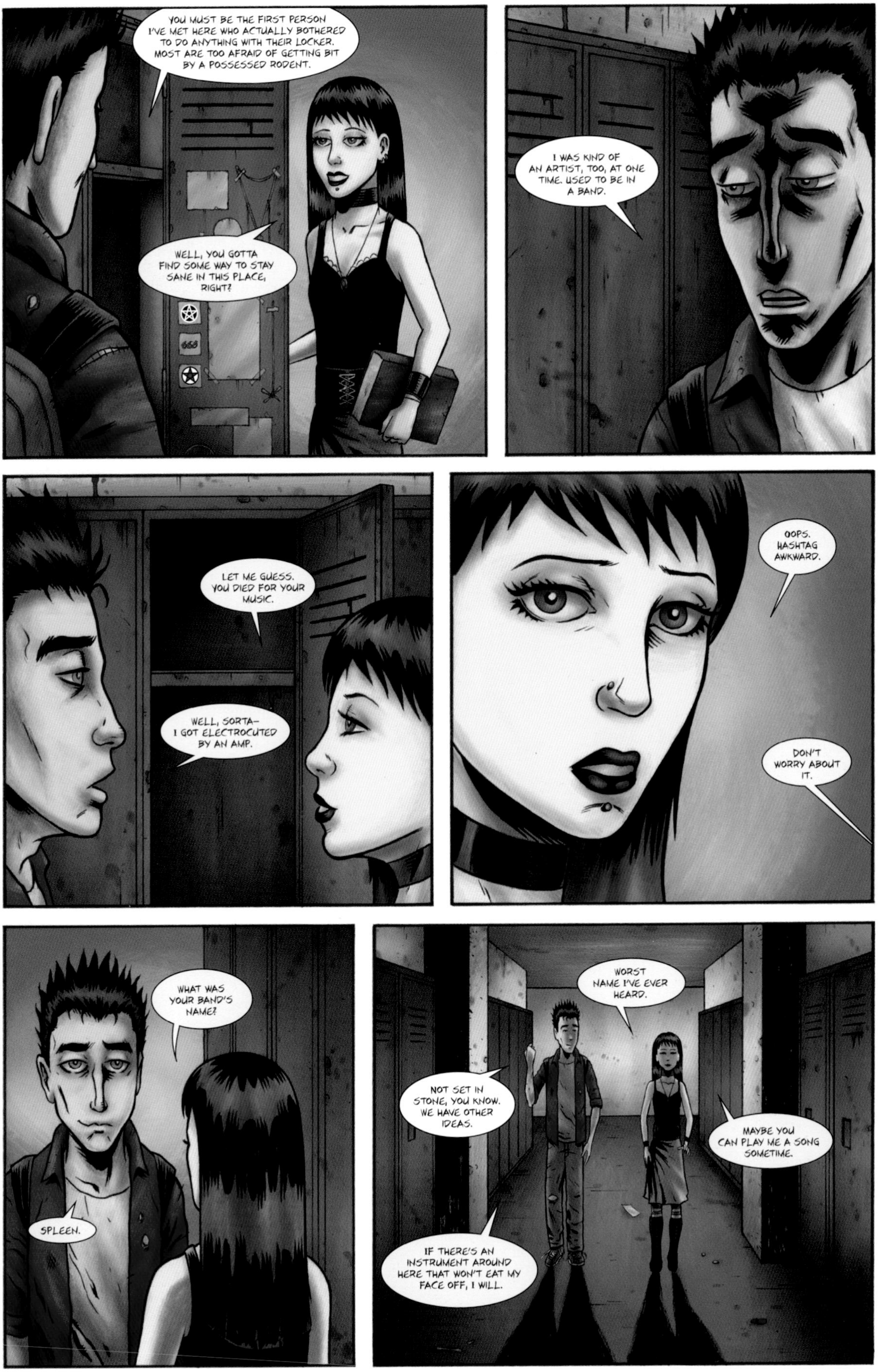
YOU MUST BE THE FIRST PERSON I'VE MET HERE WHO ACTUALLY BOTHERED TO DO ANYTHING WITH THEIR LOCKER. MOST ARE TOO AFRAID OF GETTING BIT BY A POSSESSED RODENT.
WELL, YOU GOTTA FIND SOME WAY TO STAY SANE IN THIS PLACE, RIGHT?
666
I WAS KIND OF AN ARTIST, TOO, AT ONE TIME. USED TO BE IN A BAND.
LET ME GUESS. YOU DIED FOR YOUR MUSIC.
WELL, SORTA— I GOT ELECTROCUTED BY AN AMP.
OOPS. HASHTAG AWKWARD.
DON'T WORRY ABOUT IT.
WHAT WAS YOUR BAND'S NAME?
SPLEEN.
WORST NAME I'VE EVER HEARD.
NOT SET IN STONE, YOU KNOW. WE HAVE OTHER IDEAS.
MAYBE YOU CAN PLAY ME A SONG SOMETIME.
IF THERE'S AN INSTRUMENT AROUND HERE THAT WON'T EAT MY FACE OFF, I WILL.

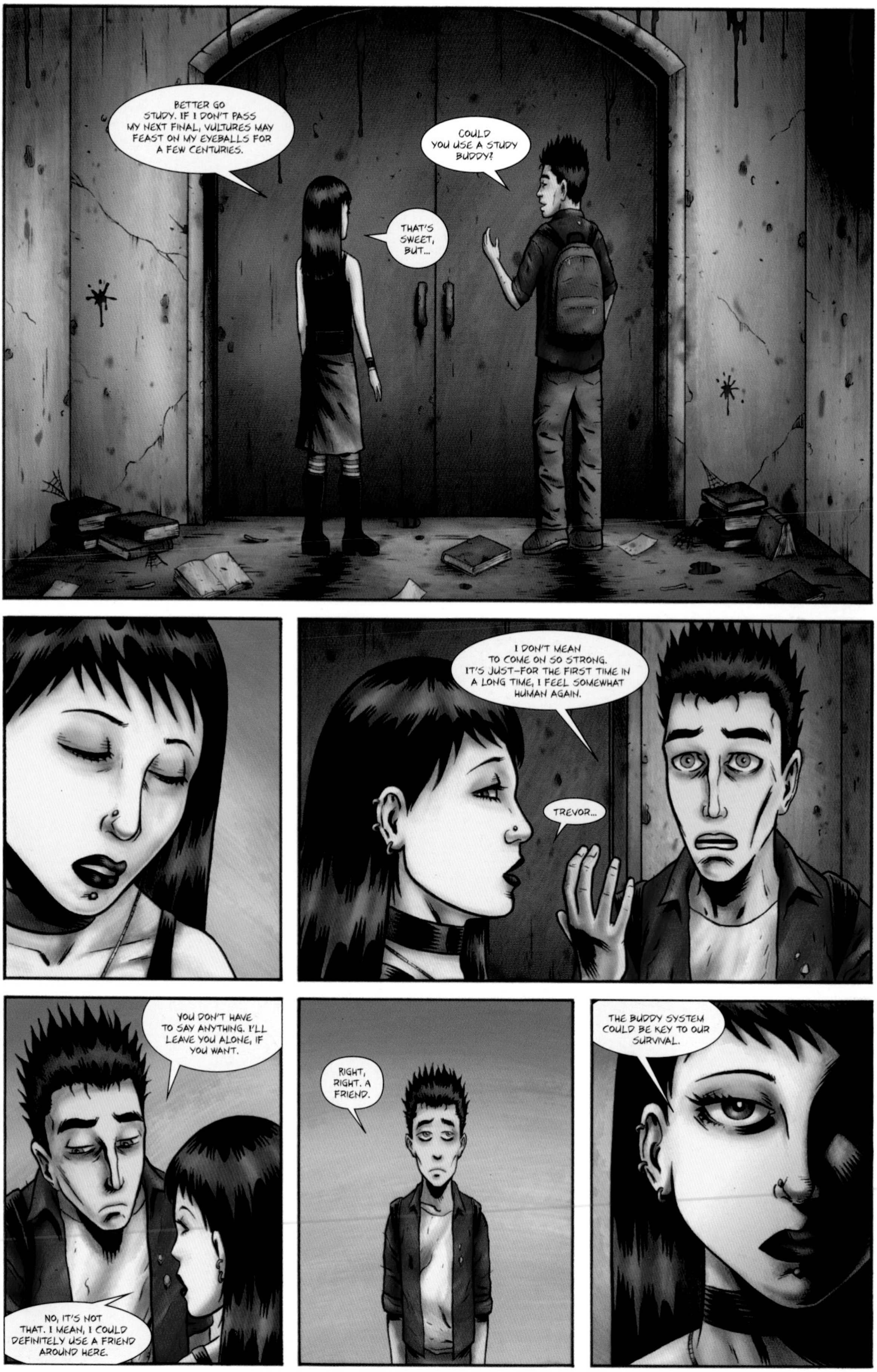
BETTER GO STUDY. IF I DON'T PASS MY NEXT FINAL, VULTURES MAY FEAST ON MY EYEBALLS FOR A FEW CENTURIES.
COULD YOU USE A STUDY BUDDY?
THAT'S SWEET, BUT...
I DON'T MEAN TO COME ON SO STRONG. IT'S JUST—FOR THE FIRST TIME IN A LONG TIME, I FEEL SOMEWHAT HUMAN AGAIN.
TREVOR...
YOU DON'T HAVE TO SAY ANYTHING. I'LL LEAVE YOU ALONE, IF YOU WANT.
NO, IT'S NOT THAT. I MEAN, I COULD DEFINITELY USE A FRIEND AROUND HERE.
RIGHT, RIGHT. A FRIEND.
THE BUDDY SYSTEM COULD BE KEY TO OUR SURVIVAL.

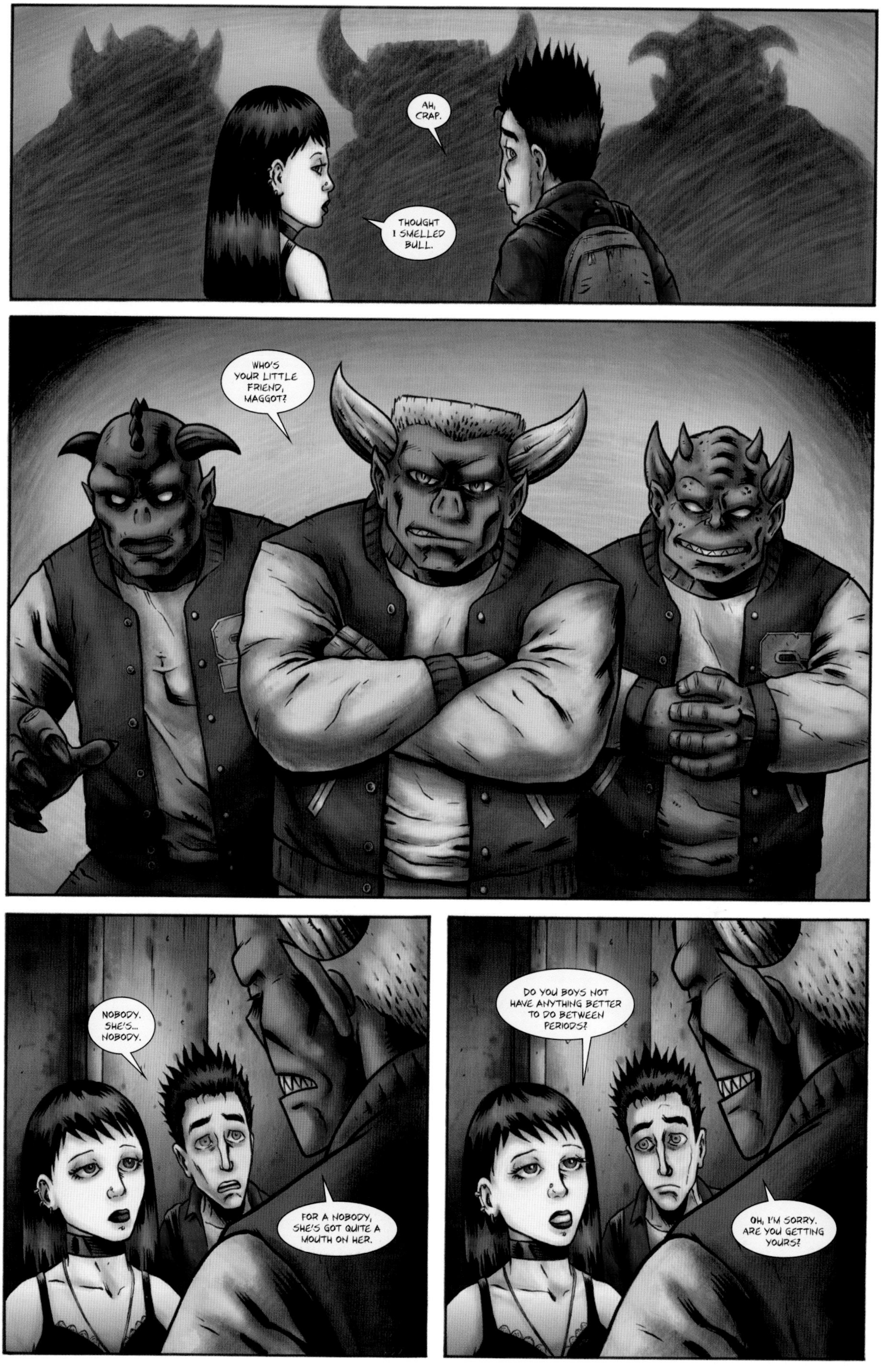
AH, CRAP.
THOUGHT I SMELLED BULL.
WHO'S YOUR LITTLE FRIEND, MAGGOT?
NOBODY. SHE'S... NOBODY.
FOR A NOBODY, SHE'S GOT QUITE A MOUTH ON HER.
DO YOU BOYS NOT HAVE ANYTHING BETTER TO DO BETWEEN PERIODS?
OH, I'M SORRY. ARE YOU GETTING YOURS?

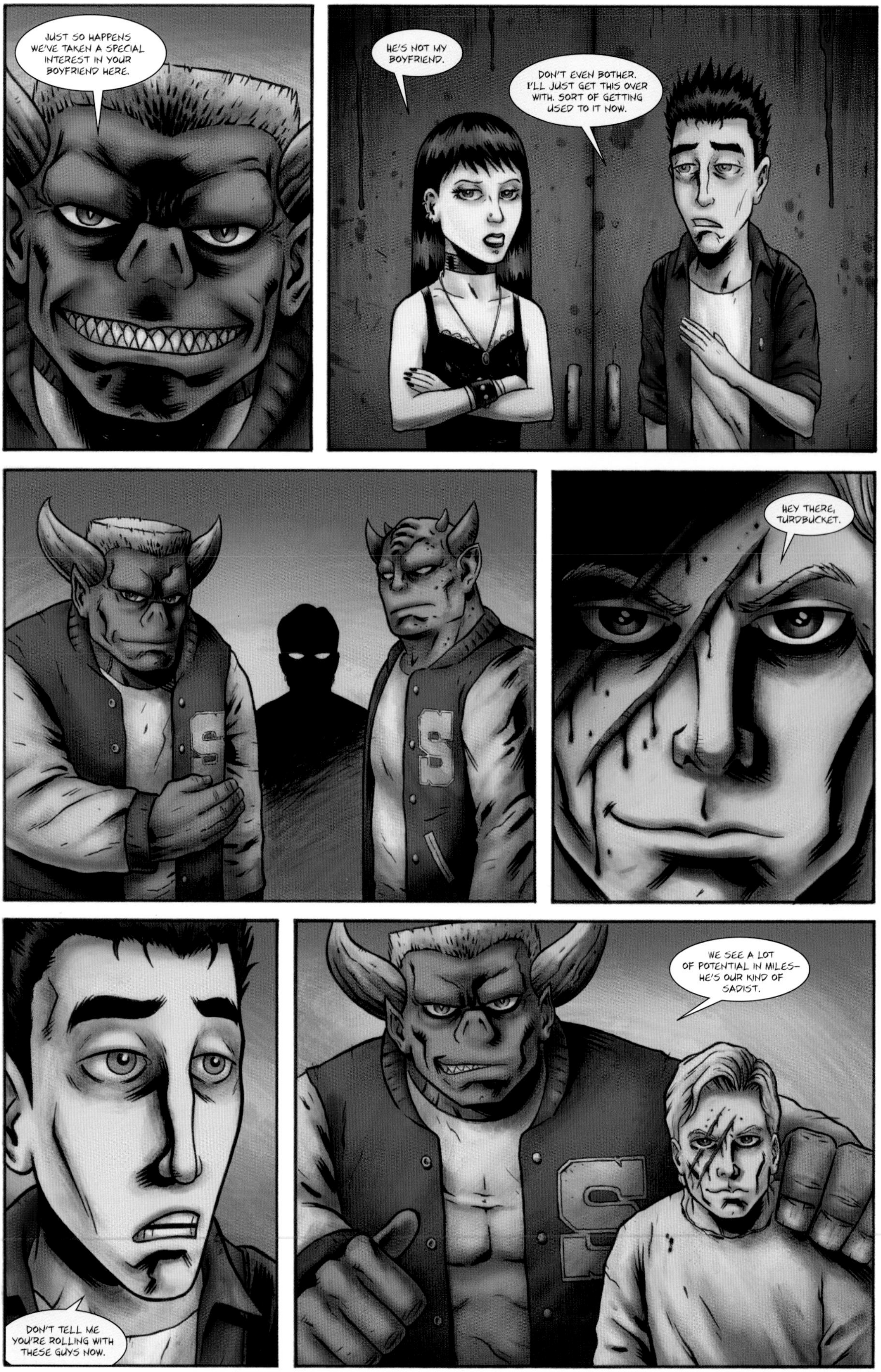
JUST SO HAPPENS WE'VE TAKEN A SPECIAL INTEREST IN YOUR BOYFRIEND HERE.
HE'S NOT MY BOYFRIEND.
DON'T EVEN BOTHER. I'LL JUST GET THIS OVER WITH. SORT OF GETTING USED TO IT NOW.
HEY THERE, TURDBUCKET.
DON'T TELL ME YOU'RE ROLLING WITH THESE GUYS NOW.
WE SEE A LOT OF POTENTIAL IN MILES– HE'S OUR KIND OF SADIST.

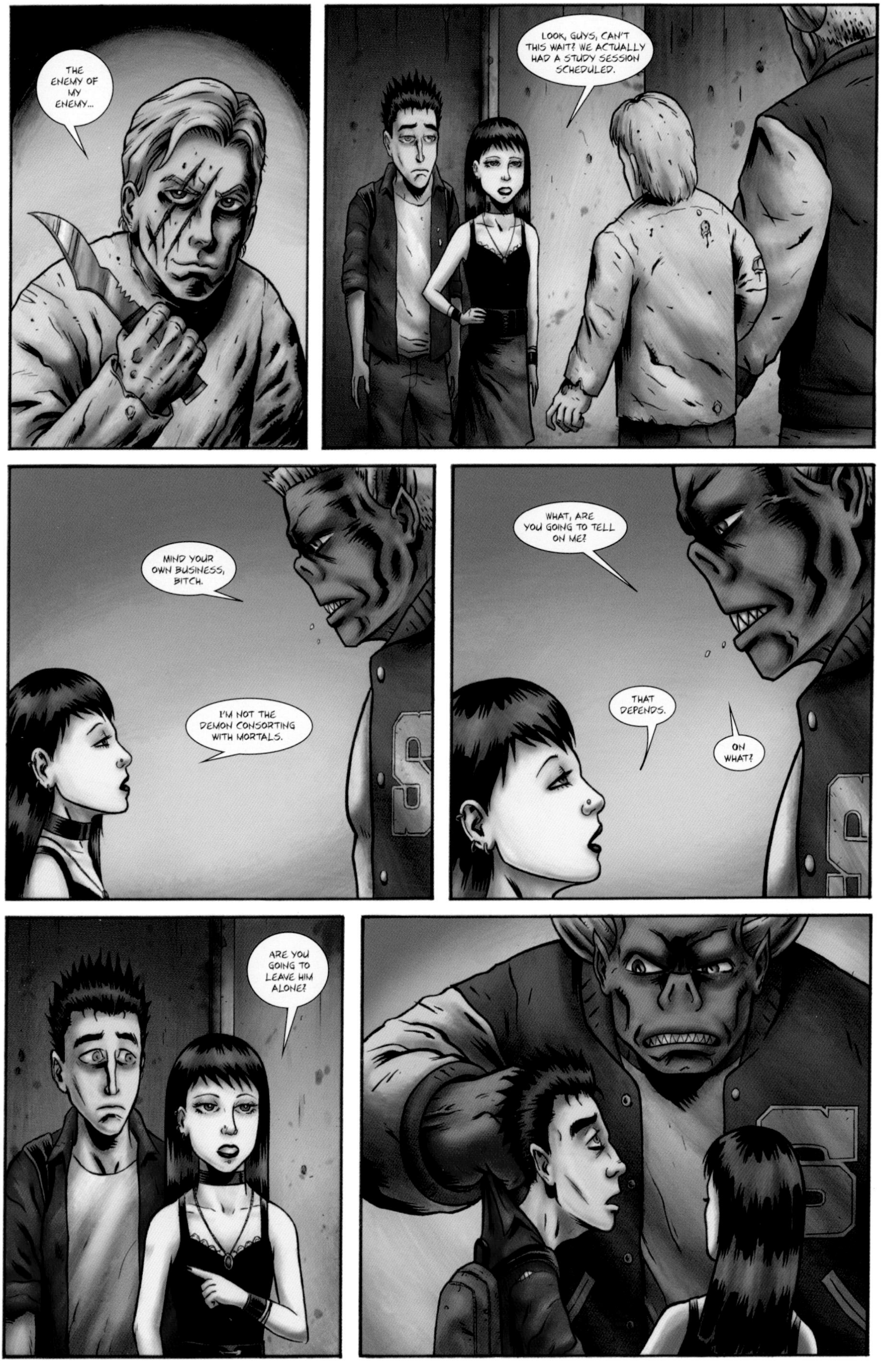
THE ENEMY OF MY ENEMY...
LOOK, GUYS, CAN'T THIS WAIT? WE ACTUALLY HAD A STUDY SESSION SCHEDULED.
MIND YOUR OWN BUSINESS, BITCH.
I'M NOT THE DEMON CONSORTING WITH MORTALS.
WHAT, ARE YOU GOING TO TELL ON ME?
THAT DEPENDS.
ON WHAT?
ARE YOU GOING TO LEAVE HIM ALONE?

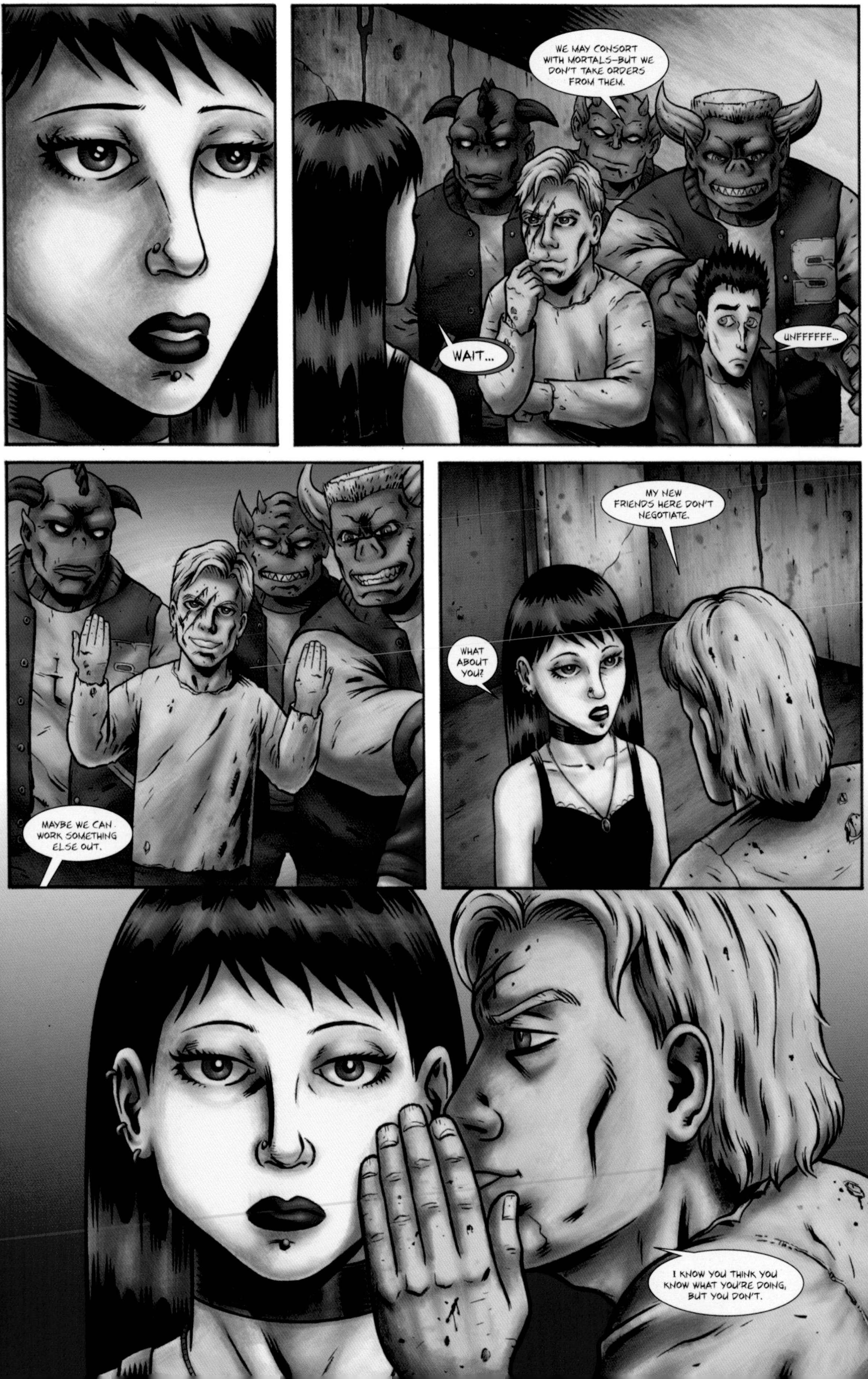
WE MAY CONSORT WITH MORTALS—BUT WE DON'T TAKE ORDERS FROM THEM.
WAIT...
UNFFFFFF...
MAYBE WE CAN WORK SOMETHING ELSE OUT.
MY NEW FRIENDS HERE DON'T NEGOTIATE.
WHAT ABOUT YOU?
I KNOW YOU THINK YOU KNOW WHAT YOU'RE DOING, BUT YOU DON'T.

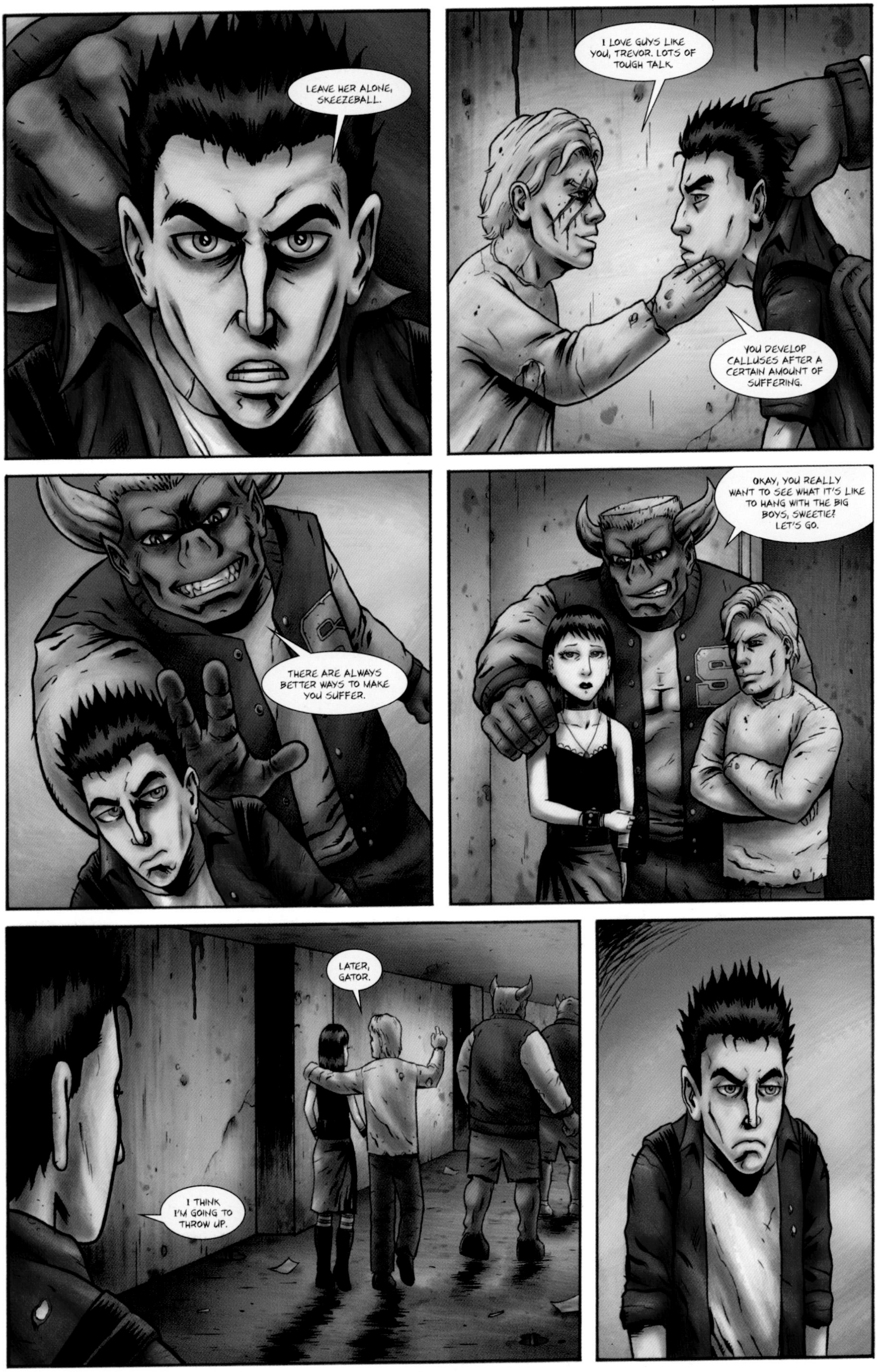
LEAVE HER ALONE, SKEEZEBALL.
I LOVE GUYS LIKE YOU, TREVOR. LOTS OF TOUGH TALK.
YOU DEVELOP CALLUSES AFTER A CERTAIN AMOUNT OF SUFFERING.
THERE ARE ALWAYS BETTER WAYS TO MAKE YOU SUFFER.
OKAY, YOU REALLY WANT TO SEE WHAT IT'S LIKE TO HANG WITH THE BIG BOYS, SWEETIE? LET'S GO.
LATER, GATOR.
I THINK I'M GOING TO THROW UP.

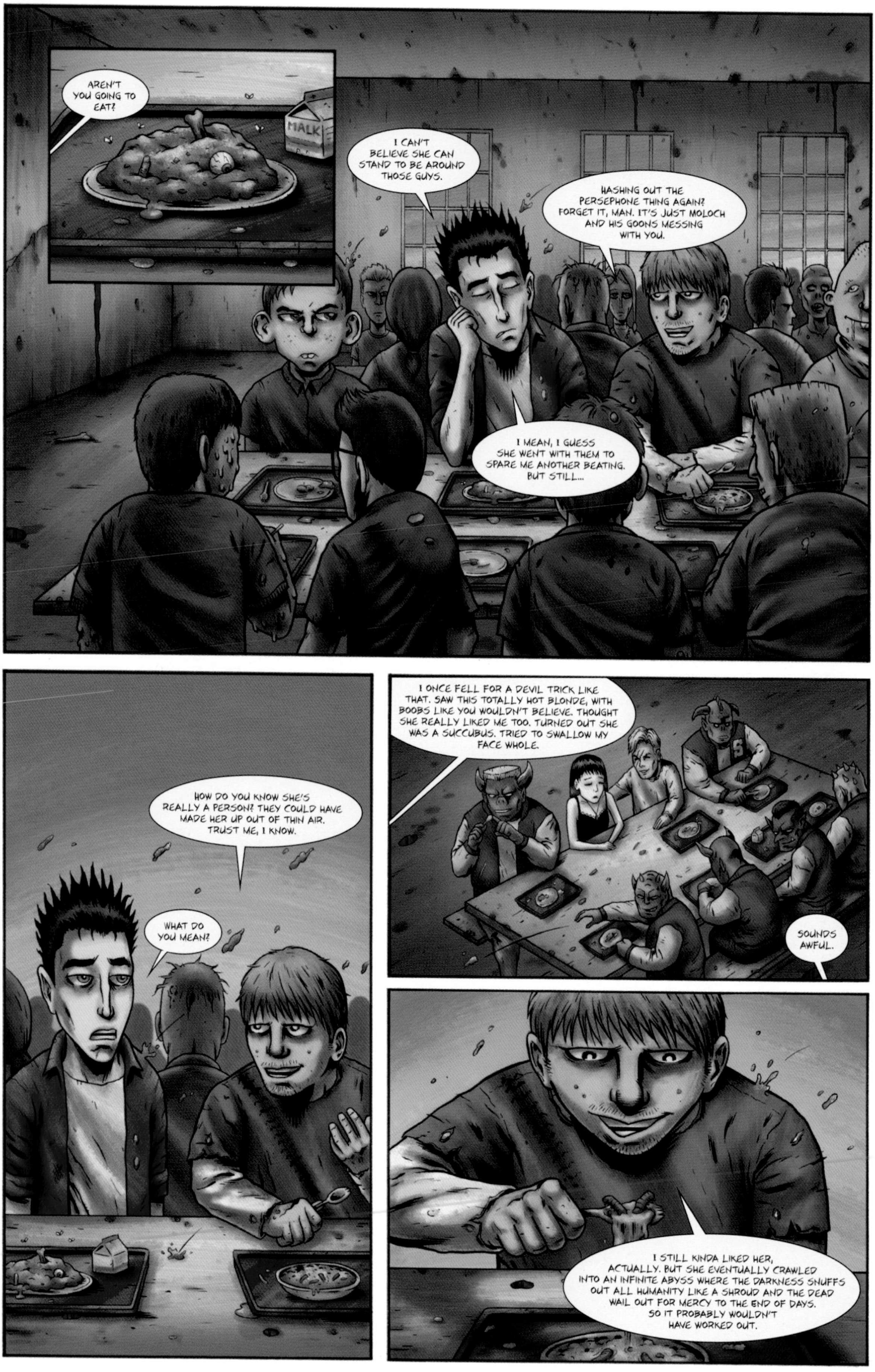
AREN'T YOU GOING TO EAT?
MALK
I CAN'T BELIEVE SHE CAN STAND TO BE AROUND THOSE GUYS.
HASHING OUT THE PERSEPHONE THING AGAIN? FORGET IT, MAN. IT'S JUST MOLOCH AND HIS GOONS MESSING WITH YOU.
I MEAN, I GUESS SHE WENT WITH THEM TO SPARE ME ANOTHER BEATING. BUT STILL...
HOW DO YOU KNOW SHE'S REALLY A PERSON? THEY COULD HAVE MADE HER UP OUT OF THIN AIR. TRUST ME, I KNOW.
WHAT DO YOU MEAN?
I ONCE FELL FOR A DEVIL TRICK LIKE THAT. SAW THIS TOTALLY HOT BLONDE, WITH BOOBS LIKE YOU WOULDN'T BELIEVE. THOUGHT SHE REALLY LIKED ME TOO. TURNED OUT SHE WAS A SUCCUBUS. TRIED TO SWALLOW MY FACE WHOLE.
SOUNDS AWFUL.
I STILL KINDA LIKED HER, ACTUALLY. BUT SHE EVENTUALLY CRAWLED INTO AN INFINITE ABYSS WHERE THE DARKNESS SNUFFS OUT ALL HUMANITY LIKE A SHROUD AND THE DEAD WAIL OUT FOR MERCY TO THE END OF DAYS. SO IT PROBABLY WOULDN'T HAVE WORKED OUT.

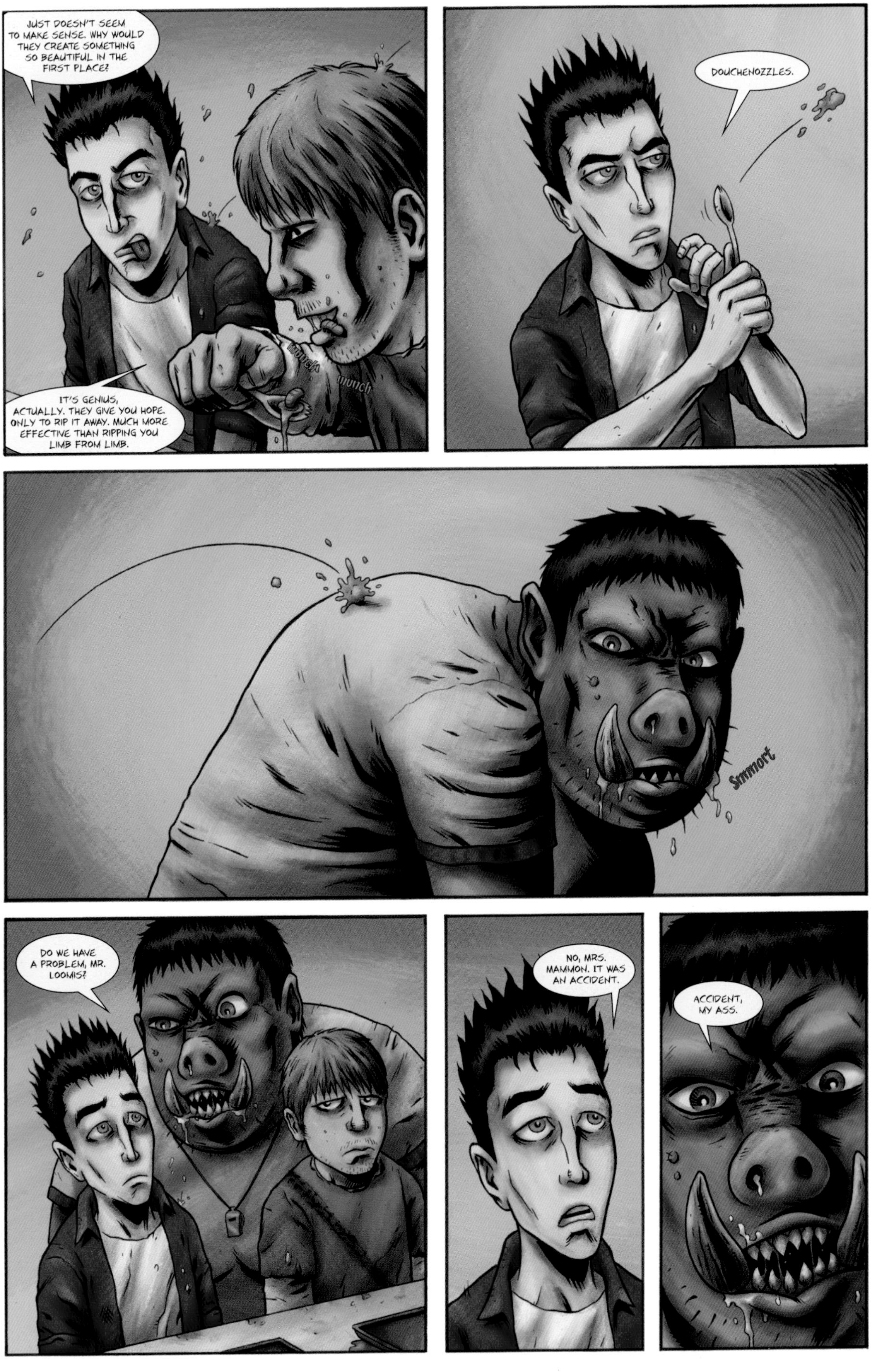
JUST DOESN'T SEEM TO MAKE SENSE. WHY WOULD THEY CREATE SOMETHING SO BEAUTIFUL IN THE FIRST PLACE?
munch
munch
IT'S GENIUS, ACTUALLY. THEY GIVE YOU HOPE. ONLY TO RIP IT AWAY. MUCH MORE EFFECTIVE THAN RIPPING YOU LIMB FROM LIMB.
DOUCHENOZZLES.
Snnort
DO WE HAVE A PROBLEM, MR. LOOMIS?
NO, MRS. MAMMON. IT WAS AN ACCIDENT.
ACCIDENT, MY ASS.

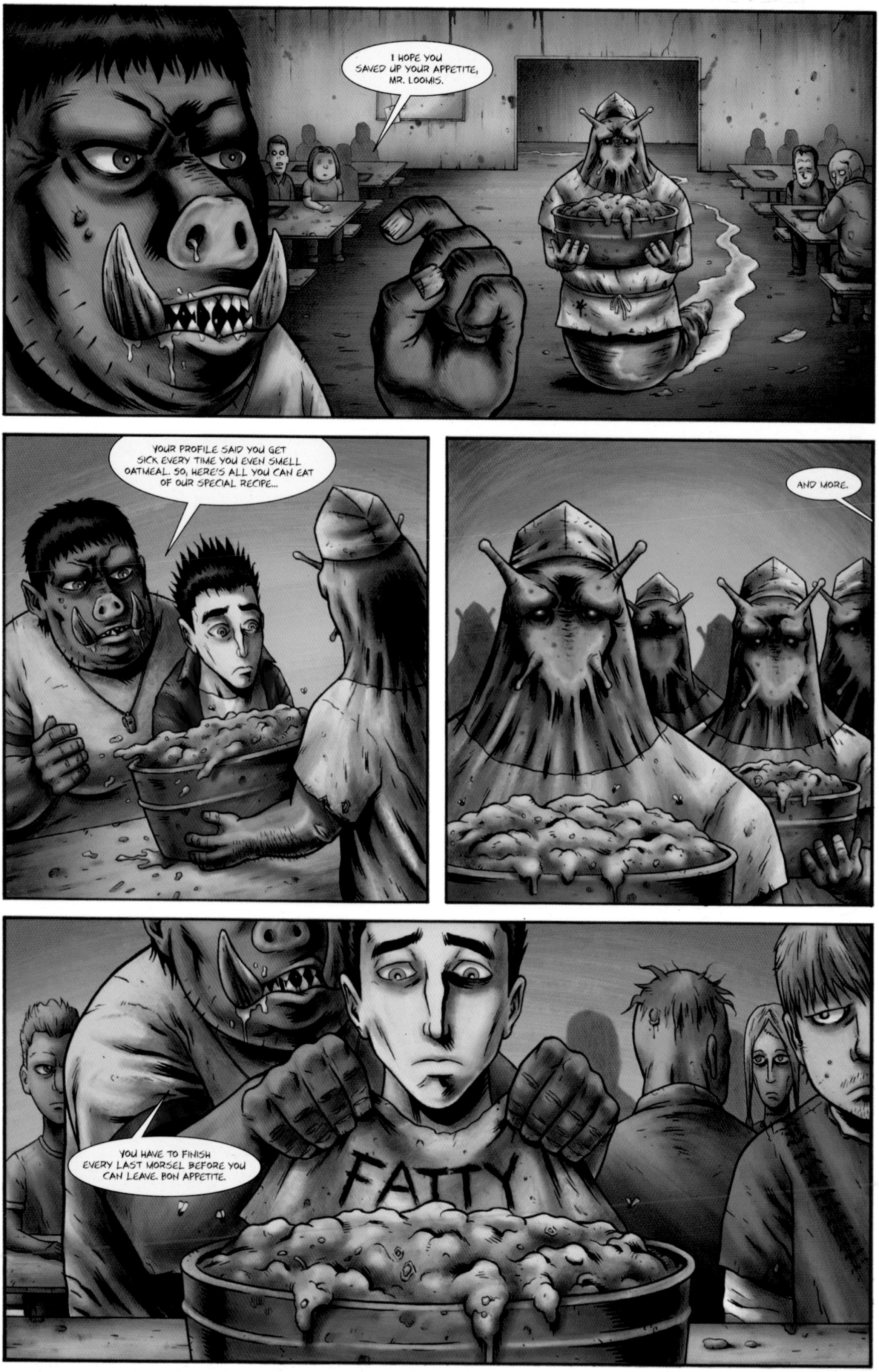
I HOPE YOU SAVED UP YOUR APPETITE, MR. LOOMIS.
YOUR PROFILE SAID YOU GET SICK EVERY TIME YOU EVEN SMELL OATMEAL. SO, HERE'S ALL YOU CAN EAT OF OUR SPECIAL RECIPE...
AND MORE.
YOU HAVE TO FINISH EVERY LAST MORSEL BEFORE YOU CAN LEAVE. BON APPETITE.
FATTY

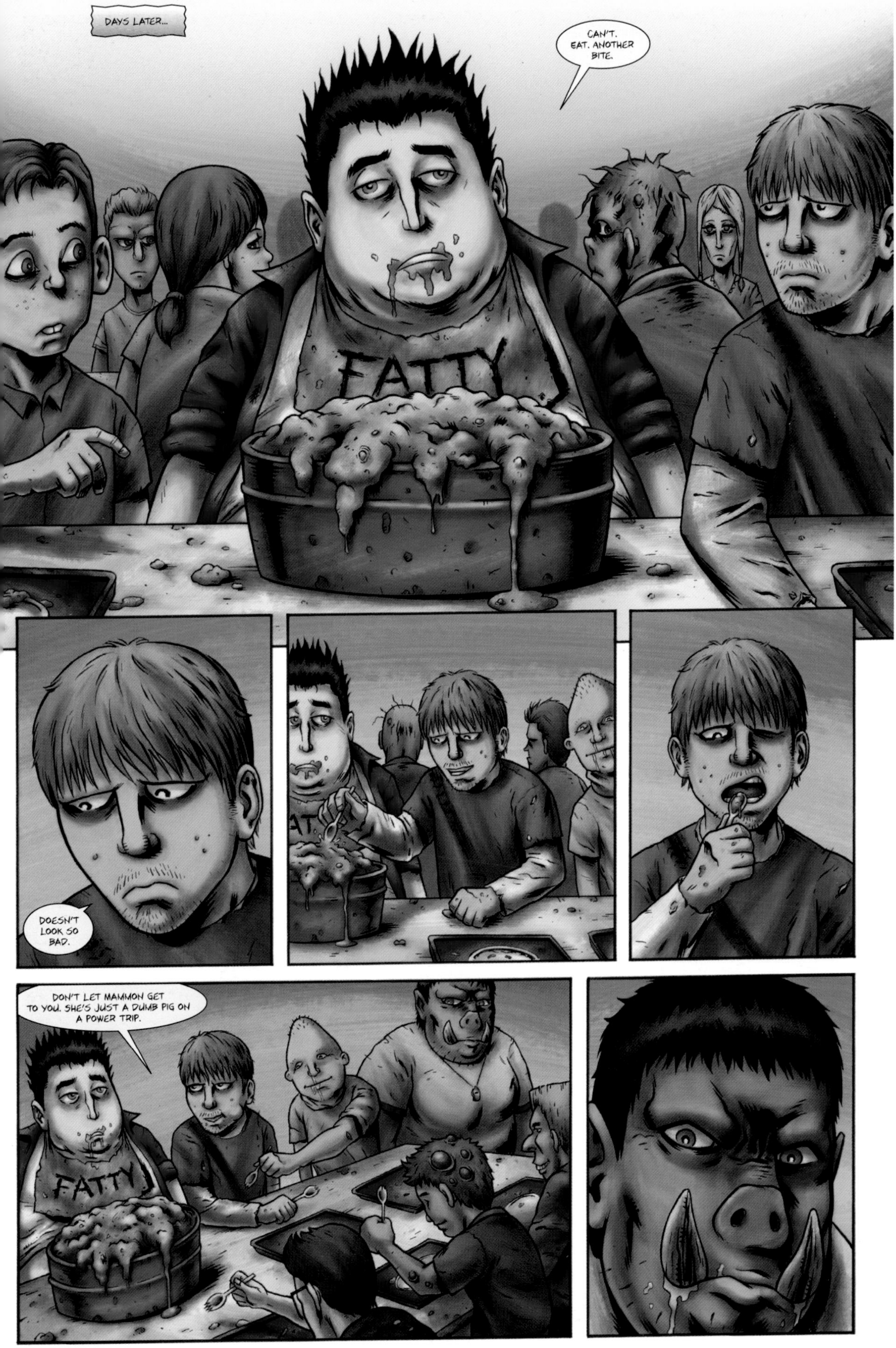
DAYS LATER...
CAN'T. EAT. ANOTHER BITE.
FATTY
DOESN'T LOOK SO BAD.
DON'T LET MAMMON GET TO YOU. SHE'S JUST A DUMB PIG ON A POWER TRIP.
FATTY

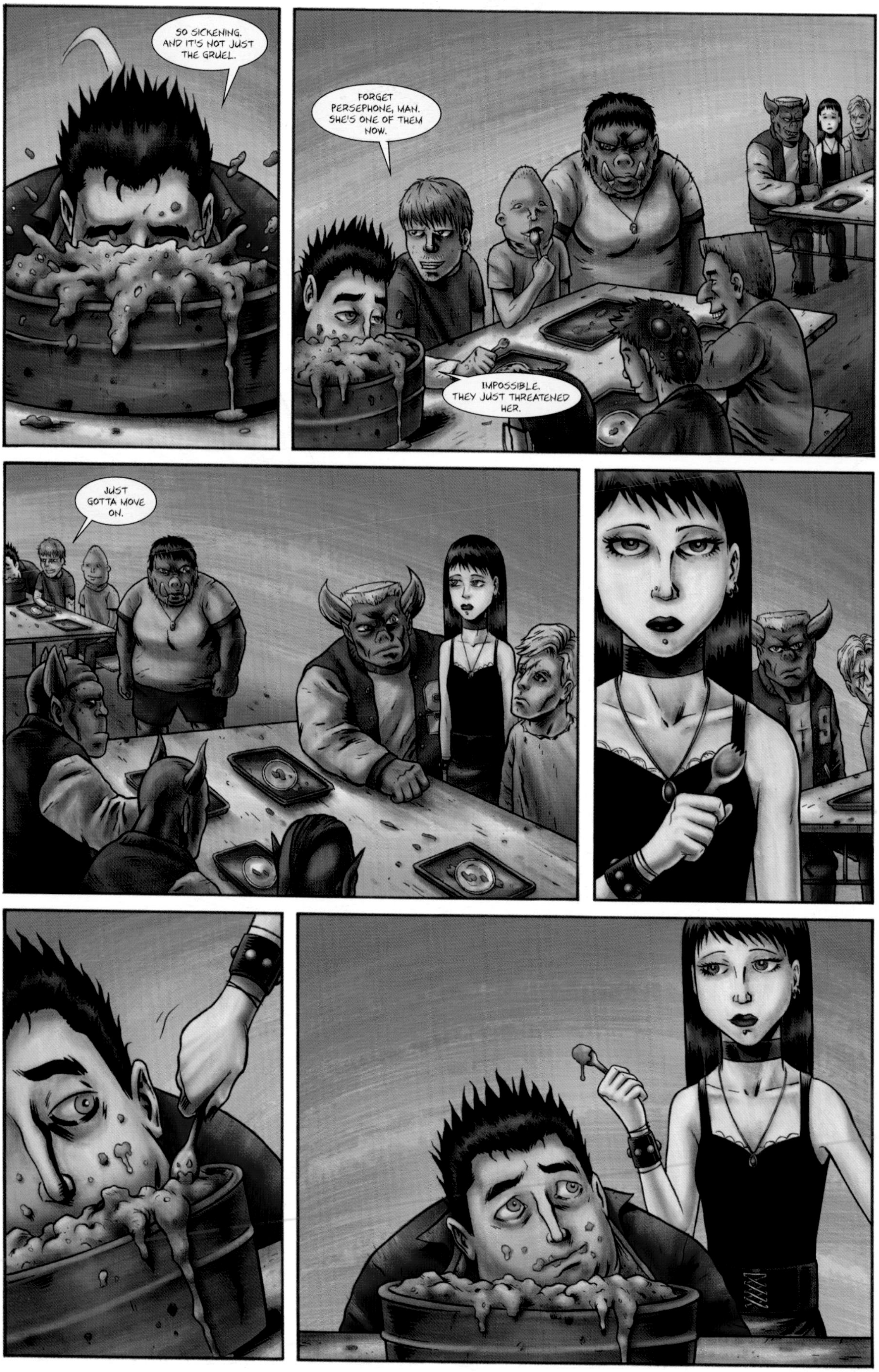
SO SICKENING. AND IT'S NOT JUST THE GRUEL.
FORGET PERSEPHONE, MAN. SHE'S ONE OF THEM NOW.
IMPOSSIBLE. THEY JUST THREATENED HER.
JUST GOTTA MOVE ON.

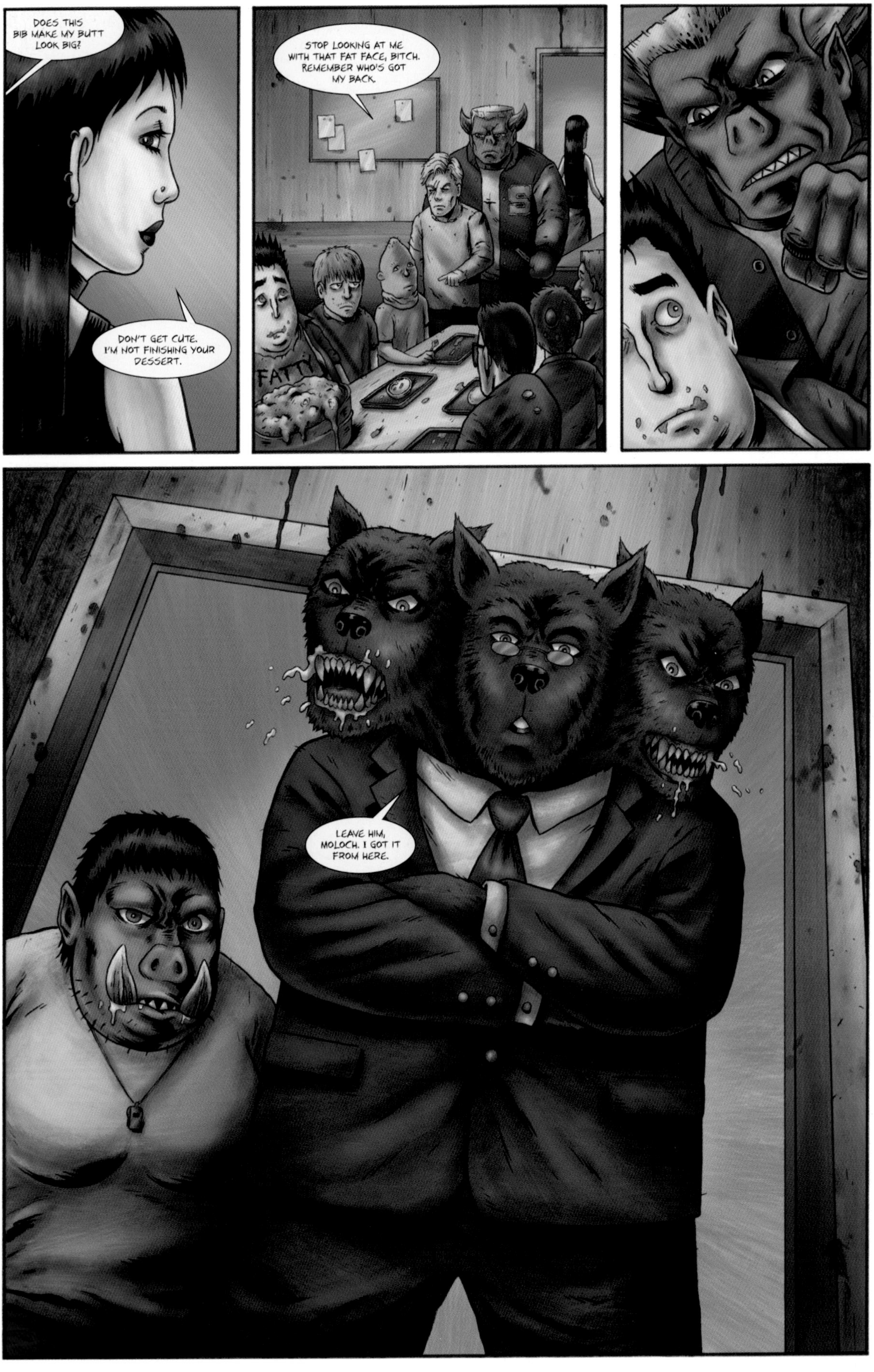
DOES THIS BIB MAKE MY BUTT LOOK BIG?
DON'T GET CUTE. I'M NOT FINISHING YOUR DESSERT.
STOP LOOKING AT ME WITH THAT FAT FACE, BITCH. REMEMBER WHO'S GOT MY BACK.
FATTY
LEAVE HIM, MOLOCH. I GOT IT FROM HERE.

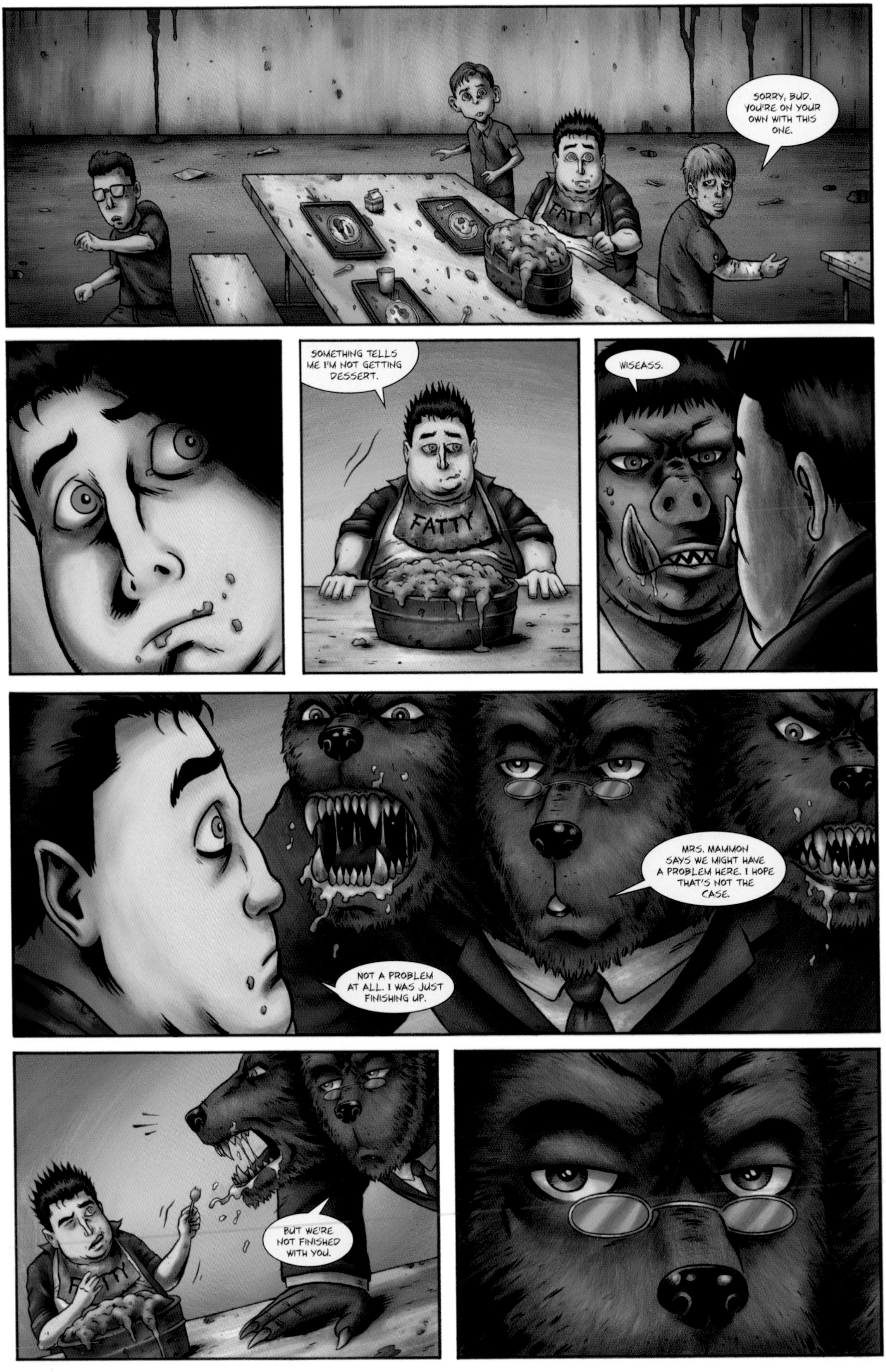
SORRY, BUD. YOU'RE ON YOUR OWN WITH THIS ONE.
SOMETHING TELLS ME I'M NOT GETTING DESSERT.
WISEASS.
MRS. MAMMON SAYS WE MIGHT HAVE A PROBLEM HERE. I HOPE THAT'S NOT THE CASE.
NOT A PROBLEM AT ALL. I WAS JUST FINISHING UP.
BUT WE'RE NOT FINISHED WITH YOU.
FATTY

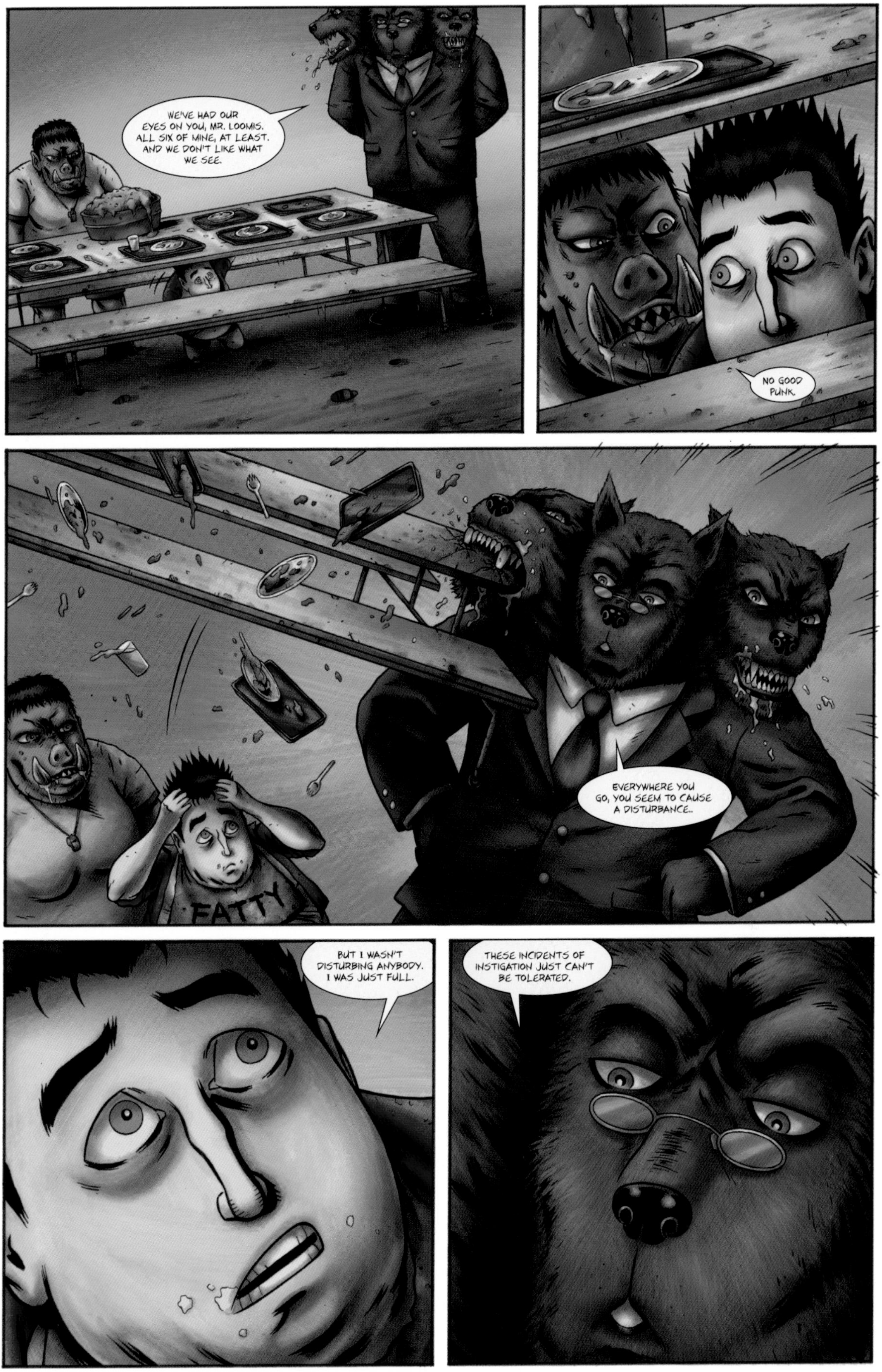
WE'VE HAD OUR EYES ON YOU, MR. LOOMIS. ALL SIX OF MINE, AT LEAST. AND WE DON'T LIKE WHAT WE SEE.
NO GOOD PUNK.
EVERYWHERE YOU GO, YOU SEEM TO CAUSE A DISTURBANCE..
FATTY
BUT I WASN'T DISTURBING ANYBODY. I WAS JUST FULL.
THESE INCIDENTS OF INSTIGATION JUST CAN'T BE TOLERATED.

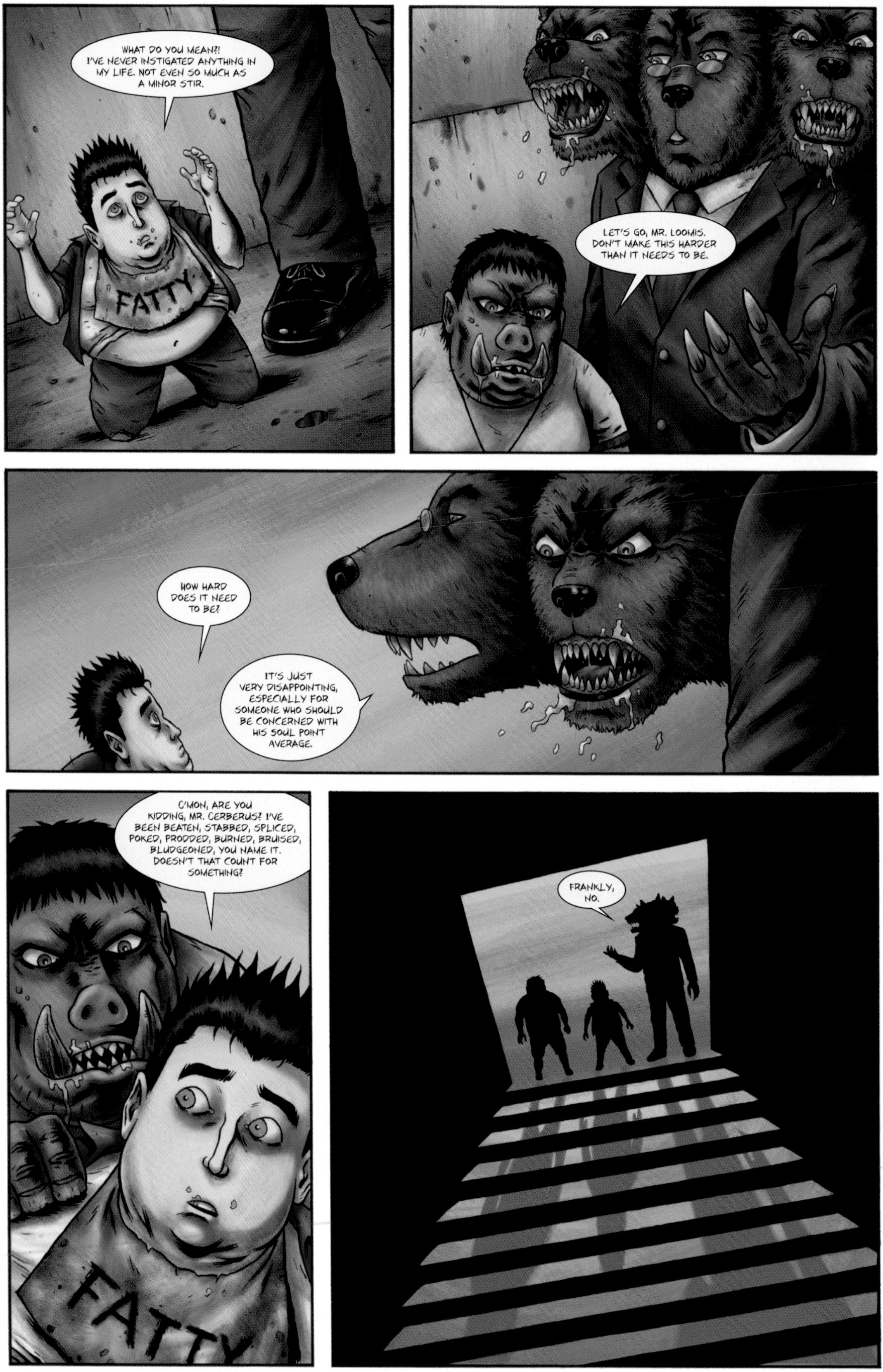
WHAT DO YOU MEAN?! I'VE NEVER INSTIGATED ANYTHING IN MY LIFE. NOT EVEN SO MUCH AS A MINOR STIR.
FATTY
LET'S GO, MR. LOOMIS. DON'T MAKE THIS HARDER THAN IT NEEDS TO BE.
HOW HARD DOES IT NEED TO BE?
IT'S JUST VERY DISAPPOINTING, ESPECIALLY FOR SOMEONE WHO SHOULD BE CONCERNED WITH HIS SOUL POINT AVERAGE.
C'MON, ARE YOU KIDDING, MR. CERBERUS? I'VE BEEN BEATEN, STABBED, SPLICED, POKED, PRODDED, BURNED, BRUISED, BLUDGEONED, YOU NAME IT. DOESN'T THAT COUNT FOR SOMETHING?
FATTY
FRANKLY, NO.

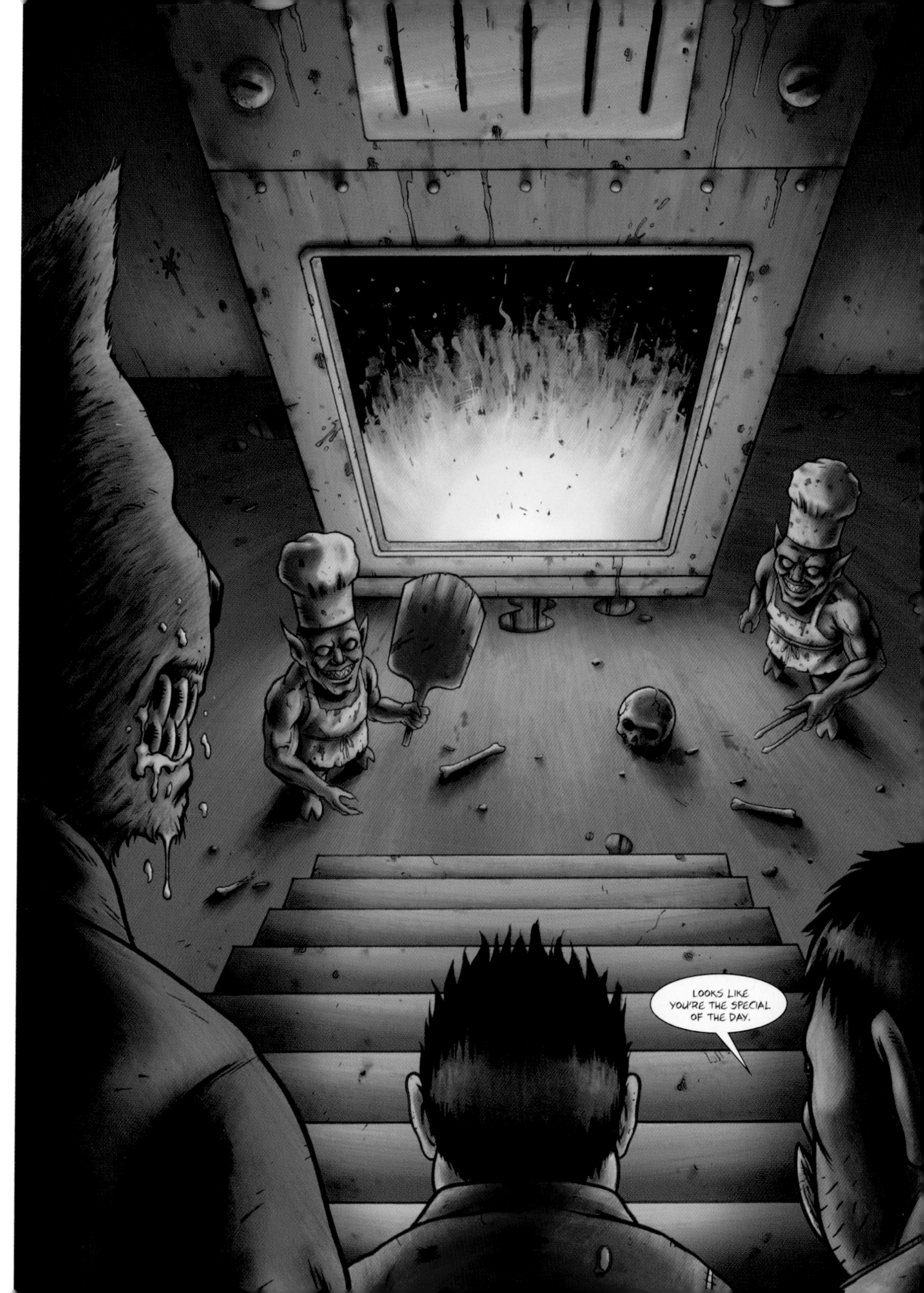
LOOKS LIKE YOU'RE THE SPECIAL OF THE DAY.

PART III

Pencils/Inks:
Luis Chichón

Colors:
Aya Ikeda-Barry
and Matthew Petz

Flats:
Keith Ikeda-Barry

Lettering:
April Brown

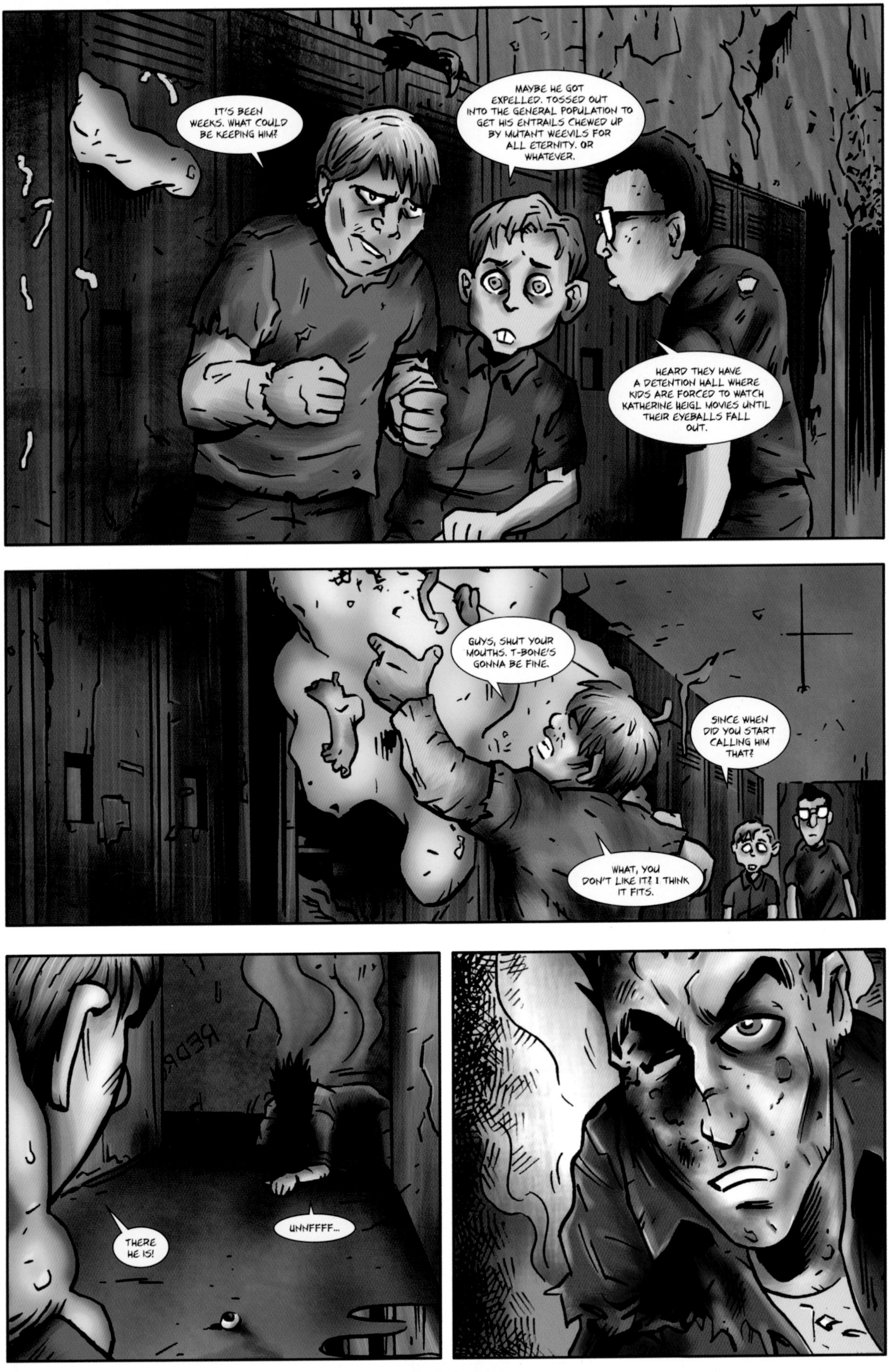
IT'S BEEN WEEKS. WHAT COULD BE KEEPING HIM?
MAYBE HE GOT EXPELLED. TOSSED OUT INTO THE GENERAL POPULATION TO GET HIS ENTRAILS CHEWED UP BY MUTANT WEEVILS FOR ALL ETERNITY. OR WHATEVER.
HEARD THEY HAVE A DETENTION HALL WHERE KIDS ARE FORCED TO WATCH KATHERINE HEIGL MOVIES UNTIL THEIR EYEBALLS FALL OUT.
GUYS, SHUT YOUR MOUTHS. T-BONE'S GONNA BE FINE.
SINCE WHEN DID YOU START CALLING HIM THAT?
WHAT, YOU DON'T LIKE IT? I THINK IT FITS.
THERE HE IS!
UNNFFFF...

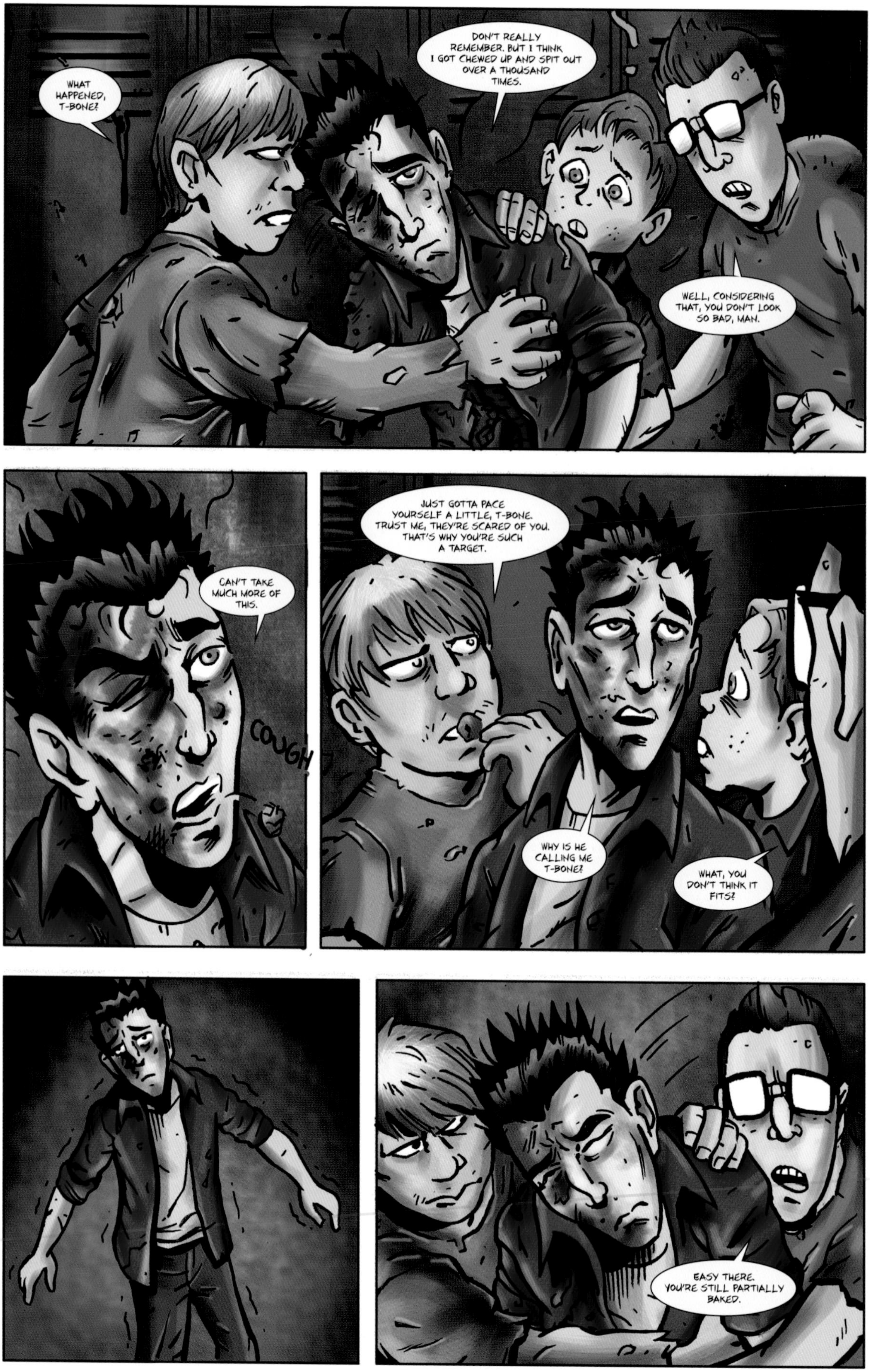
WHAT HAPPENED, T-BONE?
DON'T REALLY REMEMBER. BUT I THINK I GOT CHEWED UP AND SPIT OUT OVER A THOUSAND TIMES.
WELL, CONSIDERING THAT, YOU DON'T LOOK SO BAD, MAN.
CAN'T TAKE MUCH MORE OF THIS.
COUGH
JUST GOTTA PACE YOURSELF A LITTLE, T-BONE. TRUST ME, THEY'RE SCARED OF YOU. THAT'S WHY YOU'RE SUCH A TARGET.
WHY IS HE CALLING ME T-BONE?
WHAT, YOU DON'T THINK IT FITS?
EASY THERE. YOU'RE STILL PARTIALLY BAKED.

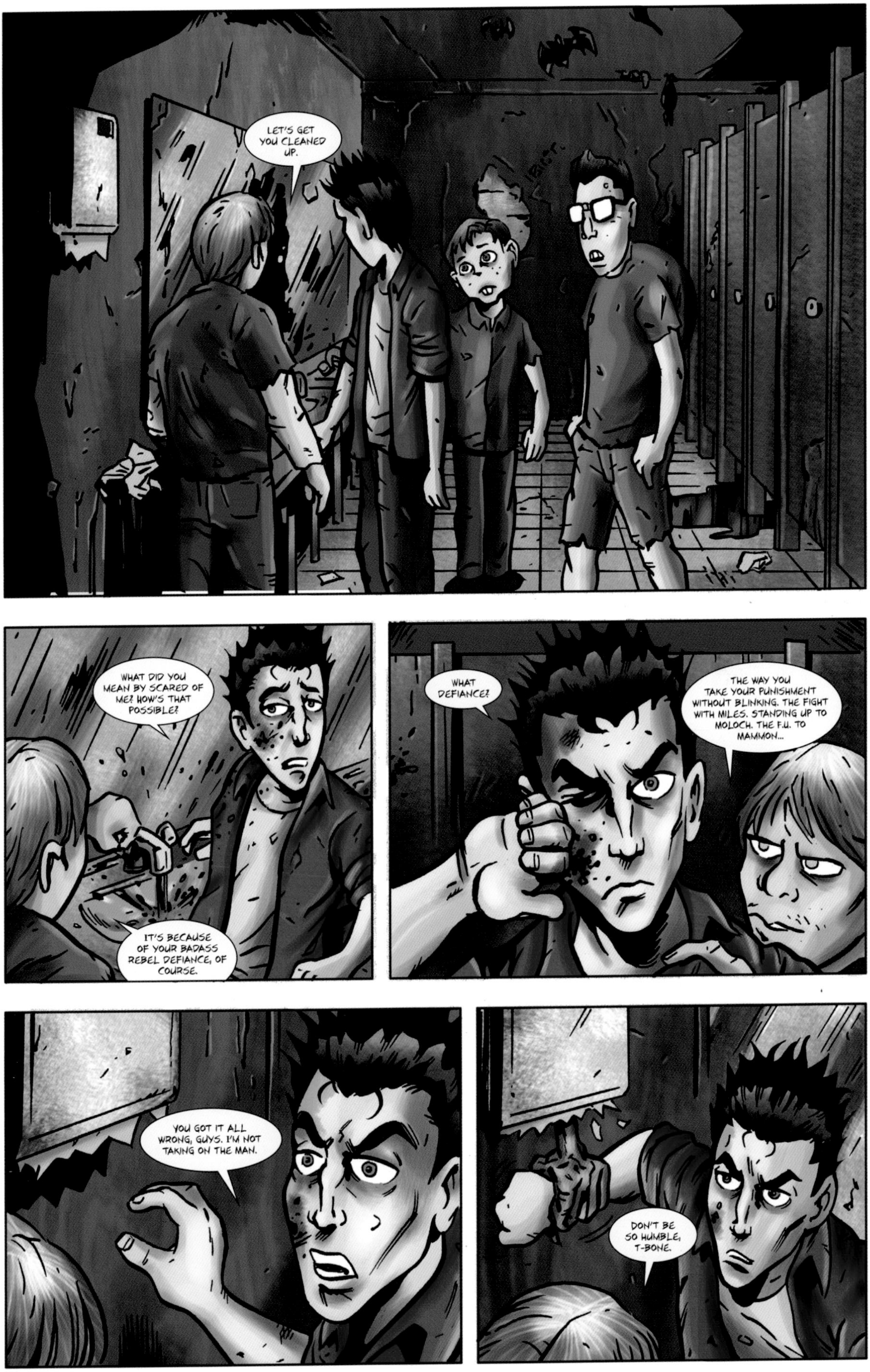
LET'S GET YOU CLEANED UP.
WHAT DID YOU MEAN BY SCARED OF ME? HOW'S THAT POSSIBLE?
IT'S BECAUSE OF YOUR BADASS REBEL DEFIANCE, OF COURSE.
WHAT DEFIANCE?
THE WAY YOU TAKE YOUR PUNISHMENT WITHOUT BLINKING. THE FIGHT WITH MILES. STANDING UP TO MOLOCH. THE F.U. TO MAMMON...
YOU GOT IT ALL WRONG, GUYS. I'M NOT TAKING ON THE MAN.
DON'T BE SO HUMBLE, T-BONE.

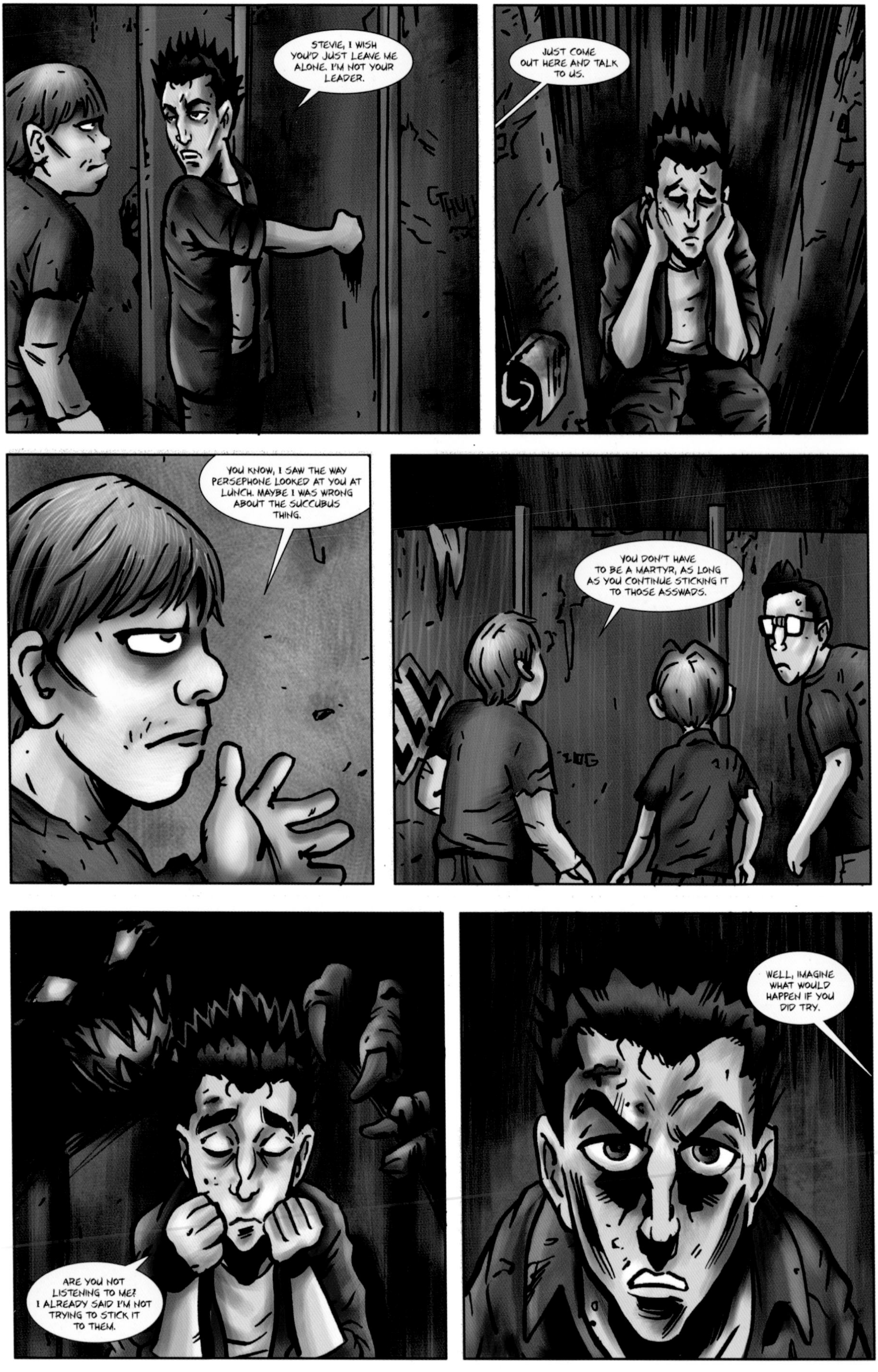
STEVIE, I WISH YOU'D JUST LEAVE ME ALONE. I'M NOT YOUR LEADER.
JUST COME OUT HERE AND TALK TO US.
YOU KNOW, I SAW THE WAY PERSEPHONE LOOKED AT YOU AT LUNCH. MAYBE I WAS WRONG ABOUT THE SUCCUBUS THING.
YOU DON'T HAVE TO BE A MARTYR, AS LONG AS YOU CONTINUE STICKING IT TO THOSE ASSWADS.
ARE YOU NOT LISTENING TO ME? I ALREADY SAID I'M NOT TRYING TO STICK IT TO THEM.
WELL, IMAGINE WHAT WOULD HAPPEN IF YOU DID TRY.

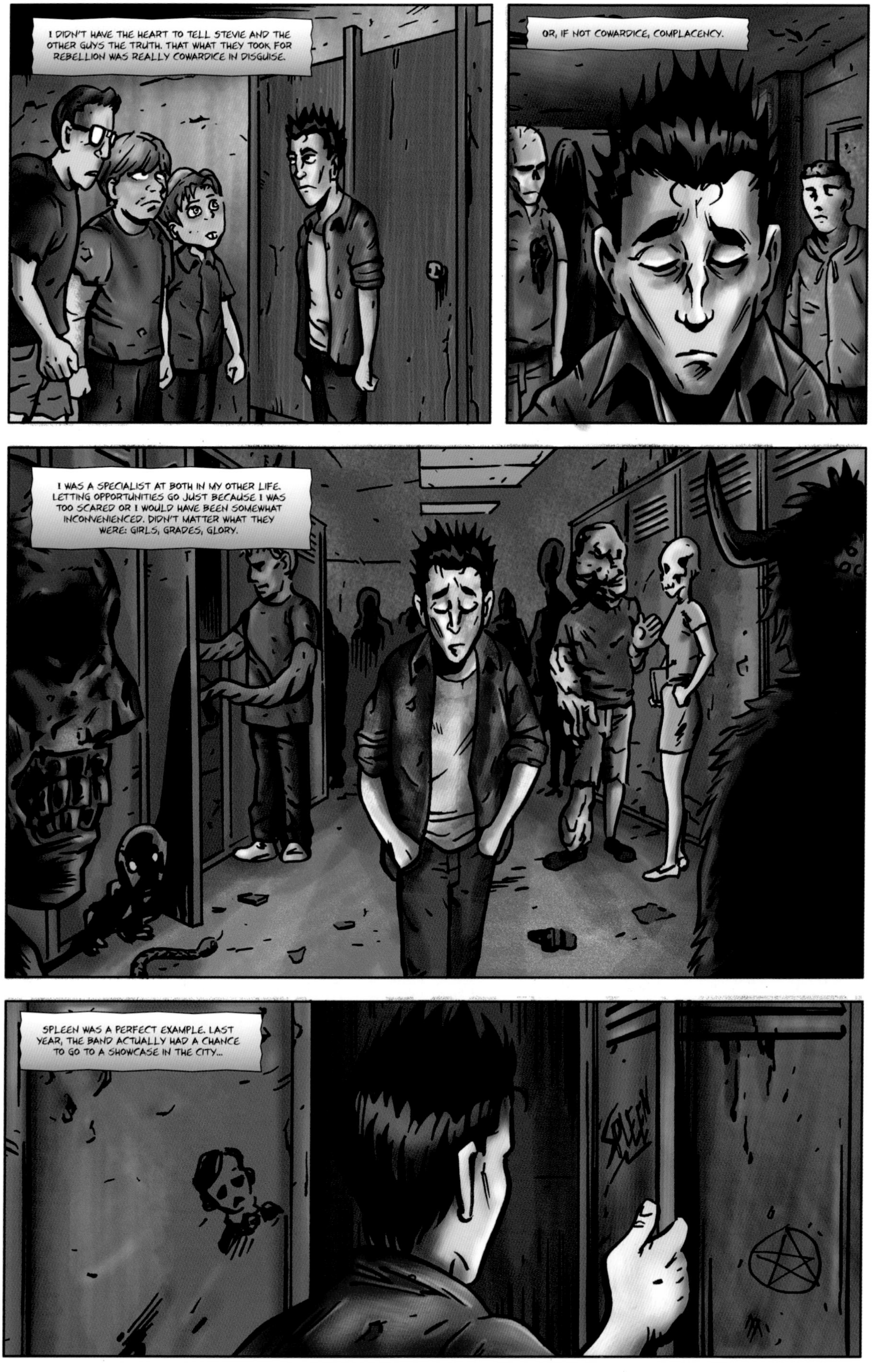
I DIDN'T HAVE THE HEART TO TELL STEVIE AND THE OTHER GUYS THE TRUTH. THAT WHAT THEY TOOK FOR REBELLION WAS REALLY COWARDICE IN DISGUISE.
OR, IF NOT COWARDICE, COMPLACENCY.
I WAS A SPECIALIST AT BOTH IN MY OTHER LIFE. LETTING OPPORTUNITIES GO JUST BECAUSE I WAS TOO SCARED OR I WOULD HAVE BEEN SOMEWHAT INCONVENIENCED. DIDN'T MATTER WHAT THEY WERE: GIRLS, GRADES, GLORY.
SPLEEN WAS A PERFECT EXAMPLE. LAST YEAR, THE BAND ACTUALLY HAD A CHANCE TO GO TO A SHOWCASE IN THE CITY...
SPLEEN

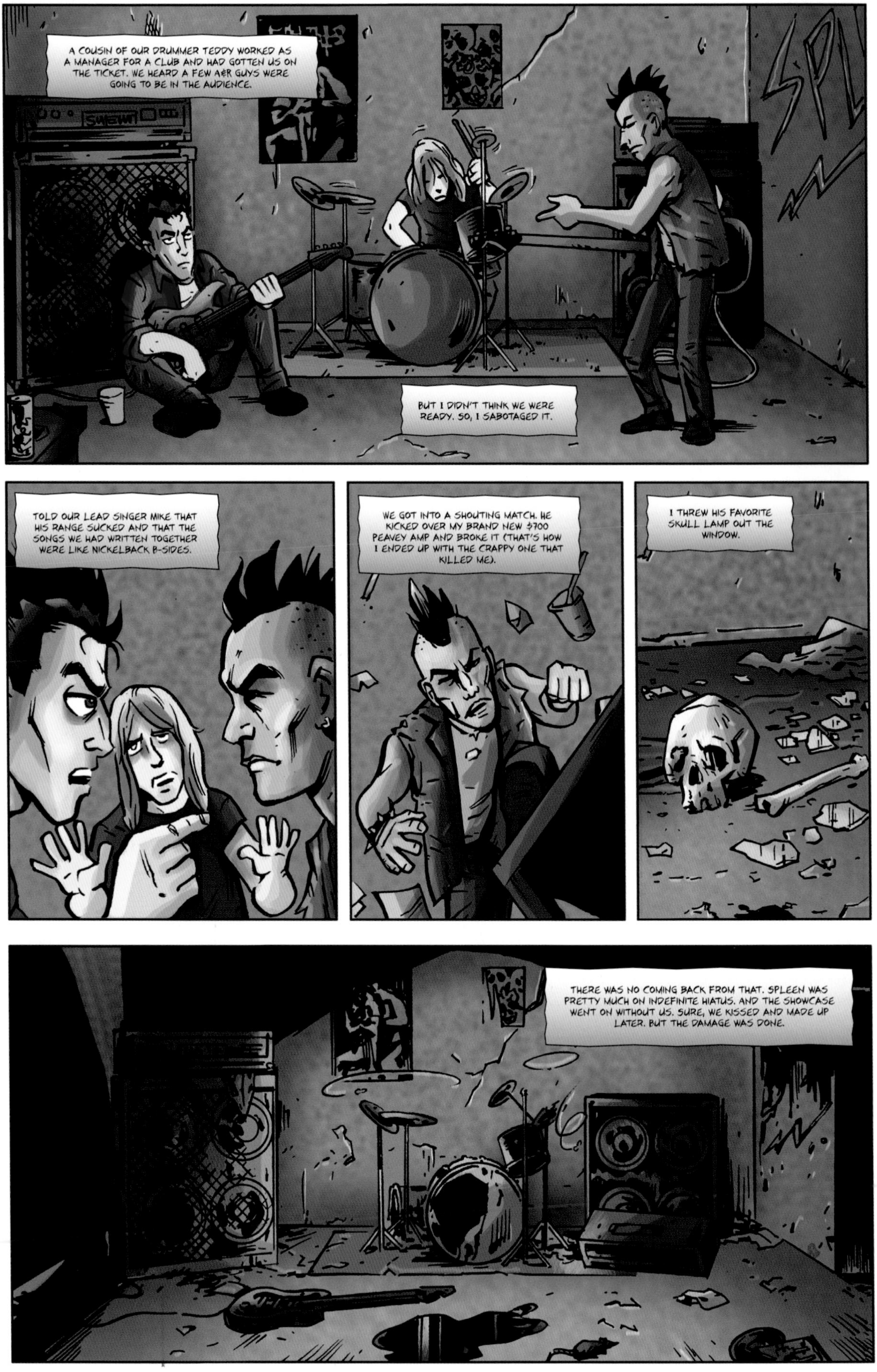

A COUSIN OF OUR DRUMMER TEDDY WORKED AS A MANAGER FOR A CLUB AND HAD GOTTEN US ON THE TICKET. WE HEARD A FEW A&R GUYS WERE GOING TO BE IN THE AUDIENCE.
BUT I DIDN'T THINK WE WERE READY. SO, I SABOTAGED IT.
TOLD OUR LEAD SINGER MIKE THAT HIS RANGE SUCKED AND THAT THE SONGS WE HAD WRITTEN TOGETHER WERE LIKE NICKELBACK B-SIDES.
WE GOT INTO A SHOUTING MATCH. HE KICKED OVER MY BRAND NEW $700 PEAVEY AMP AND BROKE IT (THAT'S HOW I ENDED UP WITH THE CRAPPY ONE THAT KILLED ME).
I THREW HIS FAVORITE SKULL LAMP OUT THE WINDOW.
THERE WAS NO COMING BACK FROM THAT. SPLEEN WAS PRETTY MUCH ON INDEFINITE HIATUS. AND THE SHOWCASE WENT ON WITHOUT US. SURE, WE KISSED AND MADE UP LATER. BUT THE DAMAGE WAS DONE.

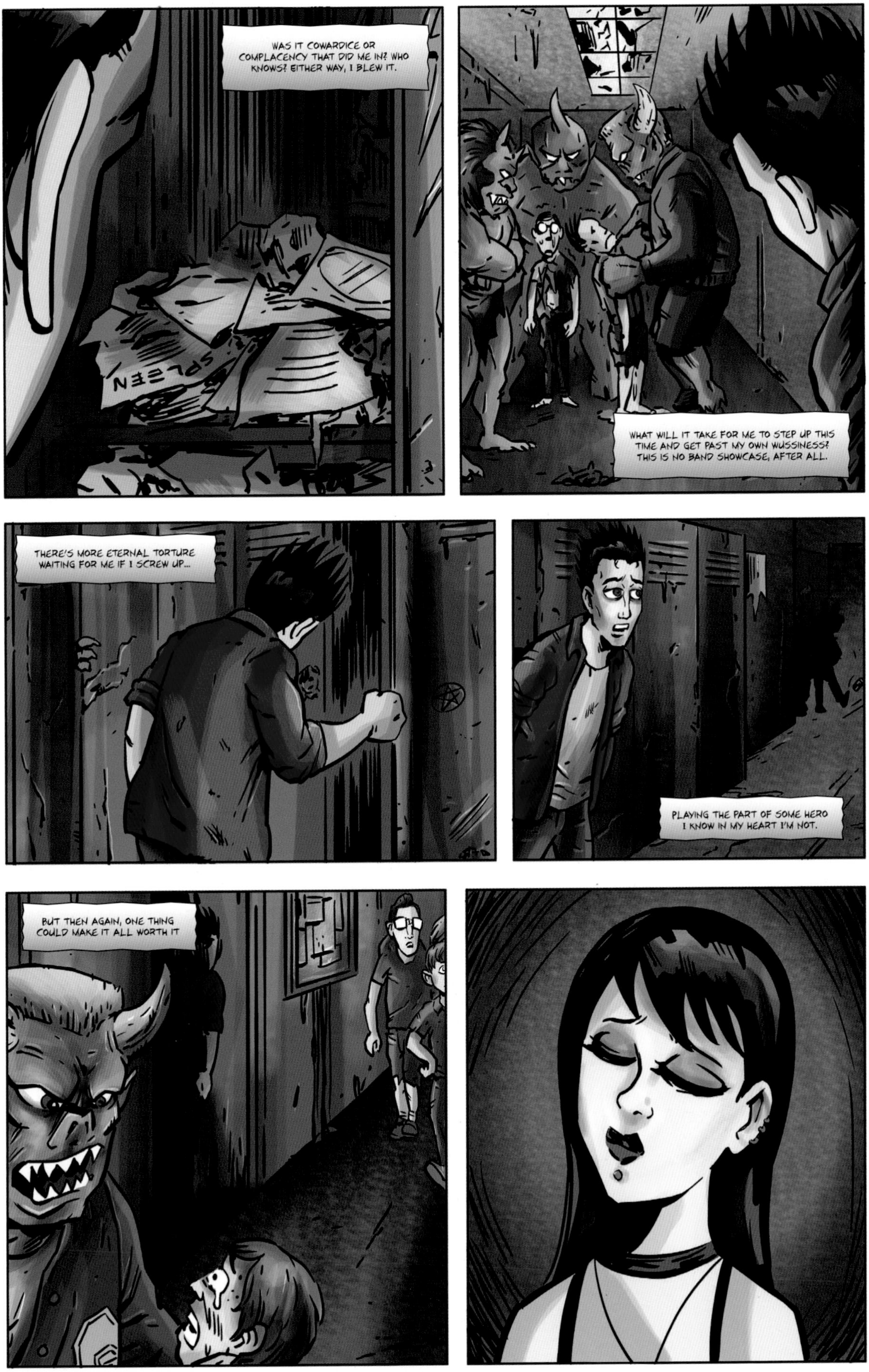
WAS IT COWARDICE OR COMPLACENCY THAT DID ME IN? WHO KNOWS? EITHER WAY, I BLEW IT.
SPLEEN
WHAT WILL IT TAKE FOR ME TO STEP UP THIS TIME AND GET PAST MY OWN WUSSINESS? THIS IS NO BAND SHOWCASE, AFTER ALL.
THERE'S MORE ETERNAL TORTURE WAITING FOR ME IF I SCREW UP...
PLAYING THE PART OF SOME HERO I KNOW IN MY HEART I'M NOT.
BUT THEN AGAIN, ONE THING COULD MAKE IT ALL WORTH IT

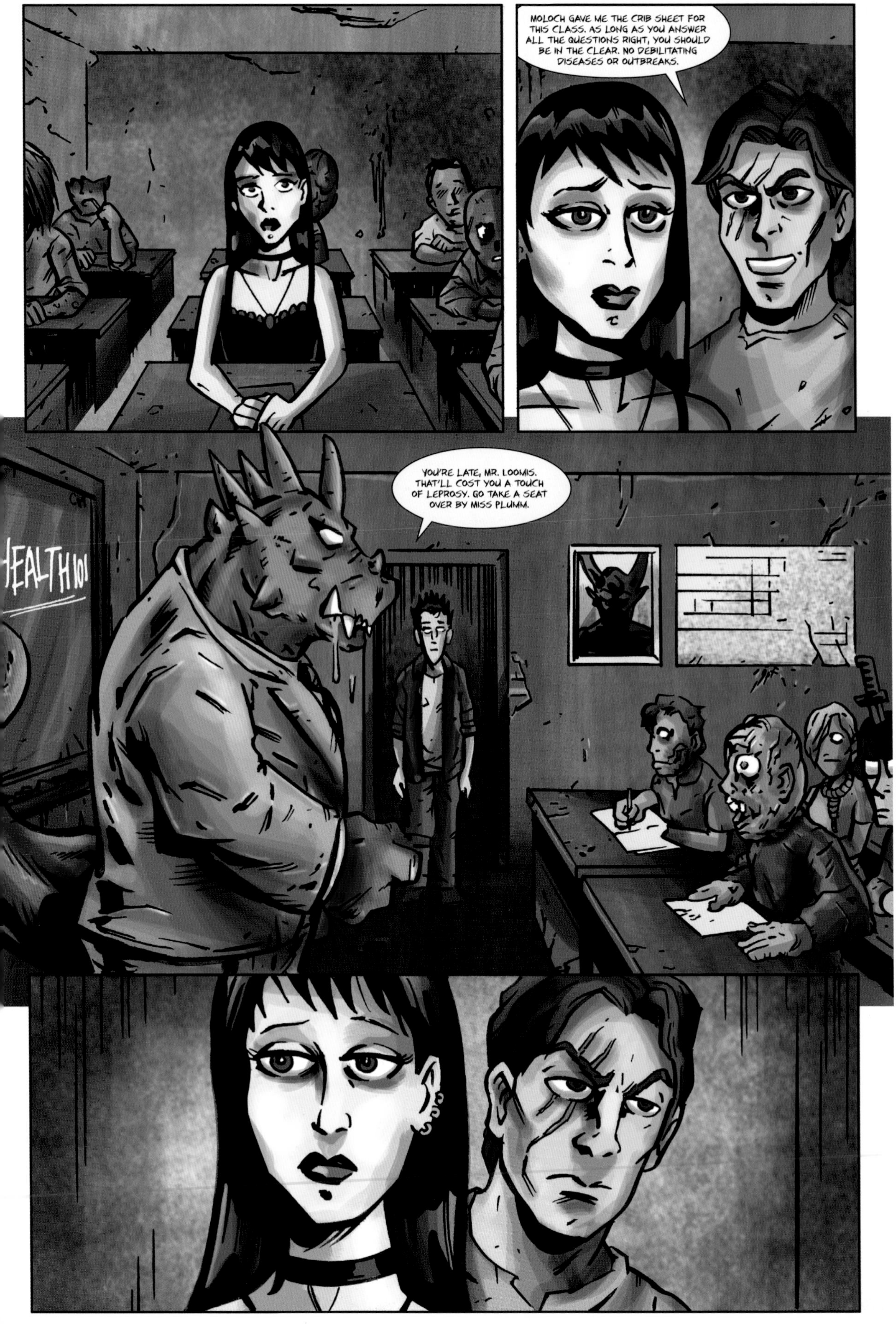
MOLOCH GAVE ME THE CRIB SHEET FOR THIS CLASS. AS LONG AS YOU ANSWER ALL THE QUESTIONS RIGHT, YOU SHOULD BE IN THE CLEAR. NO DEBILITATING DISEASES OR OUTBREAKS.
YOU'RE LATE, MR. LOOMIS. THAT'LL COST YOU A TOUCH OF LEPROSY. GO TAKE A SEAT OVER BY MISS PLUMM.
HEALTH 101

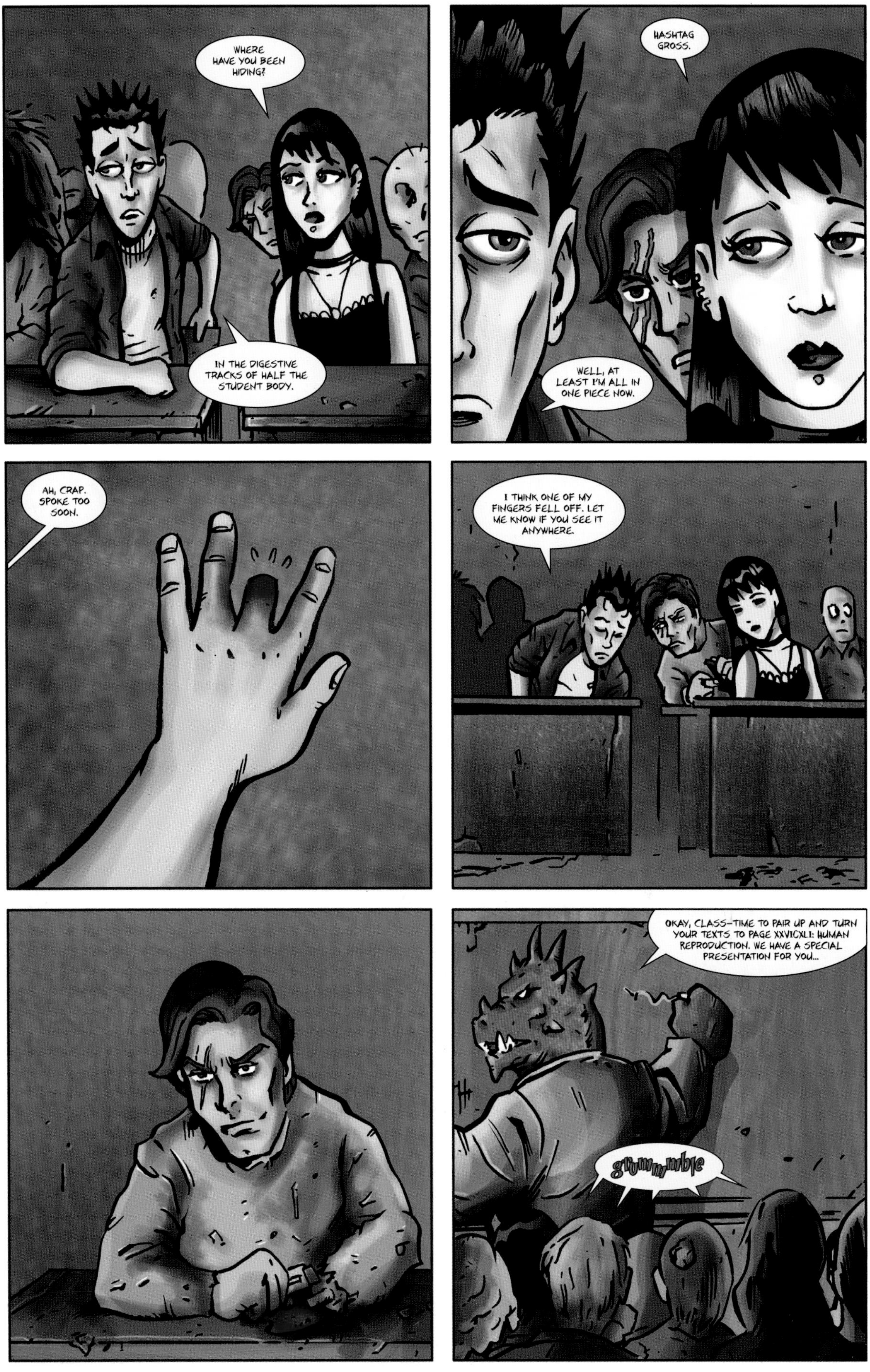
WHERE HAVE YOU BEEN HIDING?
IN THE DIGESTIVE TRACKS OF HALF THE STUDENT BODY.
HASHTAG GROSS.
WELL, AT LEAST I'M ALL IN ONE PIECE NOW.
AH, CRAP. SPOKE TOO SOON.
I THINK ONE OF MY FINGERS FELL OFF. LET ME KNOW IF YOU SEE IT ANYWHERE.
OKAY, CLASS—TIME TO PAIR UP AND TURN YOUR TEXTS TO PAGE XXVICXLI: HUMAN REPRODUCTION. WE HAVE A SPECIAL PRESENTATION FOR YOU...
grummmble

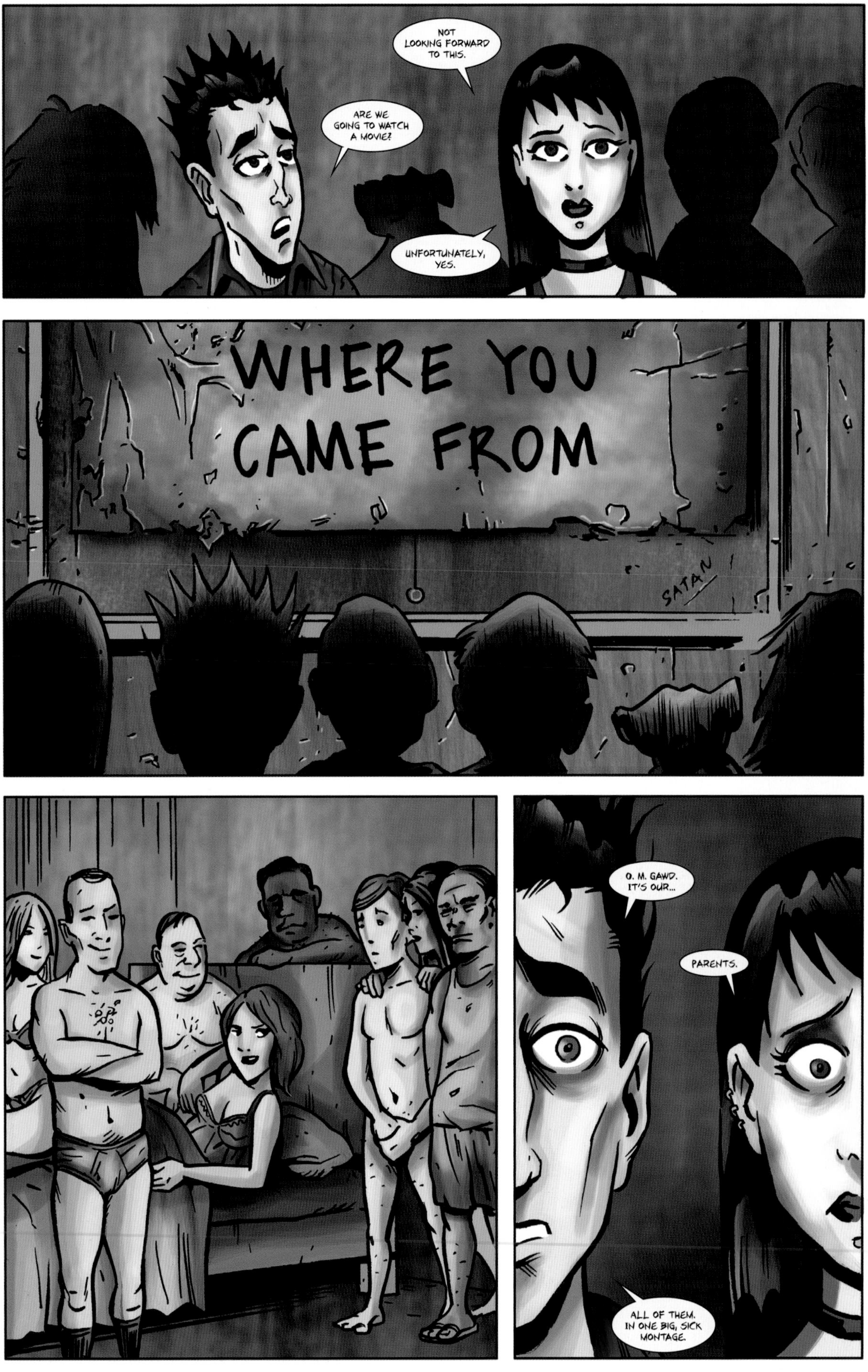
ARE WE GOING TO WATCH A MOVIE?
NOT LOOKING FORWARD TO THIS.
UNFORTUNATELY, YES.
WHERE YOU CAME FROM
SATAN
O. M. GAWD. IT'S OUR...
PARENTS.
ALL OF THEM. IN ONE BIG, SICK MONTAGE.

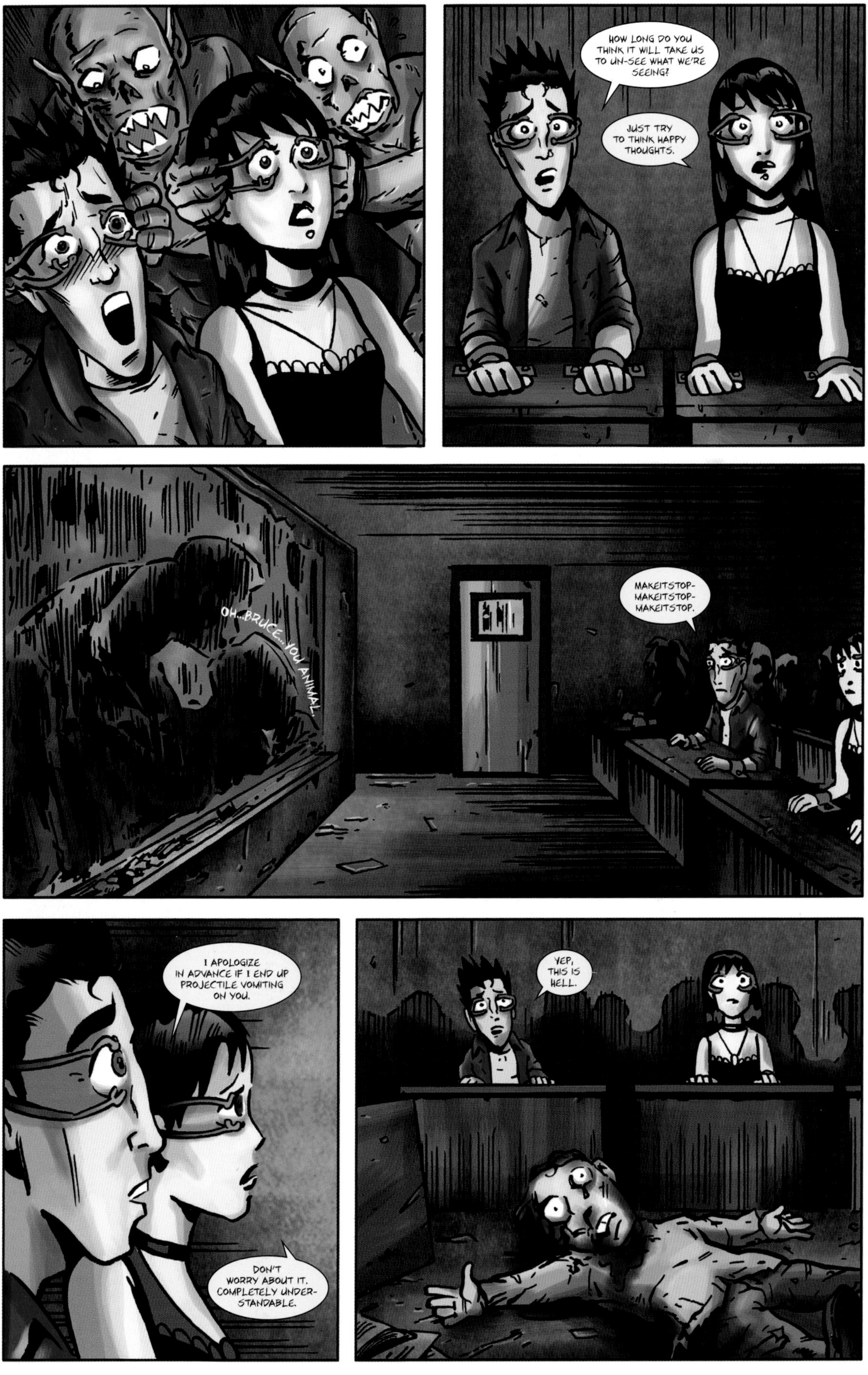
HOW LONG DO YOU THINK IT WILL TAKE US TO UN-SEE WHAT WE'RE SEEING?
JUST TRY TO THINK HAPPY THOUGHTS.
OH...BRUCE...YOU ANIMAL.
MAKEITSTOP-MAKEITSTOP-MAKEITSTOP.
I APOLOGIZE IN ADVANCE IF I END UP PROJECTILE VOMITING ON YOU.
DON'T WORRY ABOUT IT. COMPLETELY UNDER-STANDABLE.
YEP, THIS IS HELL.

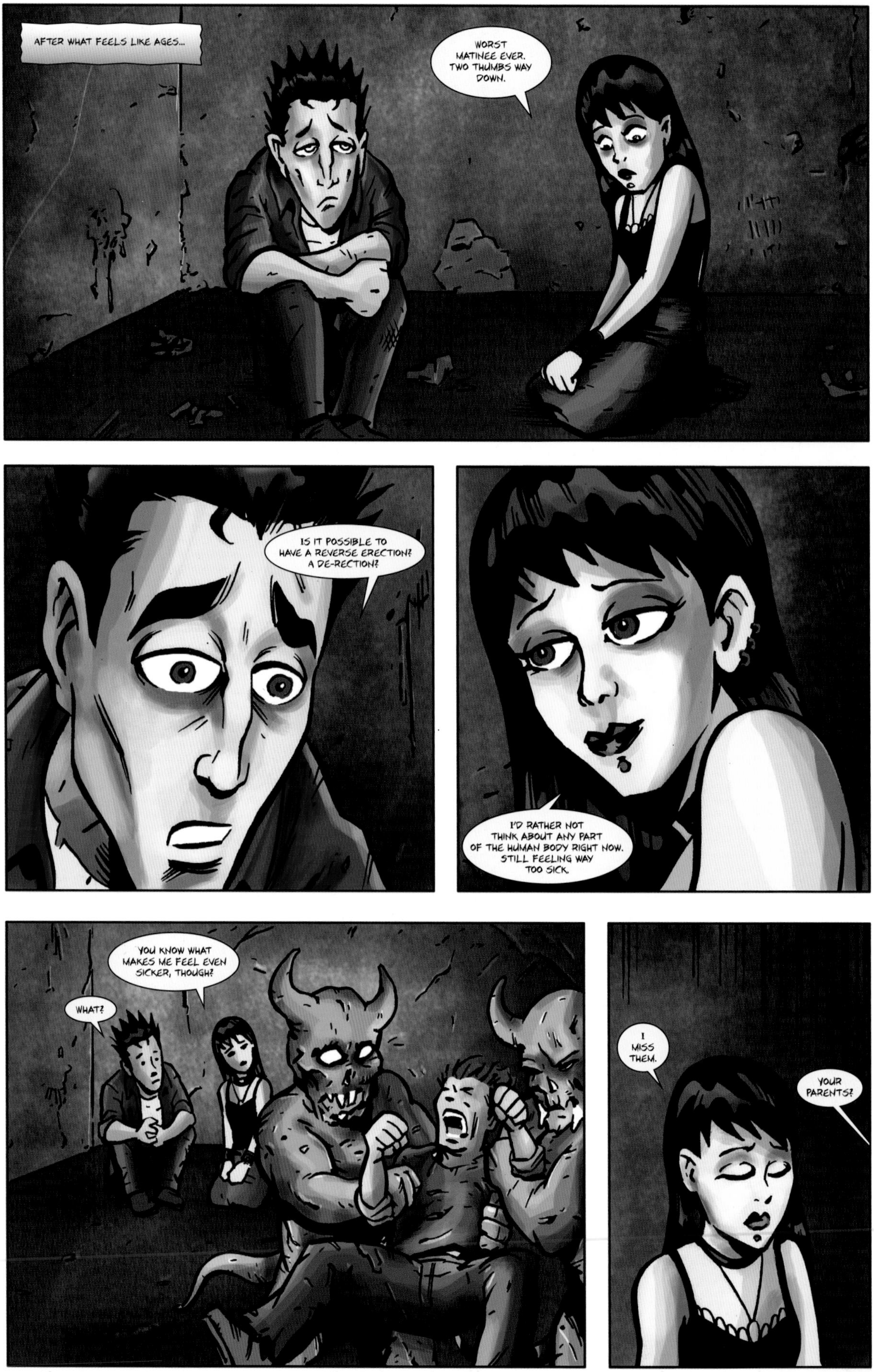
AFTER WHAT FEELS LIKE AGES...
WORST MATINEE EVER. TWO THUMBS WAY DOWN.
IS IT POSSIBLE TO HAVE A REVERSE ERECTION? A DE-RECTION?
I'D RATHER NOT THINK ABOUT ANY PART OF THE HUMAN BODY RIGHT NOW. STILL FEELING WAY TOO SICK.
YOU KNOW WHAT MAKES ME FEEL EVEN SICKER, THOUGH?
WHAT?
I MISS THEM.
YOUR PARENTS?

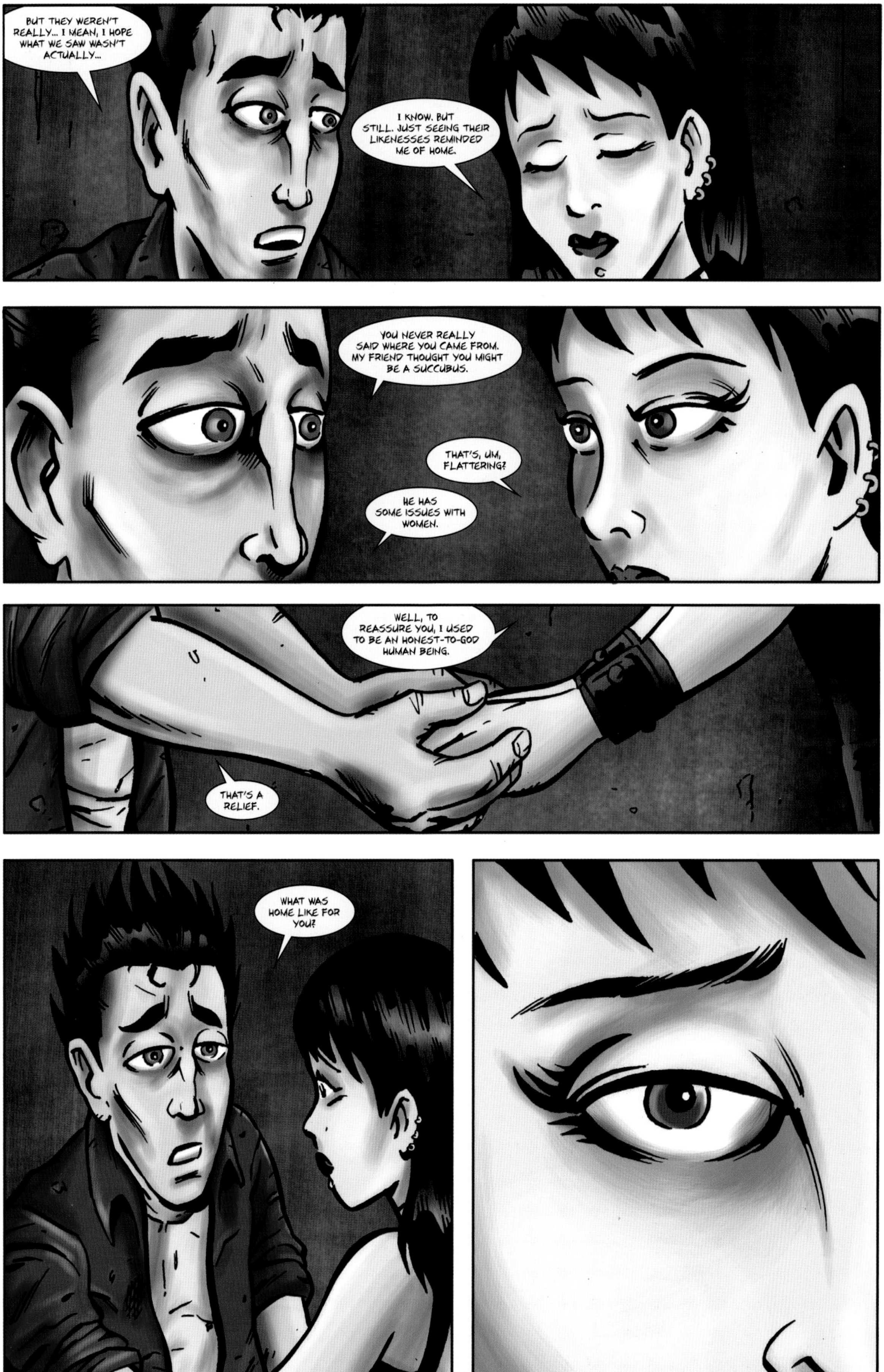
BUT THEY WEREN'T REALLY... I MEAN, I HOPE WHAT WE SAW WASN'T ACTUALLY...
I KNOW. BUT STILL. JUST SEEING THEIR LIKENESSES REMINDED ME OF HOME.
YOU NEVER REALLY SAID WHERE YOU CAME FROM. MY FRIEND THOUGHT YOU MIGHT BE A SUCCUBUS.
THAT'S, UM, FLATTERING?
HE HAS SOME ISSUES WITH WOMEN.
WELL, TO REASSURE YOU, I USED TO BE AN HONEST-TO-GOD HUMAN BEING.
THAT'S A RELIEF.
WHAT WAS HOME LIKE FOR YOU?

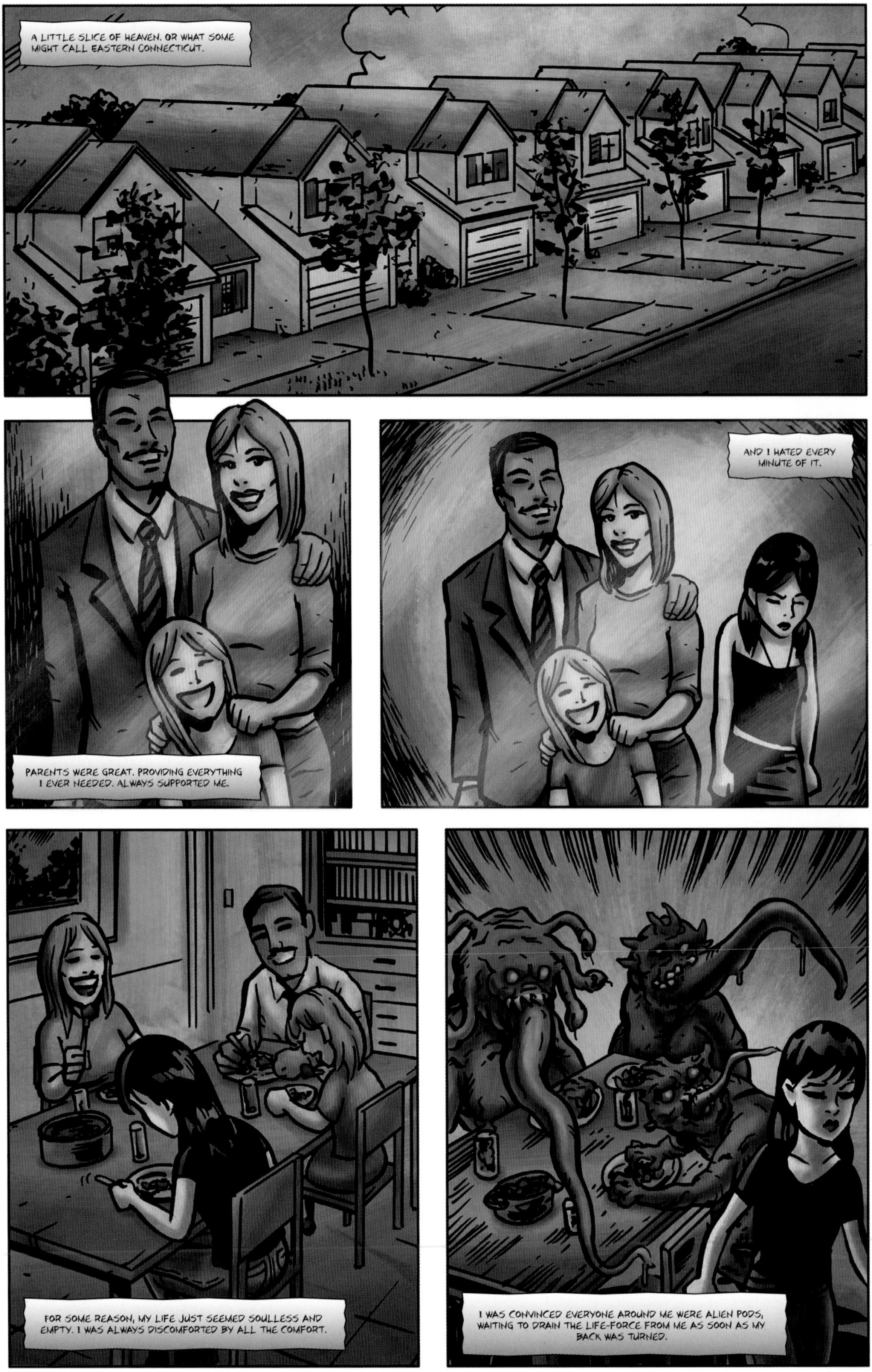
A LITTLE SLICE OF HEAVEN. OR WHAT SOME MIGHT CALL EASTERN CONNECTICUT.
PARENTS WERE GREAT. PROVIDING EVERYTHING I EVER NEEDED. ALWAYS SUPPORTED ME.
AND I HATED EVERY MINUTE OF IT.
FOR SOME REASON, MY LIFE JUST SEEMED SOULLESS AND EMPTY. I WAS ALWAYS DISCOMFORTED BY ALL THE COMFORT.
I WAS CONVINCED EVERYONE AROUND ME WERE ALIEN PODS, WAITING TO DRAIN THE LIFE-FORCE FROM ME AS SOON AS MY BACK WAS TURNED.

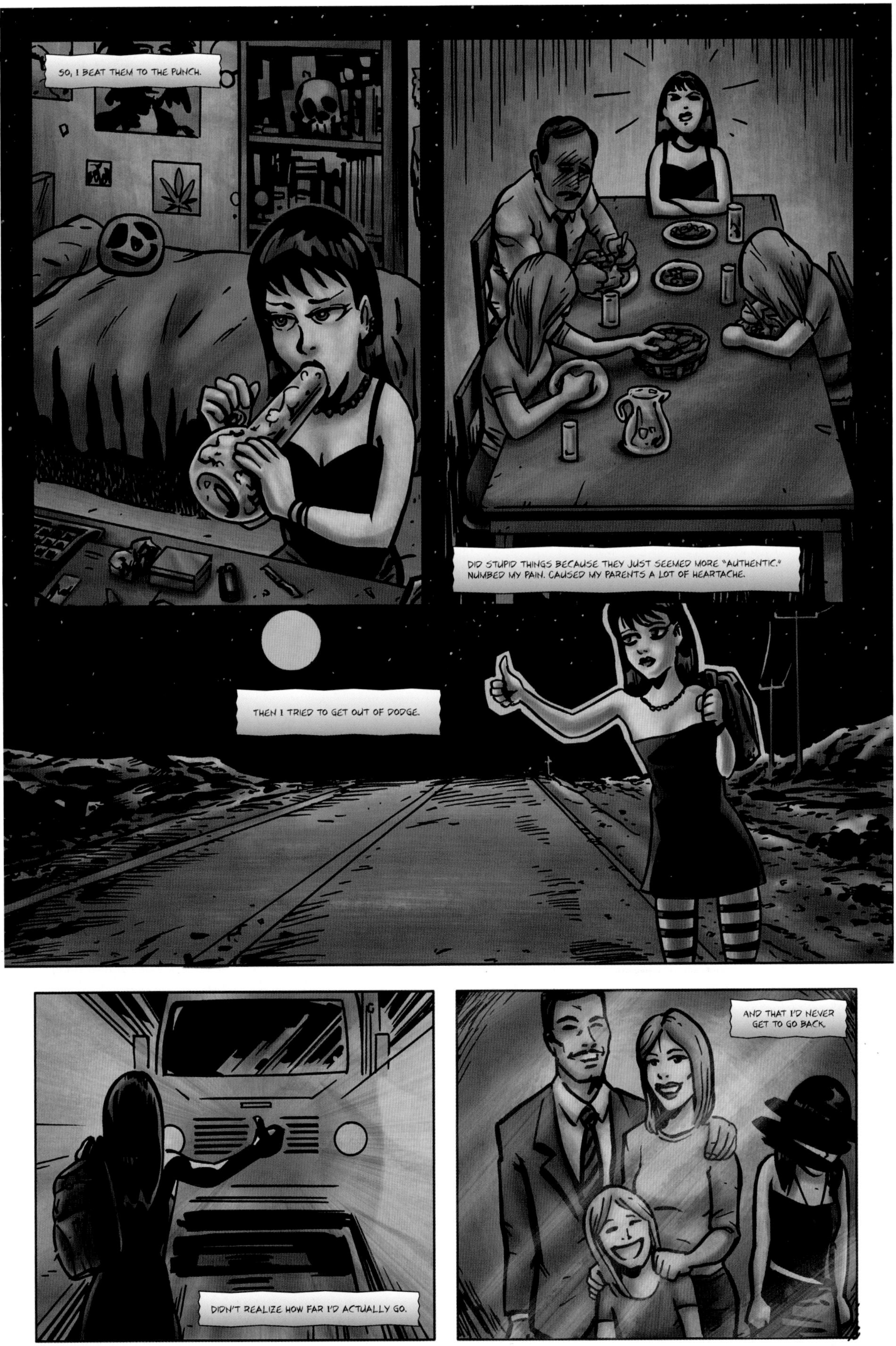
SO, I BEAT THEM TO THE PUNCH.
DID STUPID THINGS BECAUSE THEY JUST SEEMED MORE "AUTHENTIC." NUMBED MY PAIN. CAUSED MY PARENTS A LOT OF HEARTACHE.
THEN I TRIED TO GET OUT OF DODGE.
DIDN'T REALIZE HOW FAR I'D ACTUALLY GO.
AND THAT I'D NEVER GET TO GO BACK.

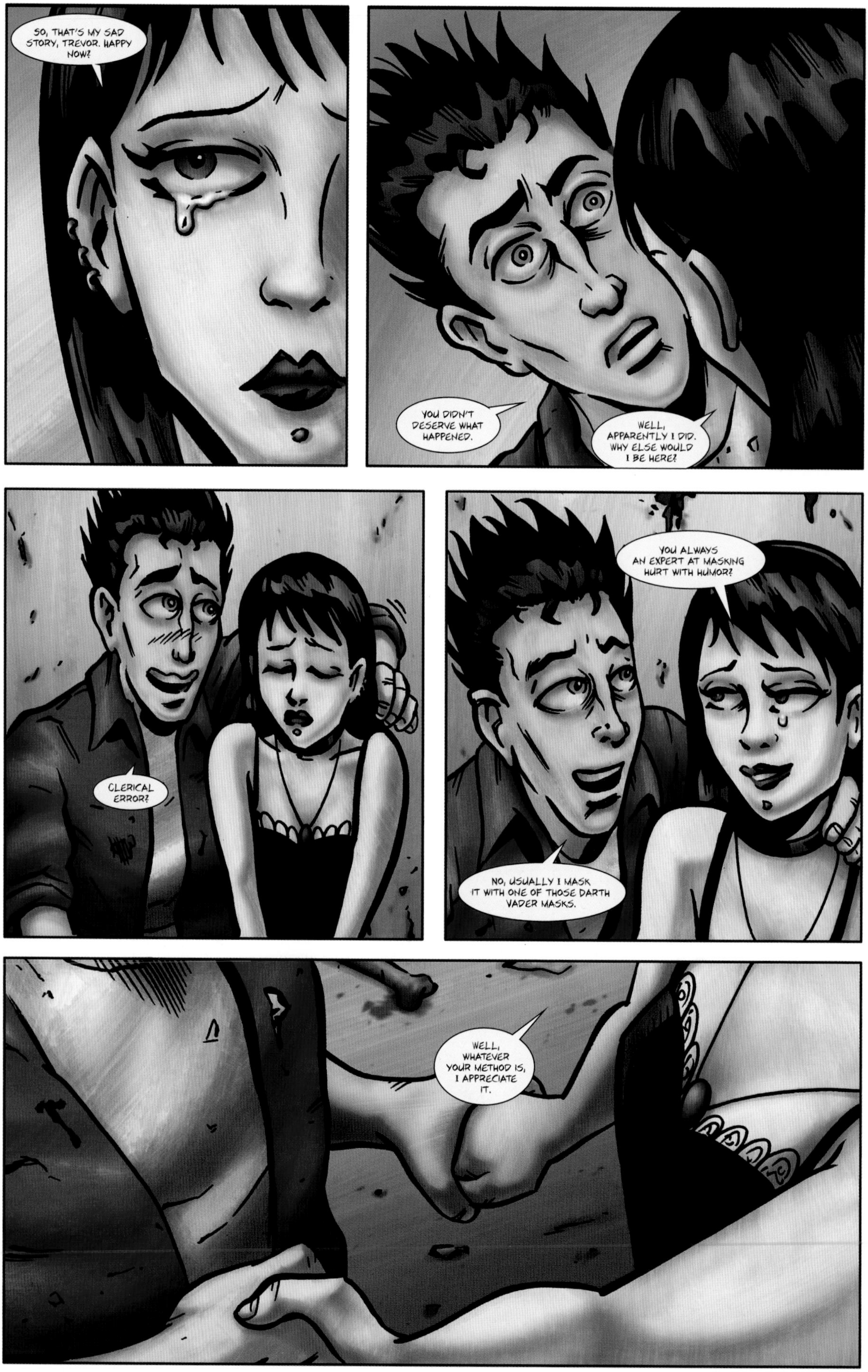
SO, THAT'S MY SAD STORY, TREVOR. HAPPY NOW?
YOU DIDN'T DESERVE WHAT HAPPENED.
WELL, APPARENTLY I DID. WHY ELSE WOULD I BE HERE?
CLERICAL ERROR?
YOU ALWAYS AN EXPERT AT MASKING HURT WITH HUMOR?
NO, USUALLY I MASK IT WITH ONE OF THOSE DARTH VADER MASKS.
WELL, WHATEVER YOUR METHOD IS, I APPRECIATE IT.

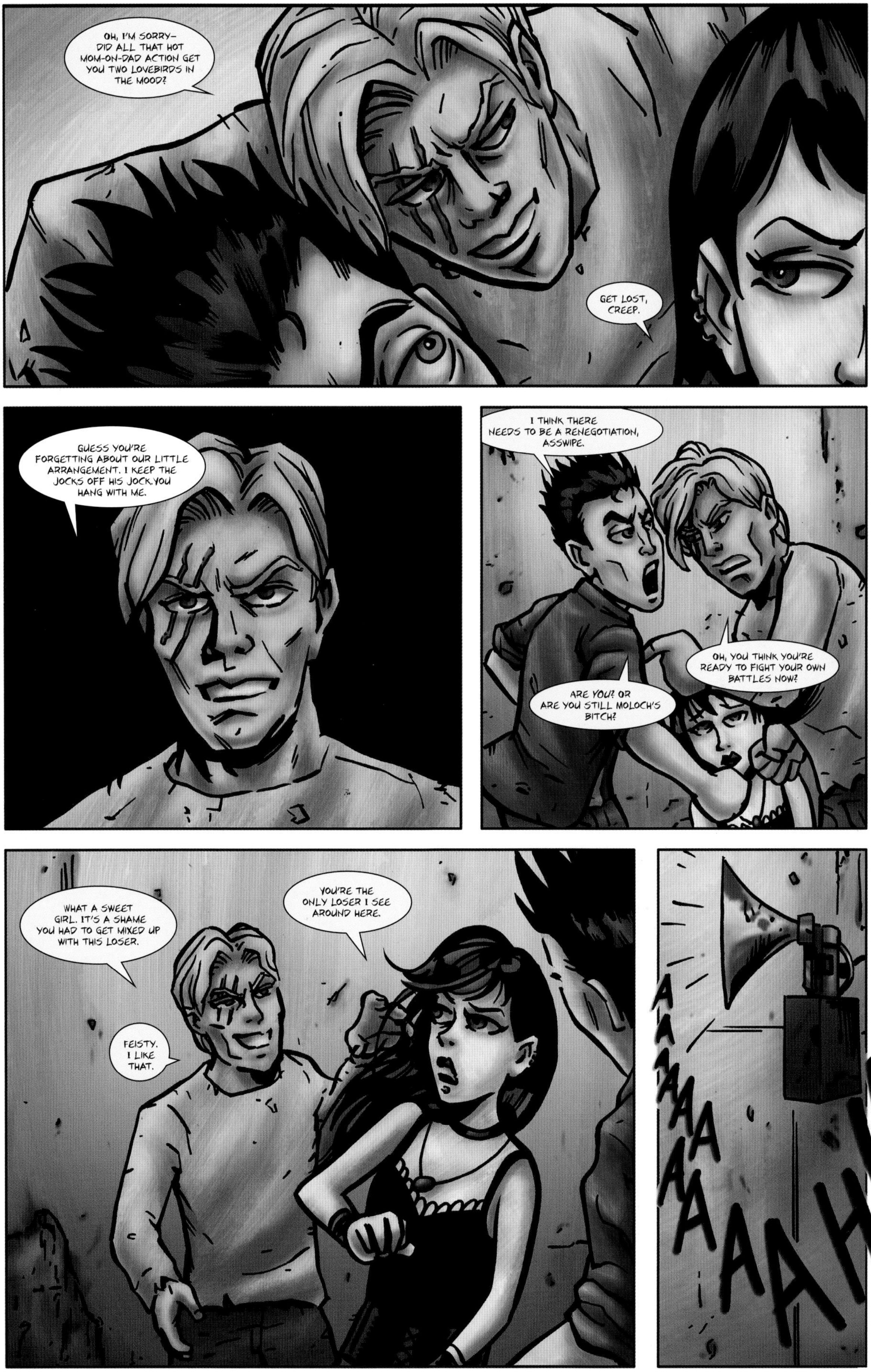
OH, I'M SORRY– DID ALL THAT HOT MOM-ON-DAD ACTION GET YOU TWO LOVEBIRDS IN THE MOOD?
GET LOST, CREEP.
GUESS YOU'RE FORGETTING ABOUT OUR LITTLE ARRANGEMENT. I KEEP THE JOCKS OFF HIS JOCK. YOU HANG WITH ME.
I THINK THERE NEEDS TO BE A RENEGOTIATION, ASSWIPE.
OH, YOU THINK YOU'RE READY TO FIGHT YOUR OWN BATTLES NOW?
ARE YOU? OR ARE YOU STILL MOLOCH'S BITCH?
WHAT A SWEET GIRL. IT'S A SHAME YOU HAD TO GET MIXED UP WITH THIS LOSER.
YOU'RE THE ONLY LOSER I SEE AROUND HERE.
FEISTY. I LIKE THAT.
AAAAAAAAAAH!!!!

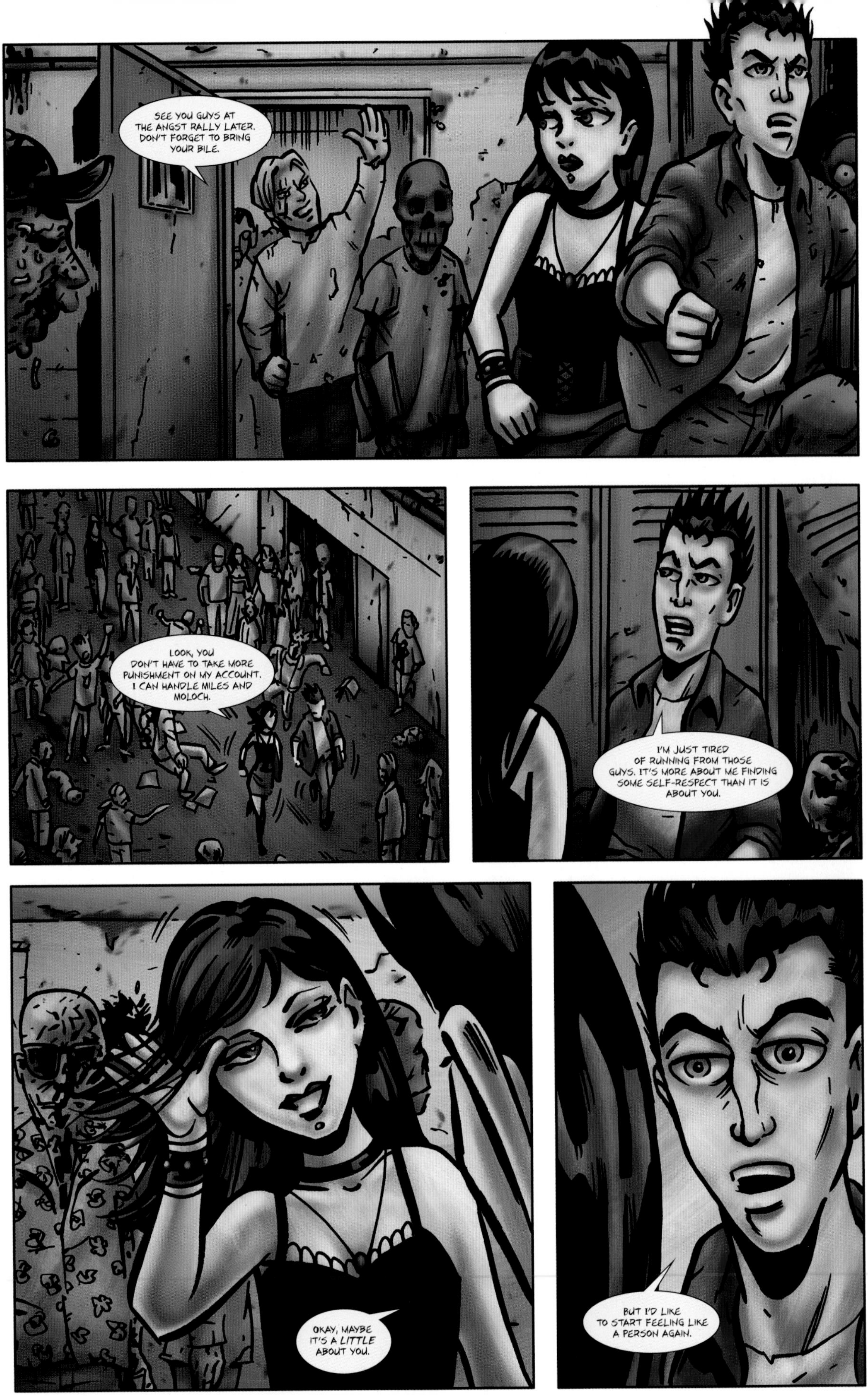
SEE YOU GUYS AT THE ANGST RALLY LATER. DON'T FORGET TO BRING YOUR BILE.
LOOK, YOU DON'T HAVE TO TAKE MORE PUNISHMENT ON MY ACCOUNT. I CAN HANDLE MILES AND MOLOCH.
I'M JUST TIRED OF RUNNING FROM THOSE GUYS. IT'S MORE ABOUT ME FINDING SOME SELF-RESPECT THAN IT IS ABOUT YOU.
OKAY, MAYBE IT'S A *LITTLE* ABOUT YOU.
BUT I'D LIKE TO START FEELING LIKE A PERSON AGAIN.

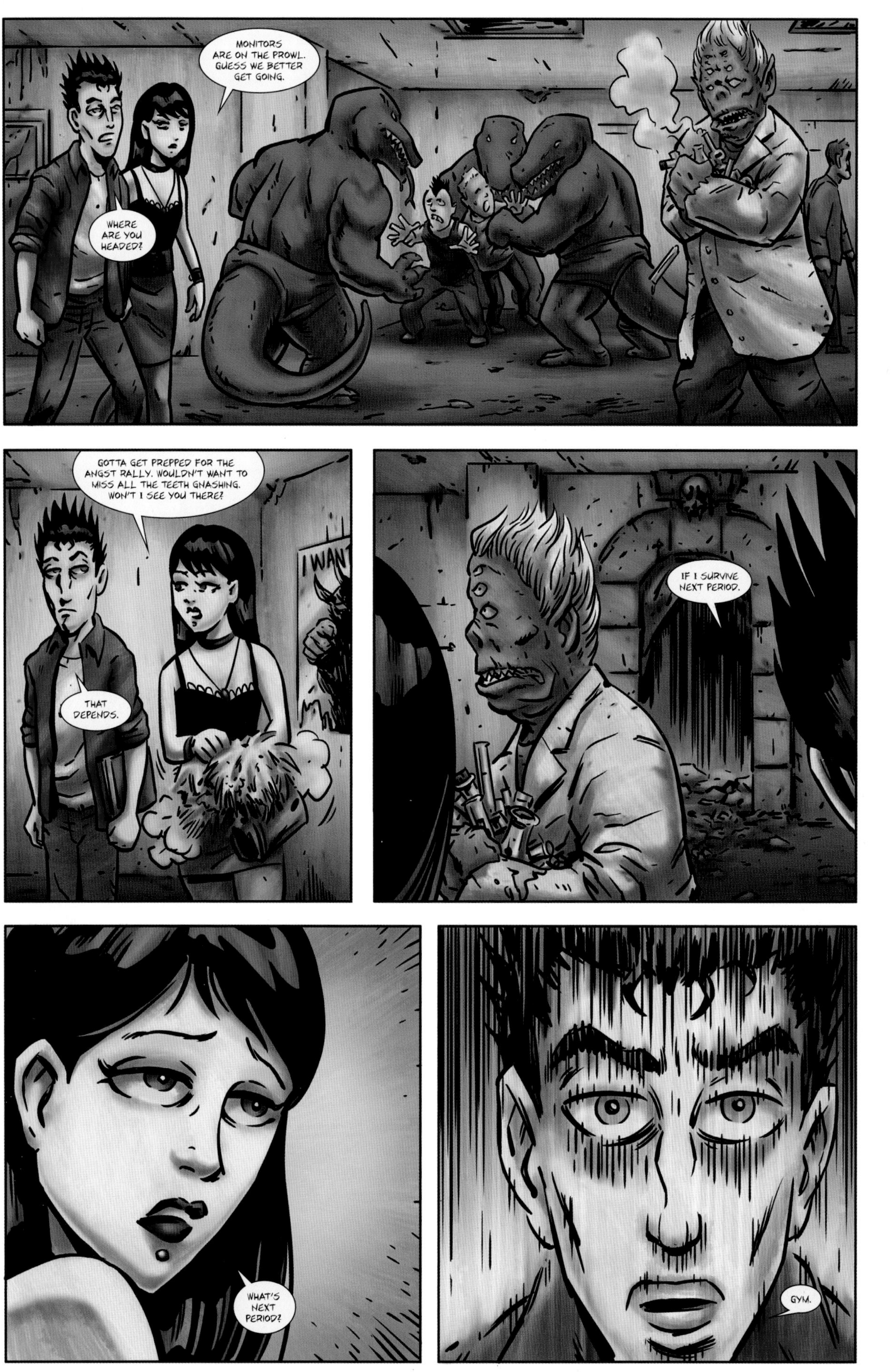
MONITORS ARE ON THE PROWL. GUESS WE BETTER GET GOING.
WHERE ARE YOU HEADED?
GOTTA GET PREPPED FOR THE ANGST RALLY. WOULDN'T WANT TO MISS ALL THE TEETH GNASHING. WON'T I SEE YOU THERE?
THAT DEPENDS.
IF I SURVIVE NEXT PERIOD.
WHAT'S NEXT PERIOD?
GYM.

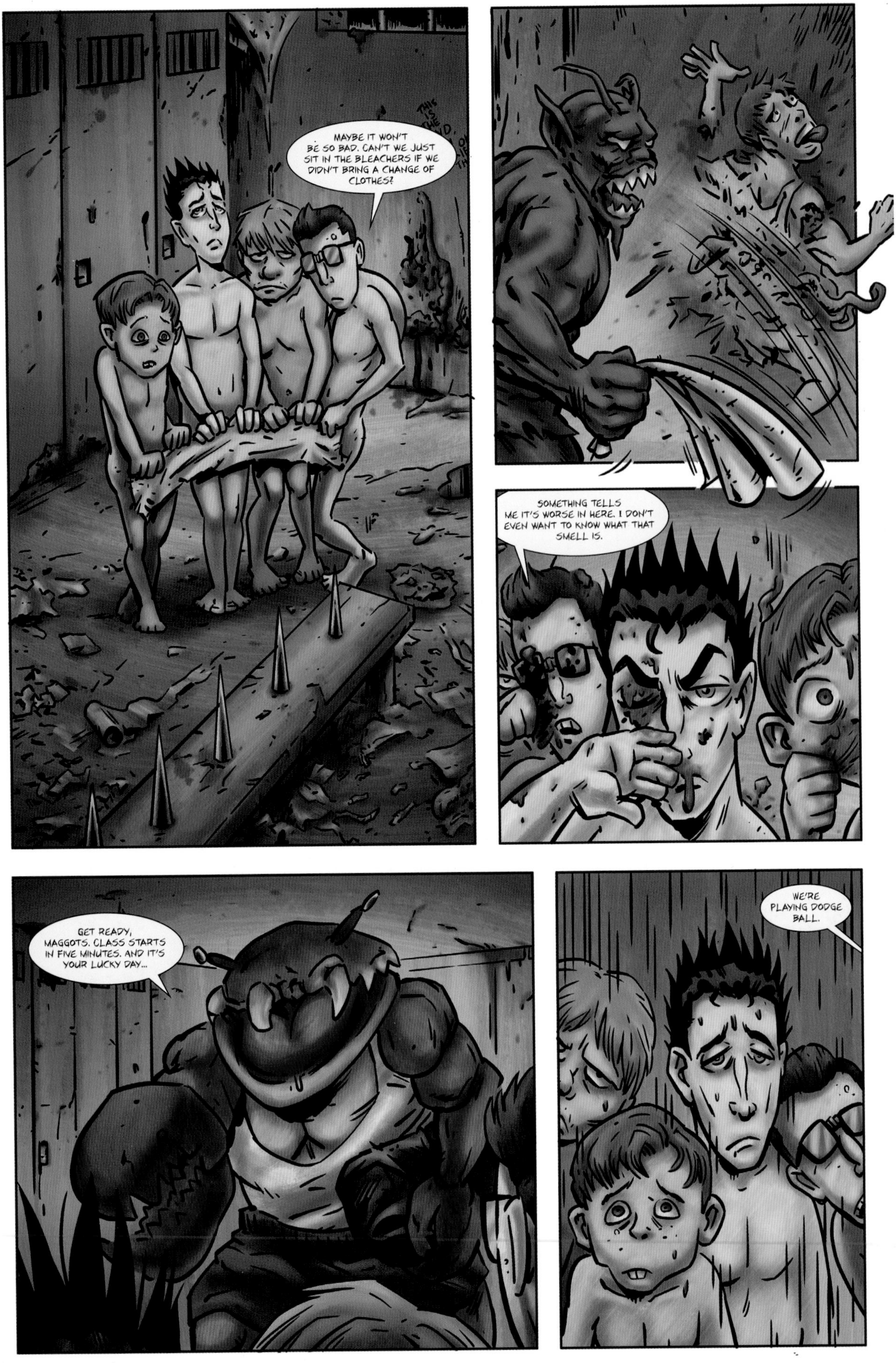
MAYBE IT WON'T BE SO BAD. CAN'T WE JUST SIT IN THE BLEACHERS IF WE DIDN'T BRING A CHANGE OF CLOTHES?
SOMETHING TELLS ME IT'S WORSE IN HERE. I DON'T EVEN WANT TO KNOW WHAT THAT SMELL IS.
GET READY, MAGGOTS. CLASS STARTS IN FIVE MINUTES. AND IT'S YOUR LUCKY DAY...
WE'RE PLAYING DODGE BALL.

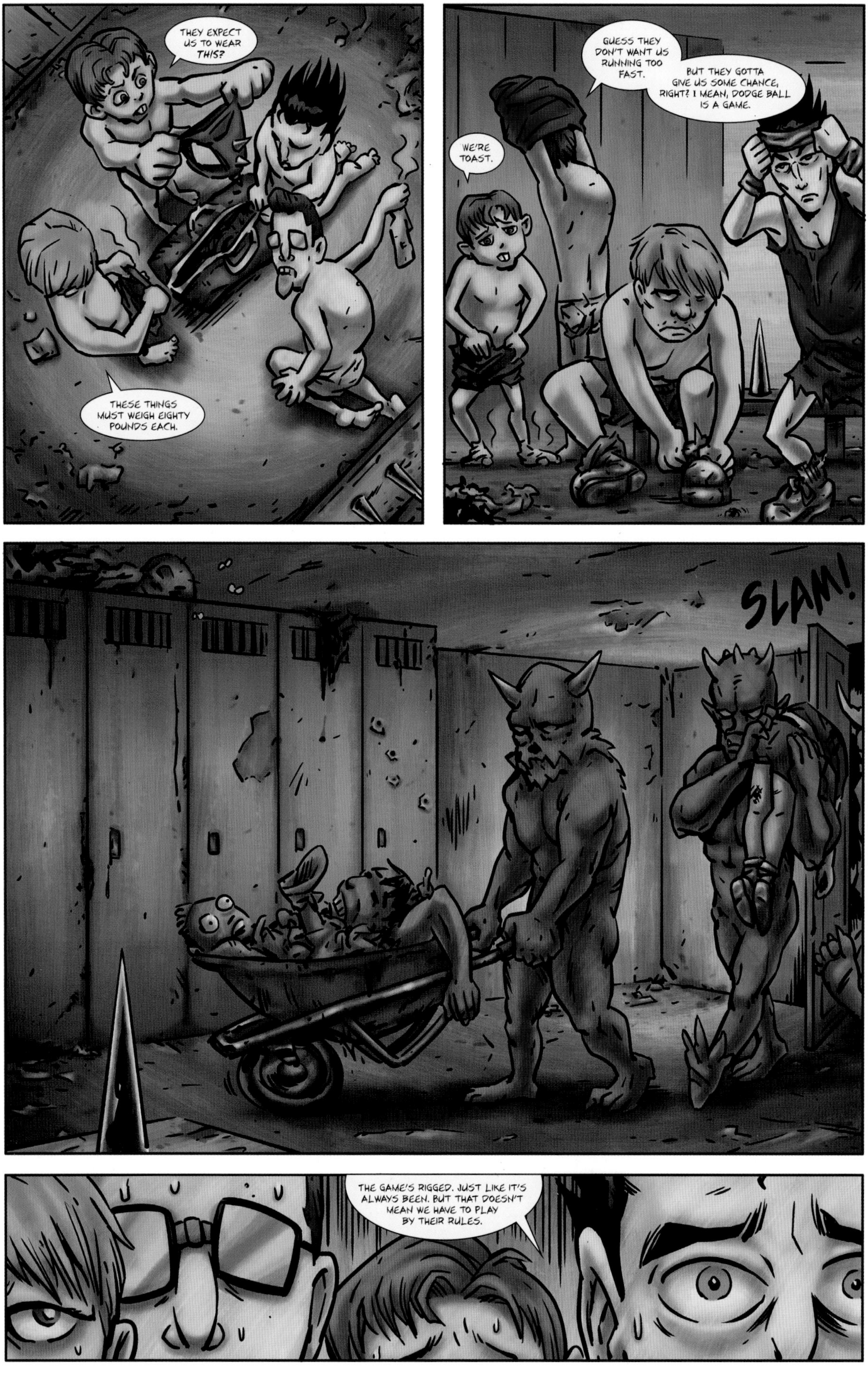
THEY EXPECT US TO WEAR *THIS?*
THESE THINGS MUST WEIGH EIGHTY POUNDS EACH.
GUESS THEY DON'T WANT US RUNNING TOO FAST.
BUT THEY GOTTA GIVE US SOME CHANCE, RIGHT? I MEAN, DODGE BALL IS A GAME.
WE'RE TOAST.
SLAM!
THE GAME'S RIGGED. JUST LIKE IT'S ALWAYS BEEN. BUT THAT DOESN'T MEAN WE HAVE TO PLAY BY THEIR RULES.

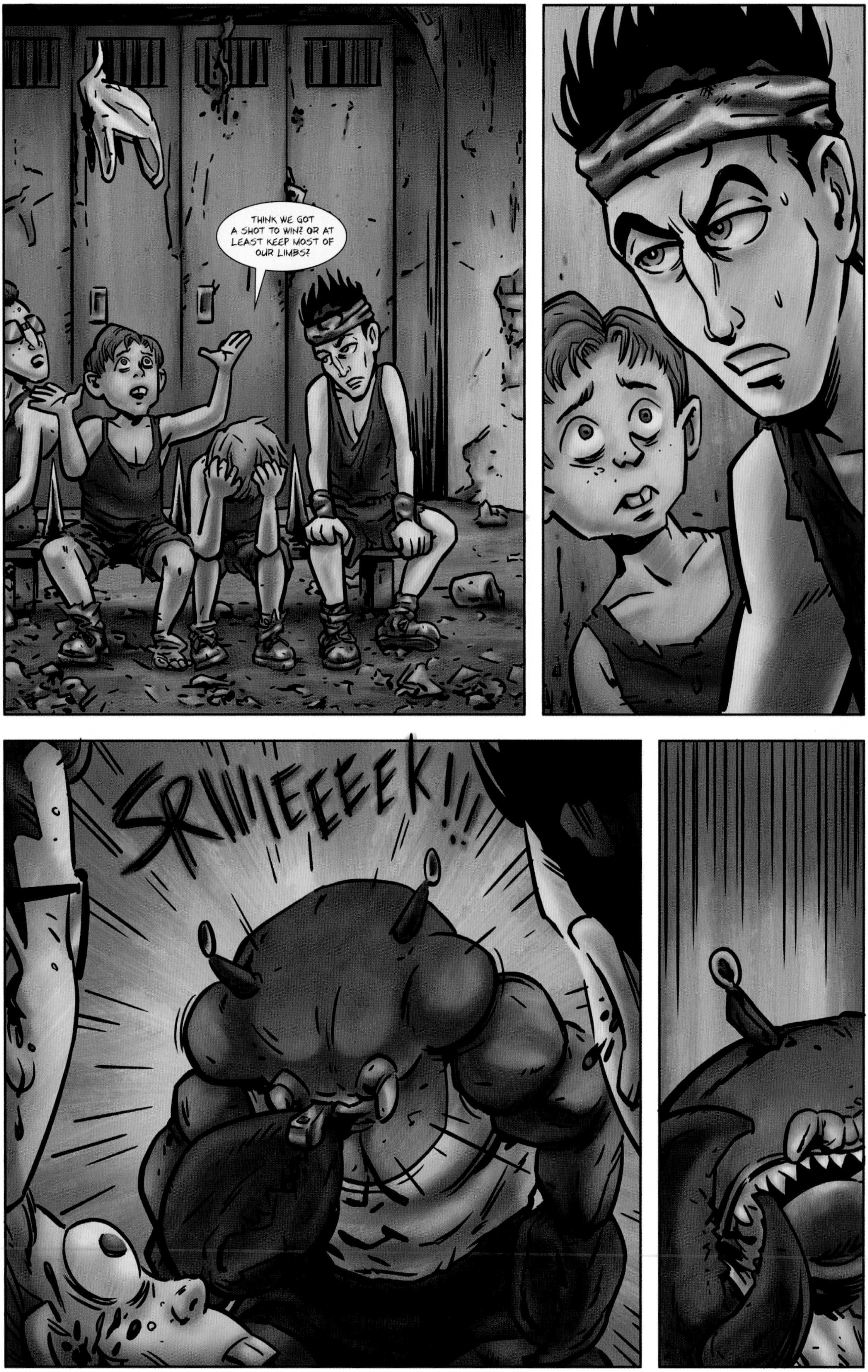
THINK WE GOT A SHOT TO WIN? OR AT LEAST KEEP MOST OF OUR LIMBS?
SRIIIIEEEEEK!!!

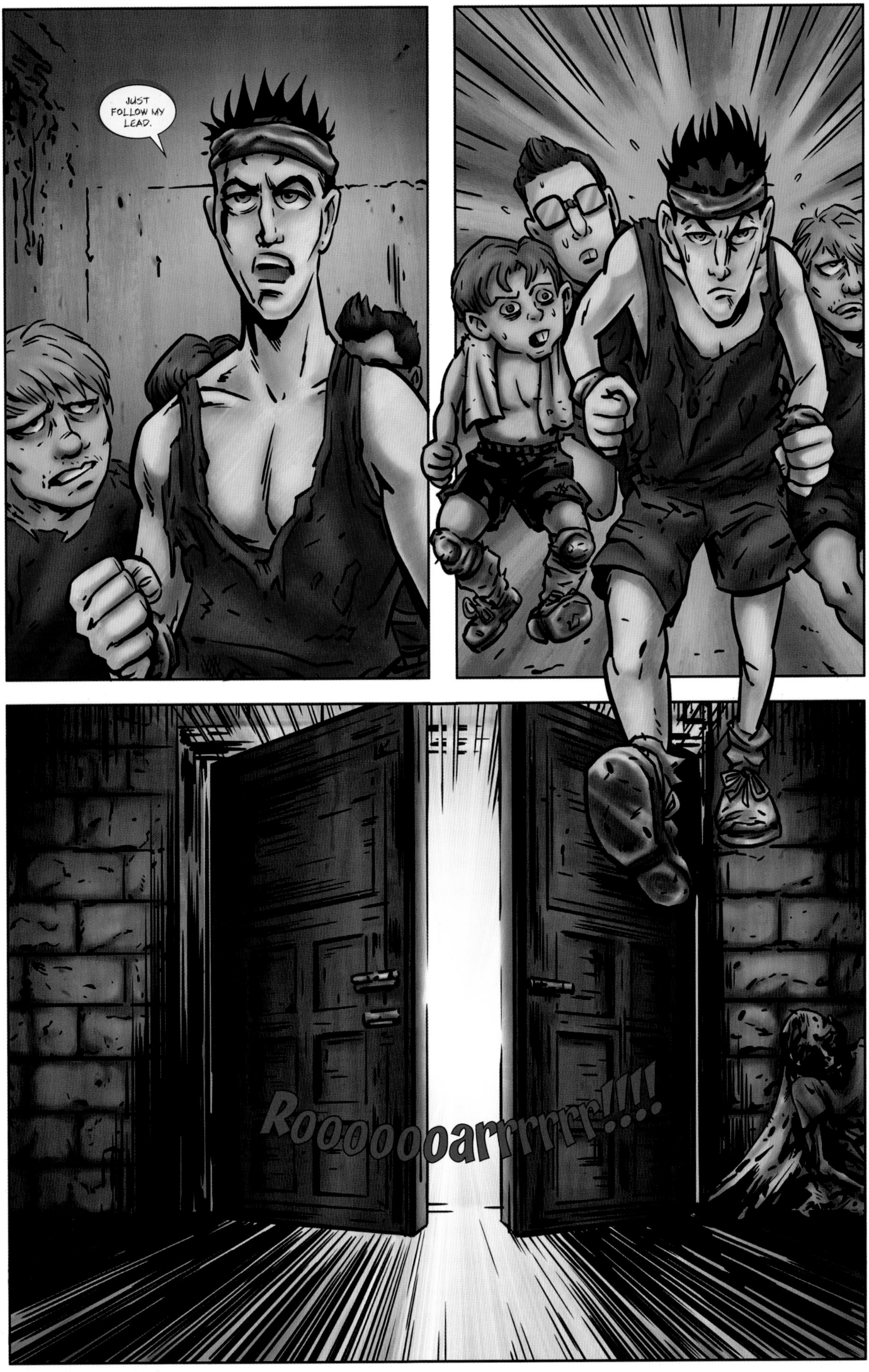
JUST FOLLOW MY LEAD.
Roooooooarrrrrrr!!!!

PART IV

Pencils/Inks:
Tricia Van den Bergh

Colors:
Aya Ikeda-Barry

Flats:
Keith Ikeda-Barry

Lettering:
April Brown

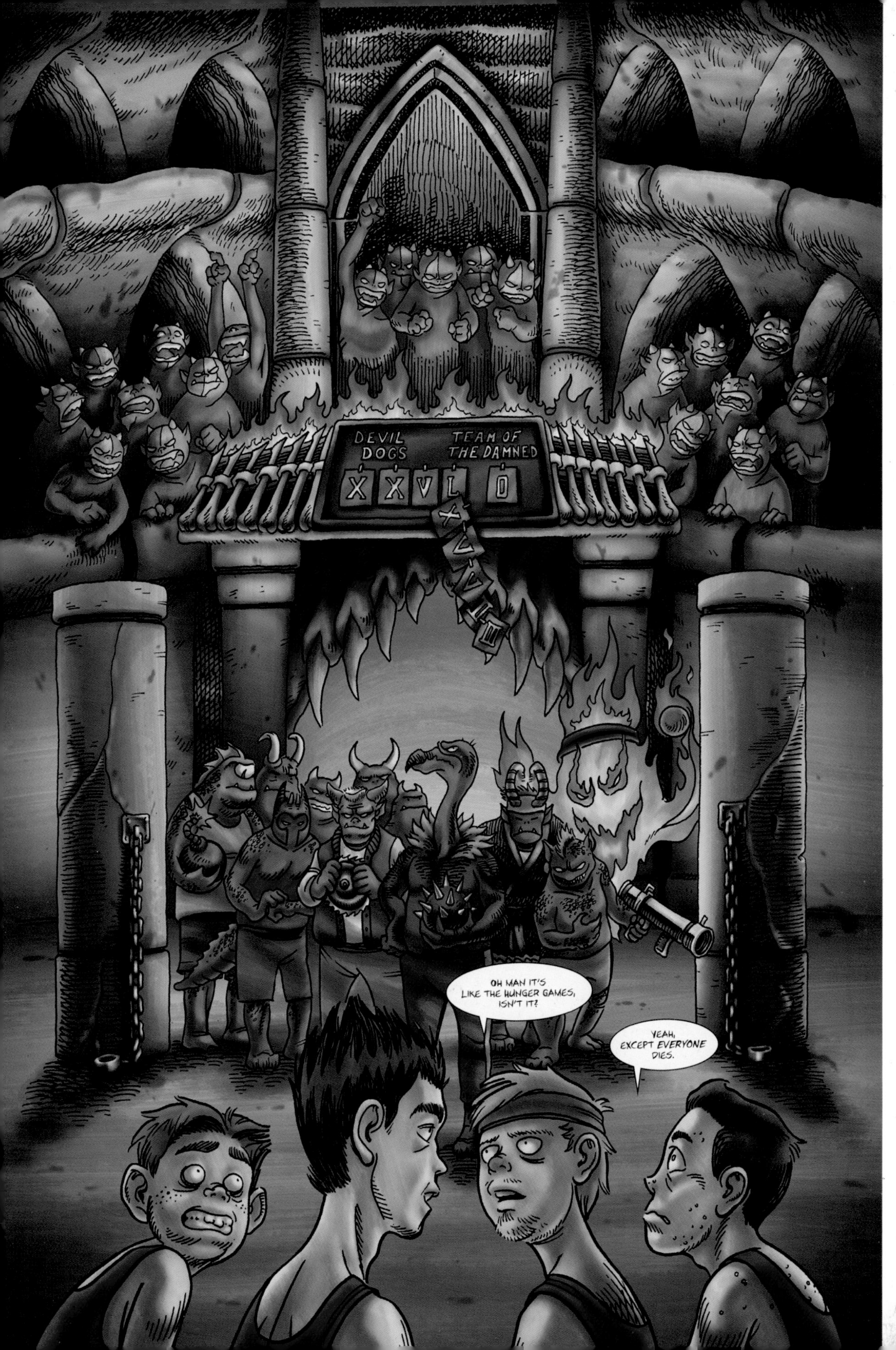
DEVIL DOGS
TEAM OF THE DAMNED
OH MAN IT'S LIKE THE HUNGER GAMES, ISN'T IT?
YEAH, EXCEPT EVERYONE DIES.

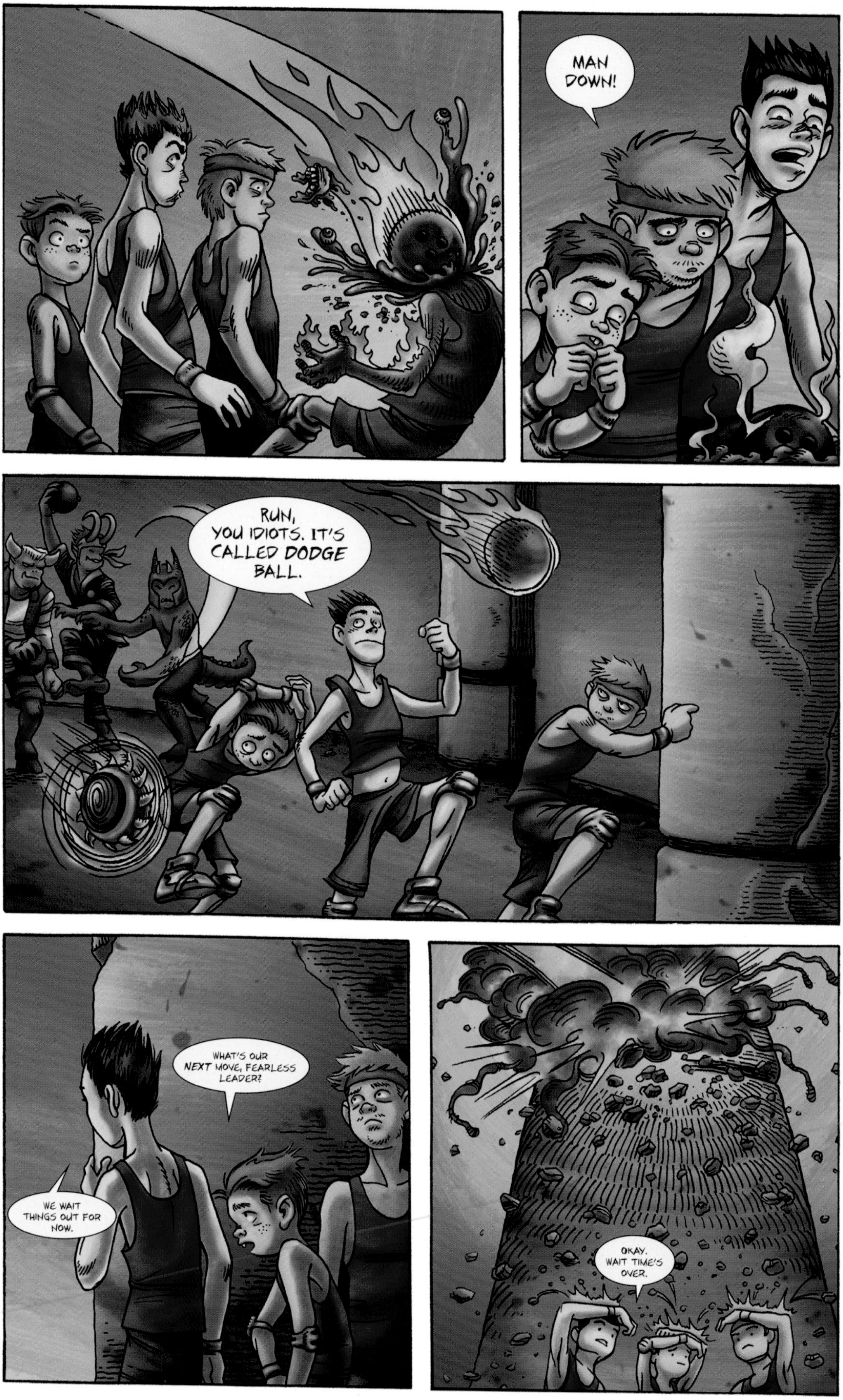
MAN DOWN!
RUN, YOU IDIOTS. IT'S CALLED DODGE BALL.
WHAT'S OUR NEXT MOVE, FEARLESS LEADER?
WE WAIT THINGS OUT FOR NOW.
OKAY. WAIT TIME'S OVER.

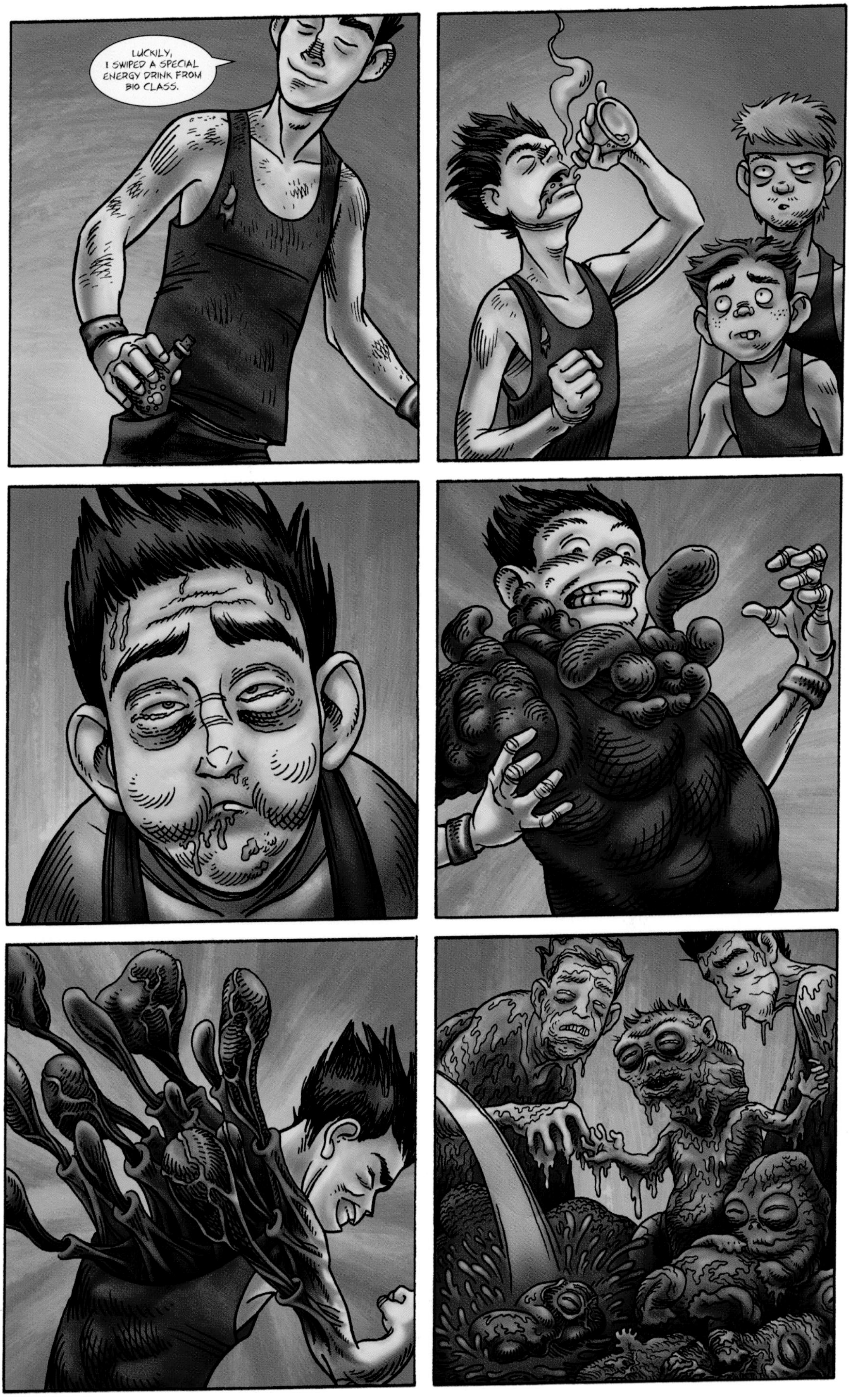
LUCKILY, I SWIPED A SPECIAL ENERGY DRINK FROM BIO CLASS.

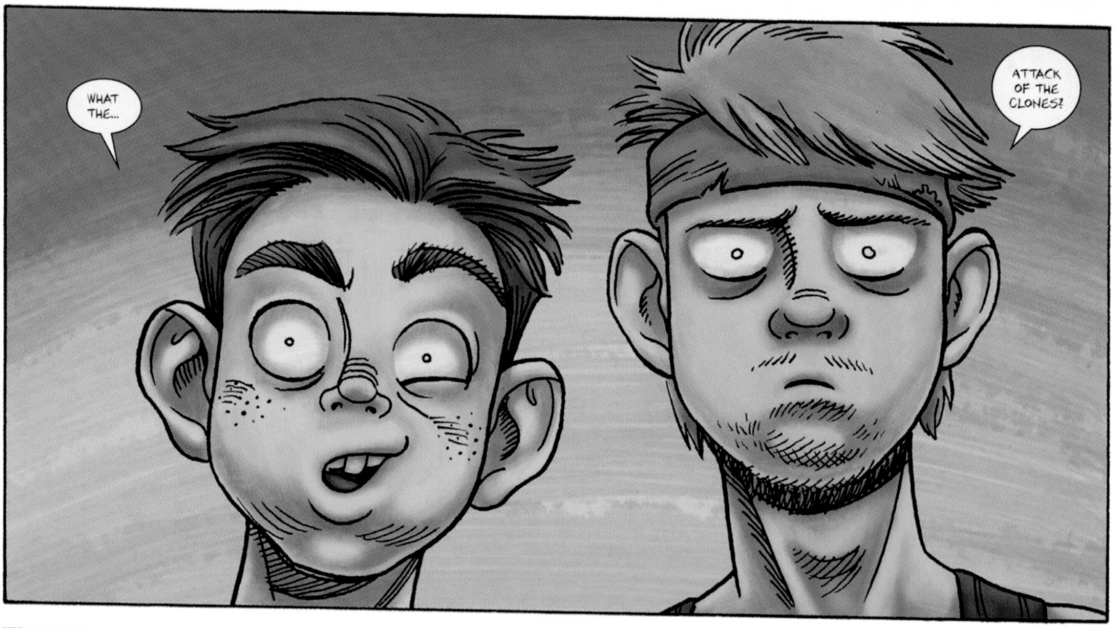
WHAT THE...
ATTACK OF THE CLONES?

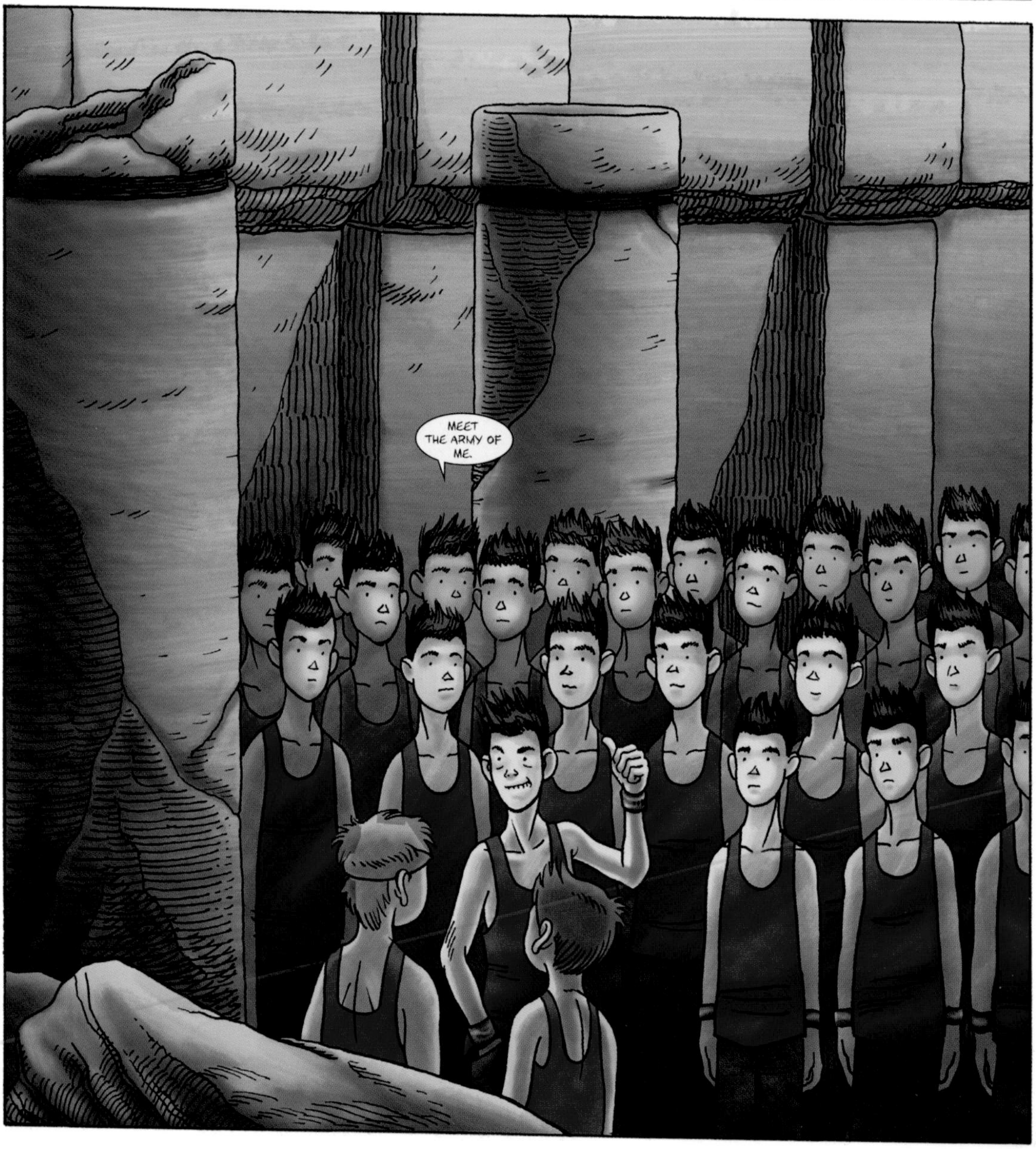
MEET THE ARMY OF ME.

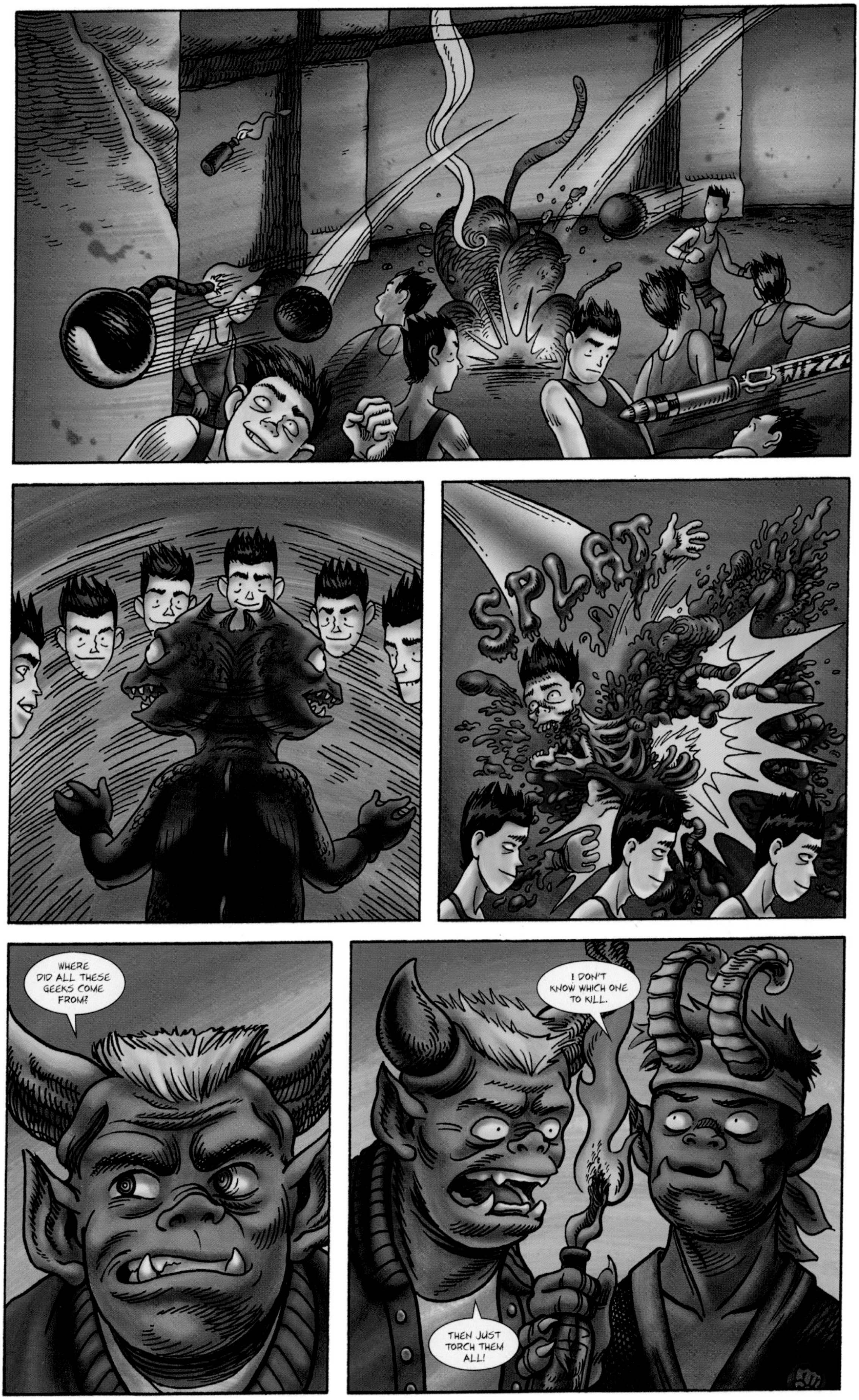
WIZZZ
SPLAT
WHERE DID ALL THESE GEEKS COME FROM?
I DON'T KNOW WHICH ONE TO KILL.
THEN JUST TORCH THEM ALL!

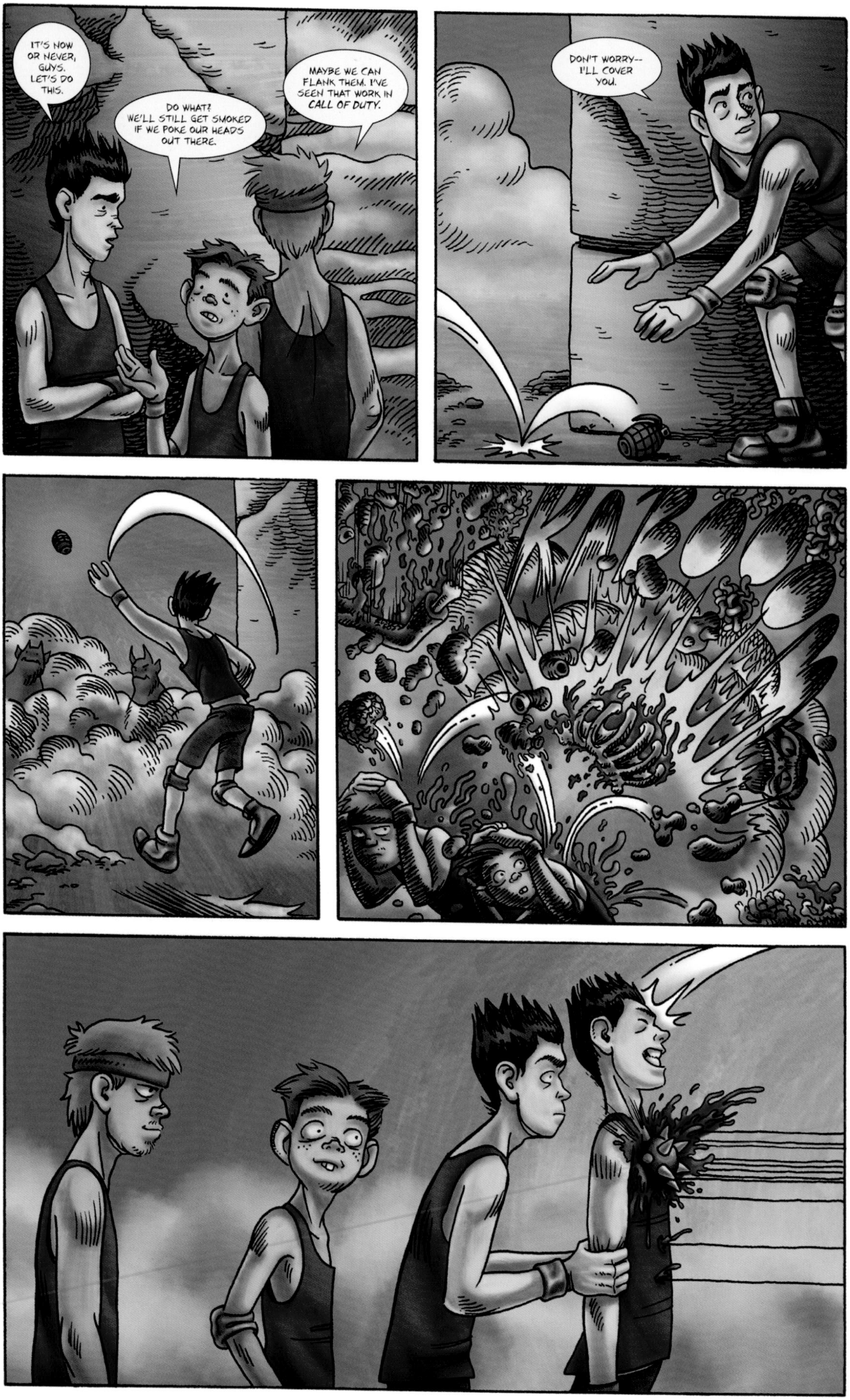
IT'S NOW OR NEVER, GUYS. LET'S DO THIS.
DO WHAT? WE'LL STILL GET SMOKED IF WE POKE OUR HEADS OUT THERE.
MAYBE WE CAN FLANK THEM. I'VE SEEN THAT WORK IN CALL OF DUTY.
DON'T WORRY-- I'LL COVER YOU.

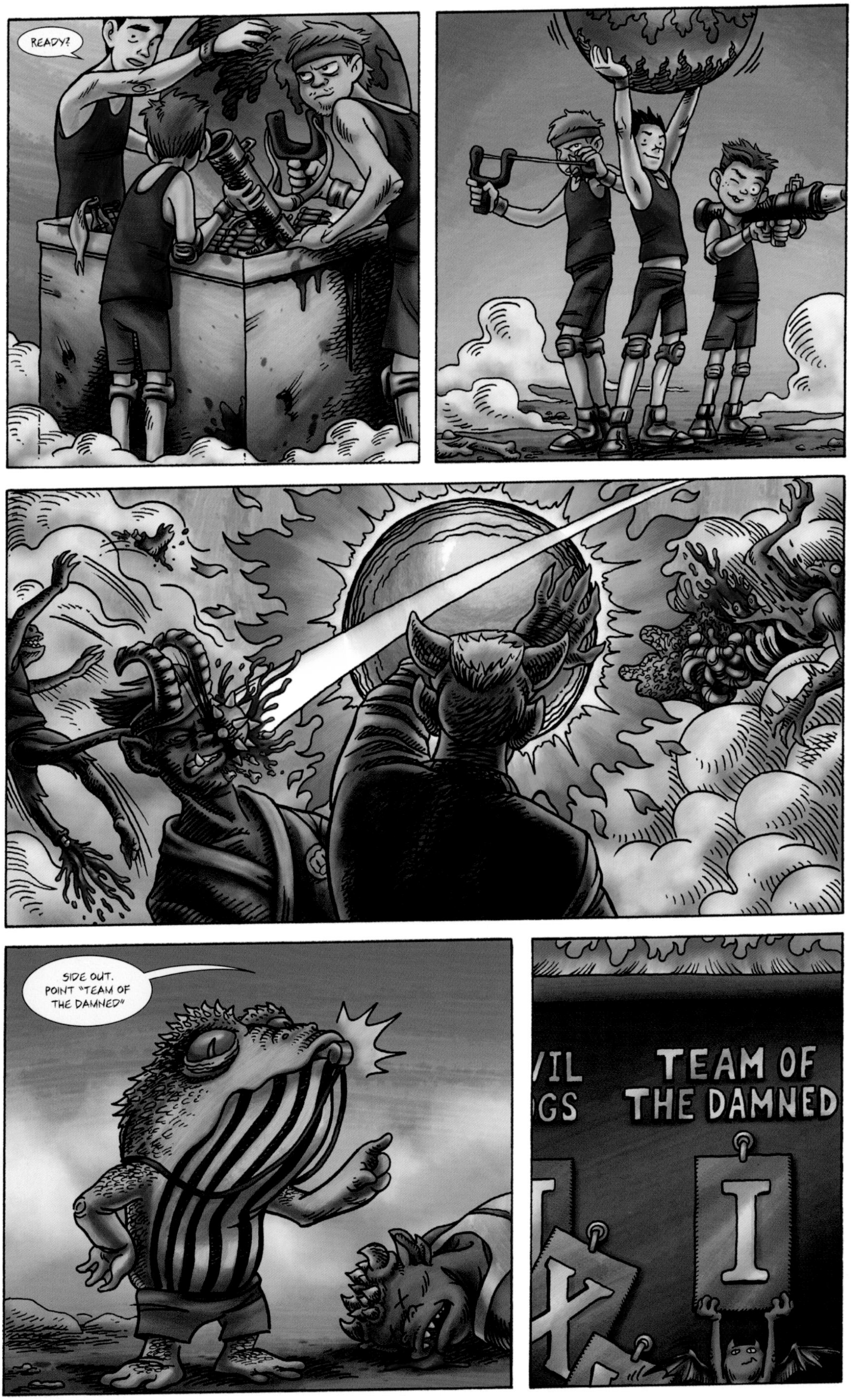
READY?
SIDE OUT.
POINT "TEAM OF
THE DAMNED"
VIL
GS
TEAM OF
THE DAMNED
I

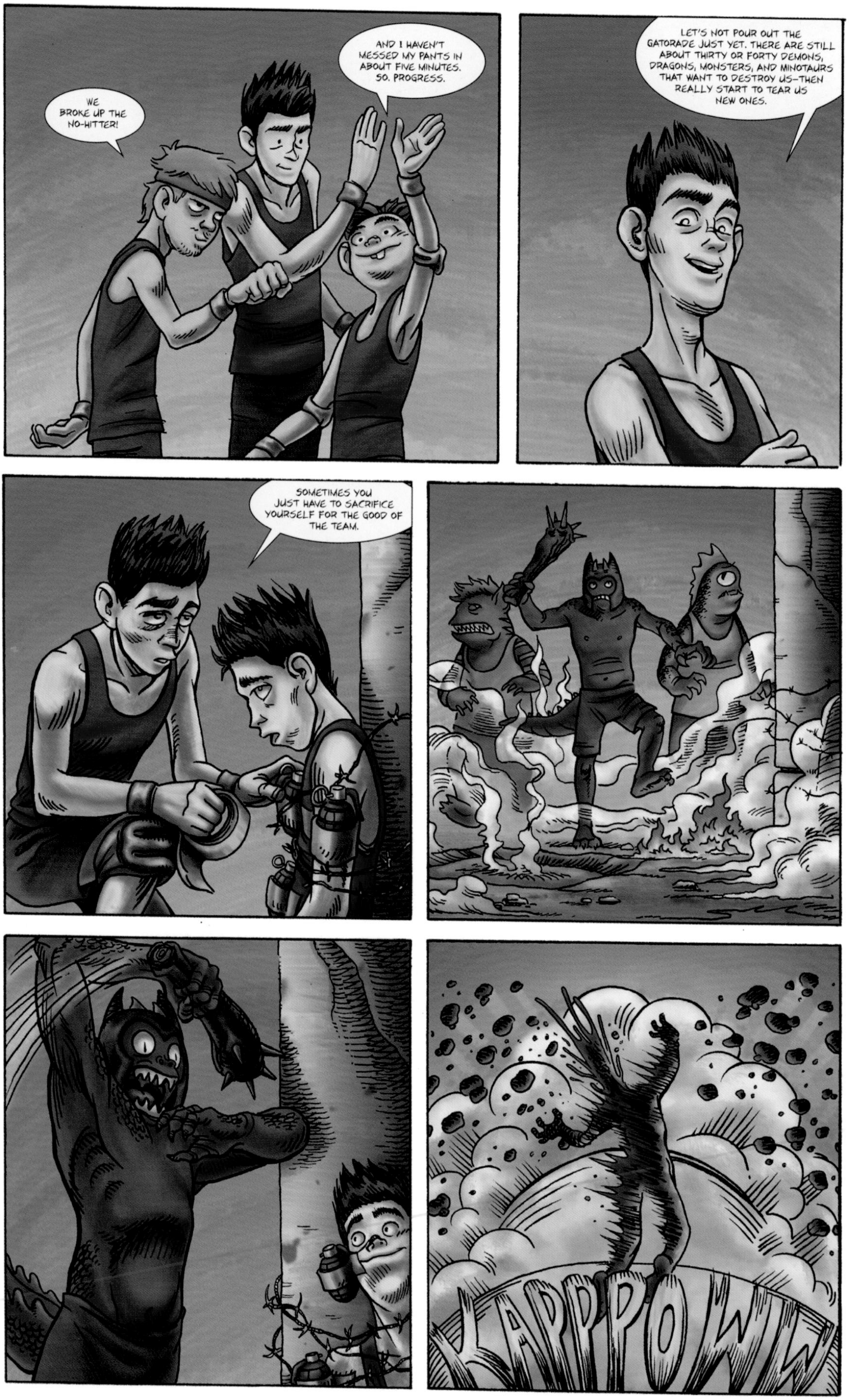
WE BROKE UP THE NO-HITTER!
AND I HAVEN'T MESSED MY PANTS IN ABOUT FIVE MINUTES. SO, PROGRESS.
LET'S NOT POUR OUT THE GATORADE JUST YET. THERE ARE STILL ABOUT THIRTY OR FORTY DEMONS, DRAGONS, MONSTERS, AND MINOTAURS THAT WANT TO DESTROY US—THEN REALLY START TO TEAR US NEW ONES.
SOMETIMES YOU JUST HAVE TO SACRIFICE YOURSELF FOR THE GOOD OF THE TEAM.

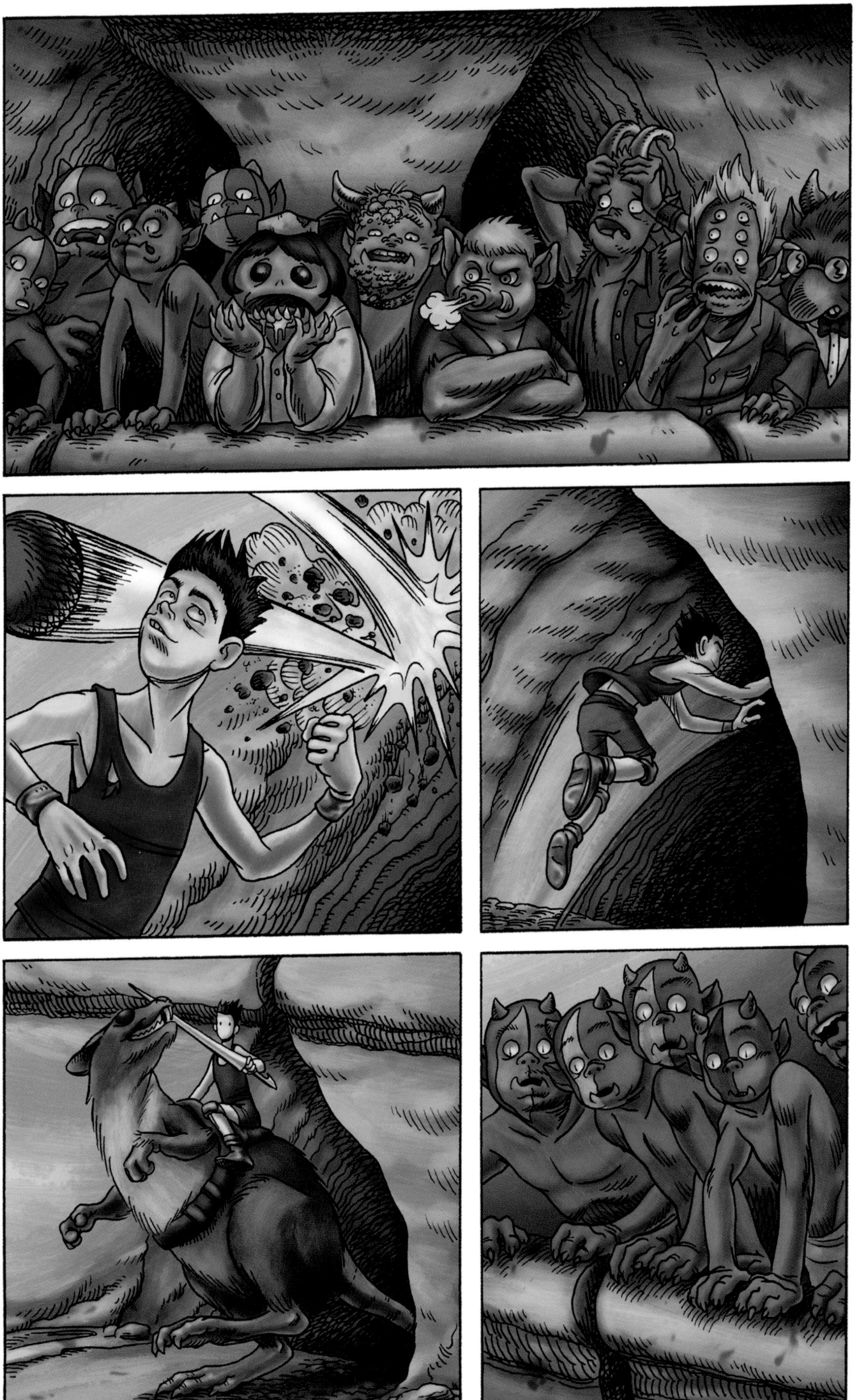

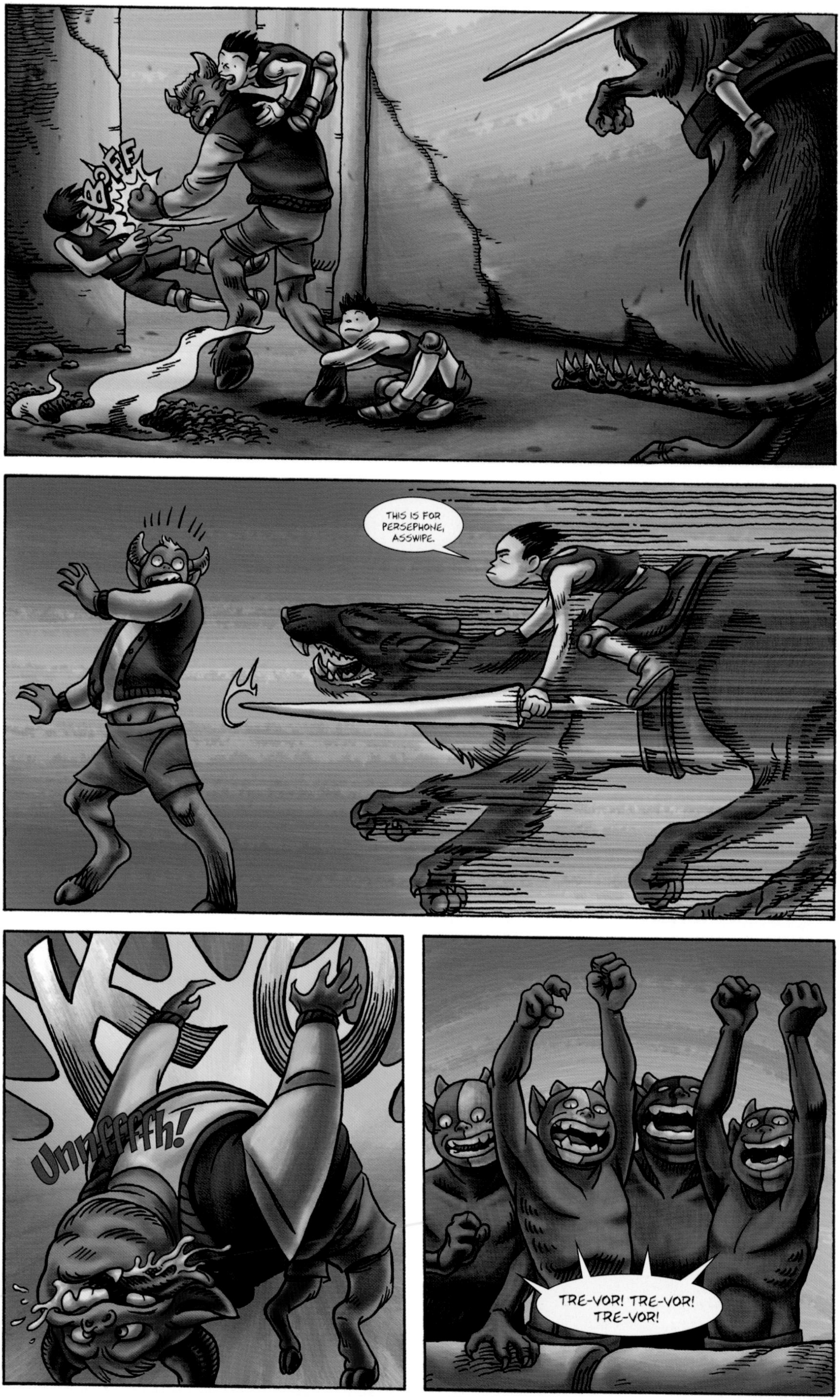
BOFF
THIS IS FOR PERSEPHONE, ASSWIPE.
Unnffffh!
TRE-VOR! TRE-VOR! TRE-VOR!

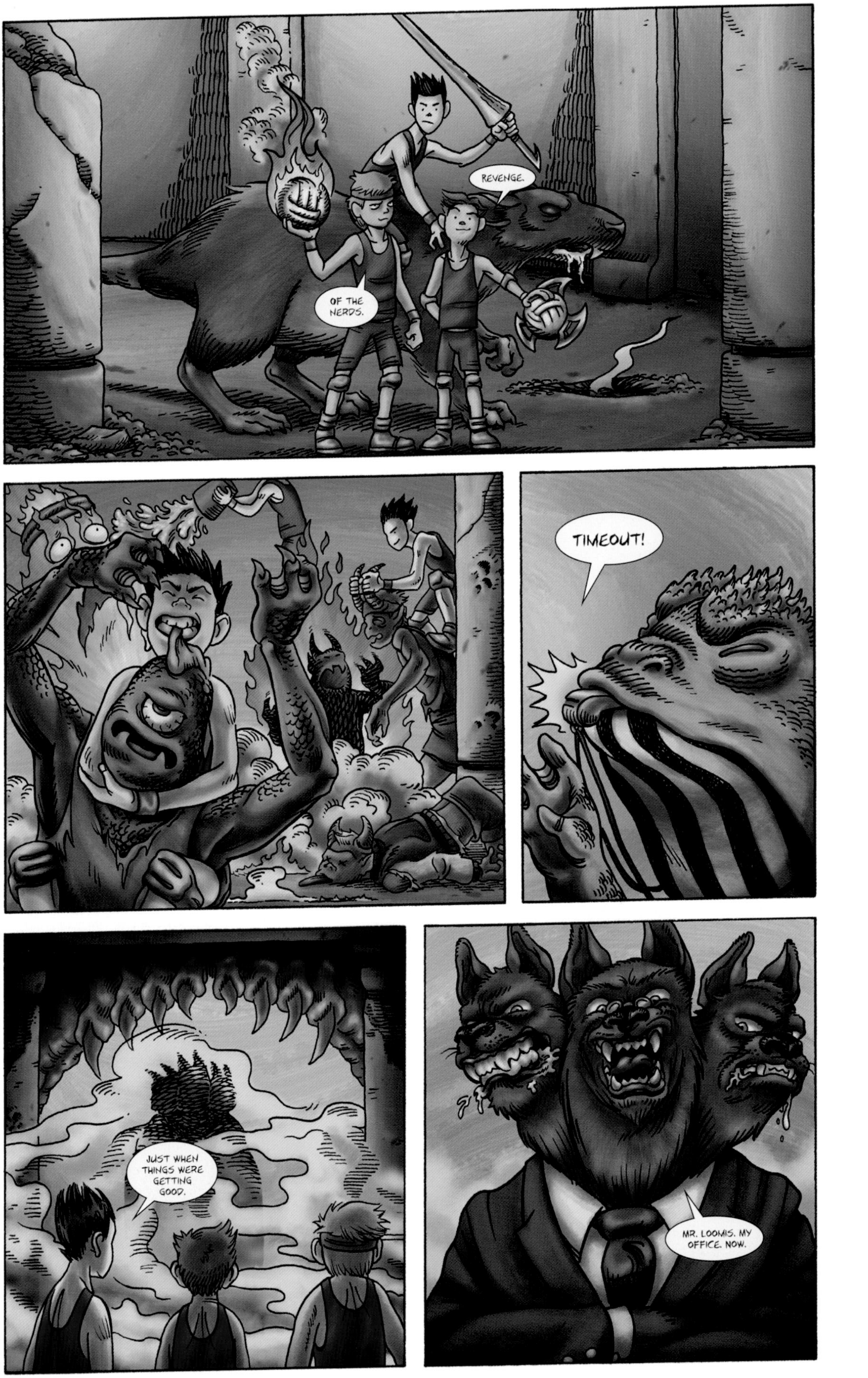
REVENGE.
OF THE NERDS.
TIMEOUT!
JUST WHEN THINGS WERE GETTING GOOD.
MR. LOOMIS. MY OFFICE. NOW.

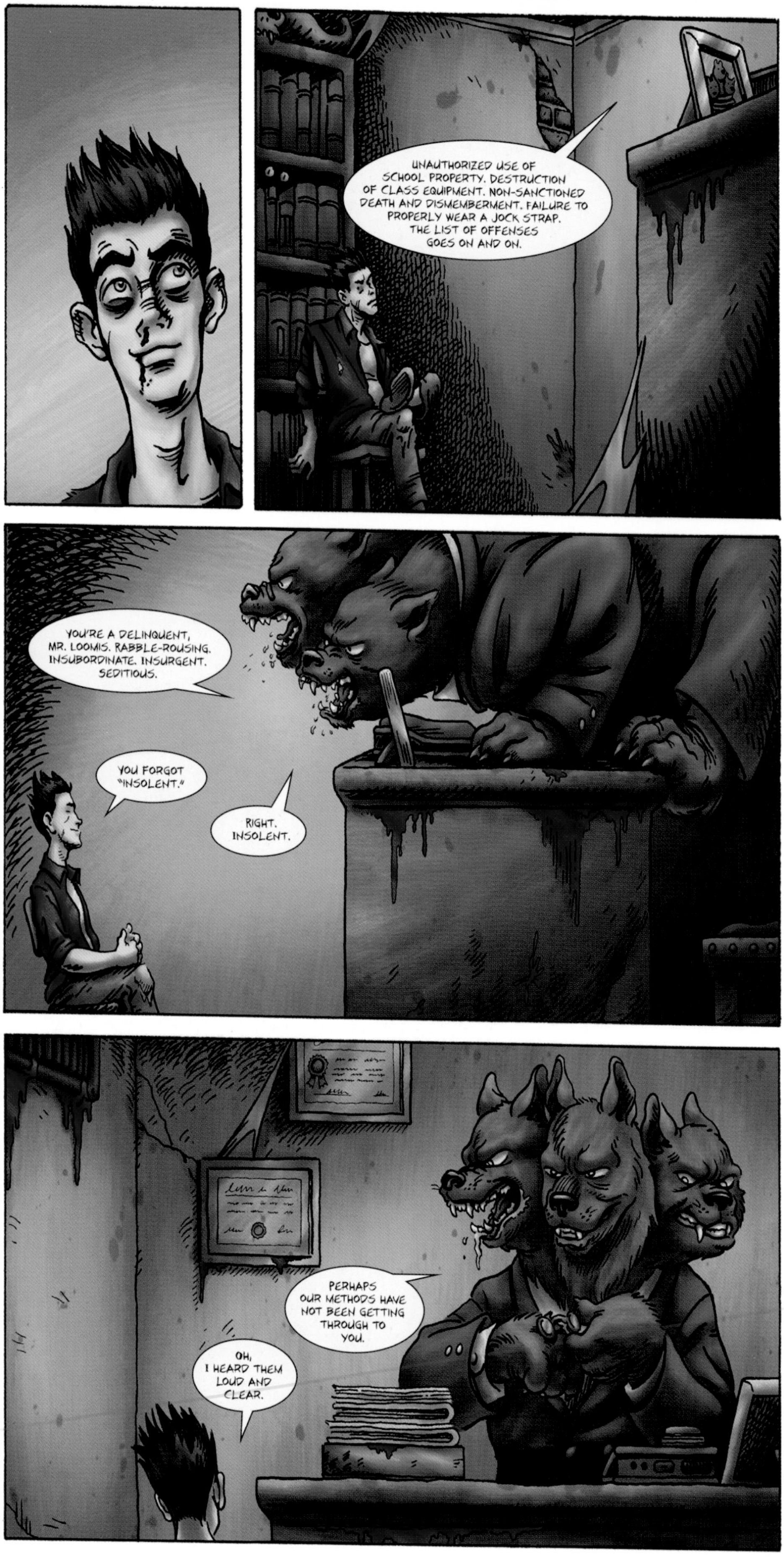
UNAUTHORIZED USE OF SCHOOL PROPERTY. DESTRUCTION OF CLASS EQUIPMENT. NON-SANCTIONED DEATH AND DISMEMBERMENT. FAILURE TO PROPERLY WEAR A JOCK STRAP. THE LIST OF OFFENSES GOES ON AND ON.
YOU'RE A DELINQUENT, MR. LOOMIS. RABBLE-ROUSING. INSUBORDINATE. INSURGENT. SEDITIOUS.
YOU FORGOT "INSOLENT."
RIGHT. INSOLENT.
PERHAPS OUR METHODS HAVE NOT BEEN GETTING THROUGH TO YOU.
OH, I HEARD THEM LOUD AND CLEAR.

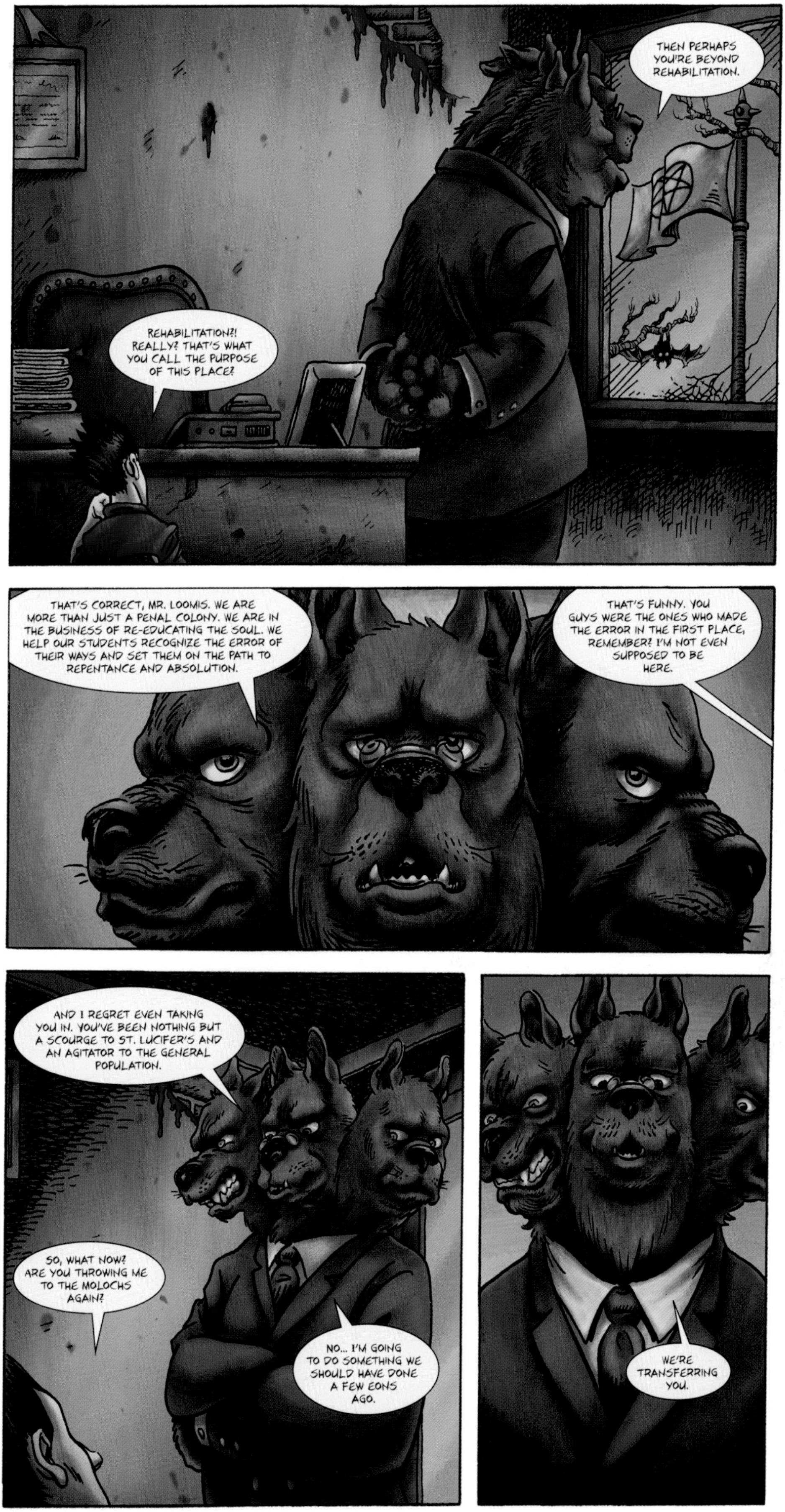
THEN PERHAPS YOU'RE BEYOND REHABILITATION.
REHABILITATION?! REALLY? THAT'S WHAT YOU CALL THE PURPOSE OF THIS PLACE?
THAT'S CORRECT, MR. LOOMIS. WE ARE MORE THAN JUST A PENAL COLONY. WE ARE IN THE BUSINESS OF RE-EDUCATING THE SOUL. WE HELP OUR STUDENTS RECOGNIZE THE ERROR OF THEIR WAYS AND SET THEM ON THE PATH TO REPENTANCE AND ABSOLUTION.
THAT'S FUNNY. YOU GUYS WERE THE ONES WHO MADE THE ERROR IN THE FIRST PLACE, REMEMBER? I'M NOT EVEN SUPPOSED TO BE HERE.
AND I REGRET EVEN TAKING YOU IN. YOU'VE BEEN NOTHING BUT A SCOURGE TO ST. LUCIFER'S AND AN AGITATOR TO THE GENERAL POPULATION.
SO, WHAT NOW? ARE YOU THROWING ME TO THE MOLOCHS AGAIN?
NO... I'M GOING TO DO SOMETHING WE SHOULD HAVE DONE A FEW EONS AGO.
WE'RE TRANSFERRING YOU.

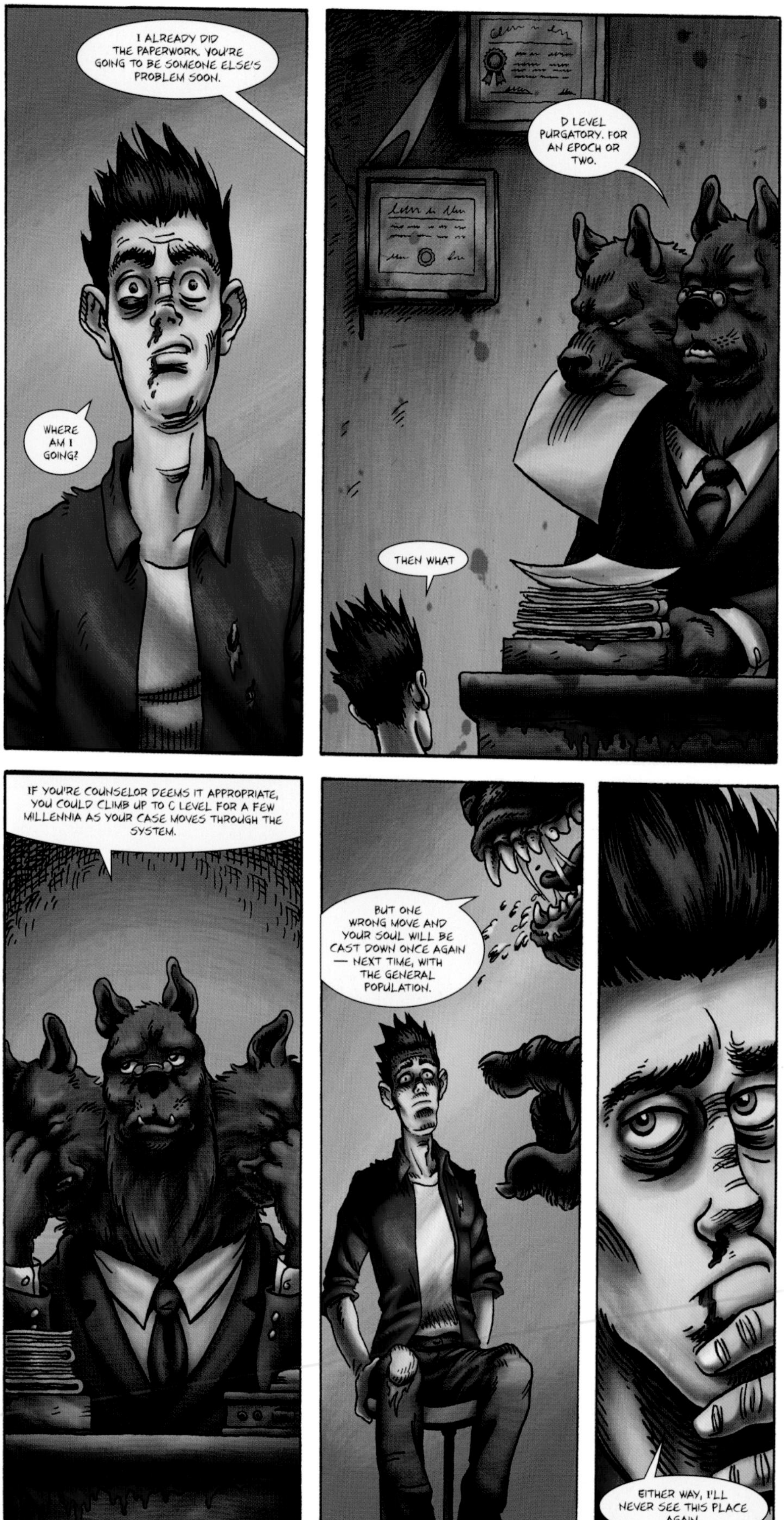

I ALREADY DID THE PAPERWORK. YOU'RE GOING TO BE SOMEONE ELSE'S PROBLEM SOON.
WHERE AM I GOING?
D LEVEL PURGATORY. FOR AN EPOCH OR TWO.
THEN WHAT
IF YOU'RE COUNSELOR DEEMS IT APPROPRIATE, YOU COULD CLIMB UP TO C LEVEL FOR A FEW MILLENNIA AS YOUR CASE MOVES THROUGH THE SYSTEM.
BUT ONE WRONG MOVE AND YOUR SOUL WILL BE CAST DOWN ONCE AGAIN — NEXT TIME, WITH THE GENERAL POPULATION.
EITHER WAY, I'LL NEVER SEE THIS PLACE AGAIN.

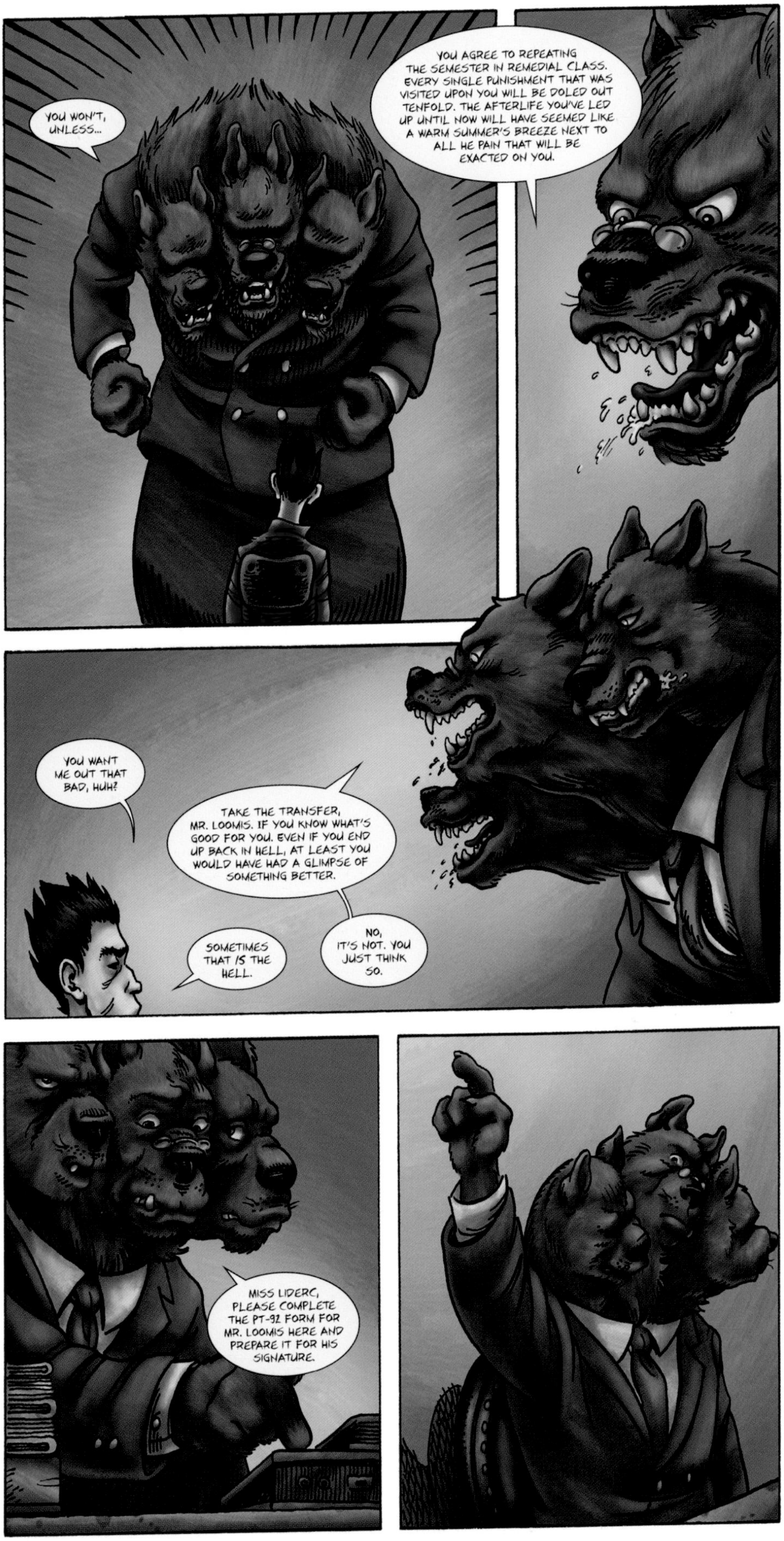
YOU WON'T, UNLESS...
YOU AGREE TO REPEATING THE SEMESTER IN REMEDIAL CLASS. EVERY SINGLE PUNISHMENT THAT WAS VISITED UPON YOU WILL BE DOLED OUT TENFOLD. THE AFTERLIFE YOU'VE LED UP UNTIL NOW WILL HAVE SEEMED LIKE A WARM SUMMER'S BREEZE NEXT TO ALL HE PAIN THAT WILL BE EXACTED ON YOU.
YOU WANT ME OUT THAT BAD, HUH?
TAKE THE TRANSFER, MR. LOOMIS. IF YOU KNOW WHAT'S GOOD FOR YOU. EVEN IF YOU END UP BACK IN HELL, AT LEAST YOU WOULD HAVE HAD A GLIMPSE OF SOMETHING BETTER.
SOMETIMES THAT IS THE HELL.
NO, IT'S NOT. YOU JUST THINK SO.
MISS LIDERC, PLEASE COMPLETE THE PT-92 FORM FOR MR. LOOMIS HERE AND PREPARE IT FOR HIS SIGNATURE.

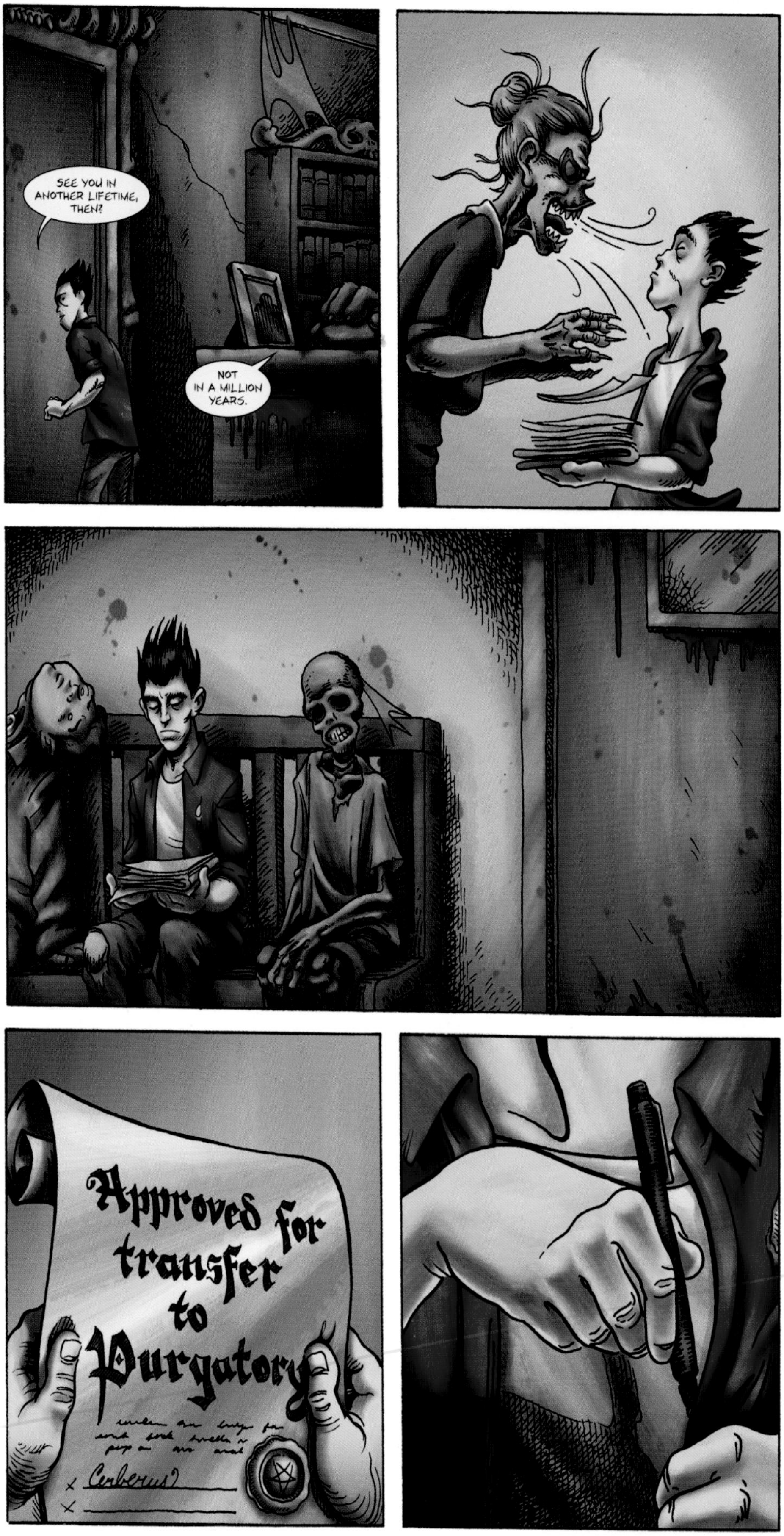
SEE YOU IN ANOTHER LIFETIME, THEN?
NOT IN A MILLION YEARS.
Approved for transfer to Purgatory
Cerberus

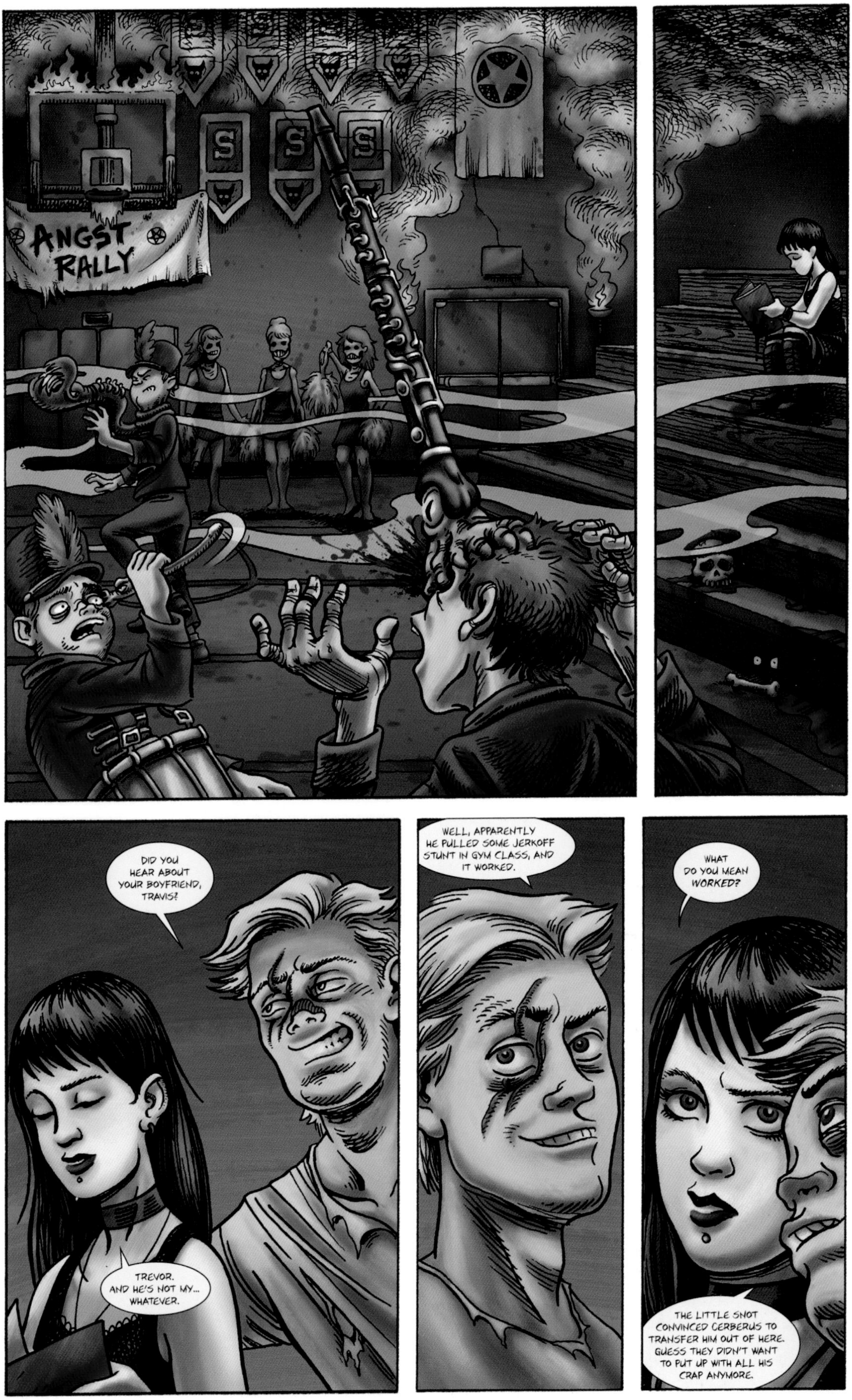
ANGST RALLY
DID YOU HEAR ABOUT YOUR BOYFRIEND, TRAVIS?
TREVOR. AND HE'S NOT MY... WHATEVER.
WELL, APPARENTLY HE PULLED SOME JERKOFF STUNT IN GYM CLASS, AND IT WORKED.
WHAT DO YOU MEAN *WORKED?*
THE LITTLE SNOT CONVINCED CERBERUS TO TRANSFER HIM OUT OF HERE. GUESS THEY DIDN'T WANT TO PUT UP WITH ALL HIS CRAP ANYMORE.

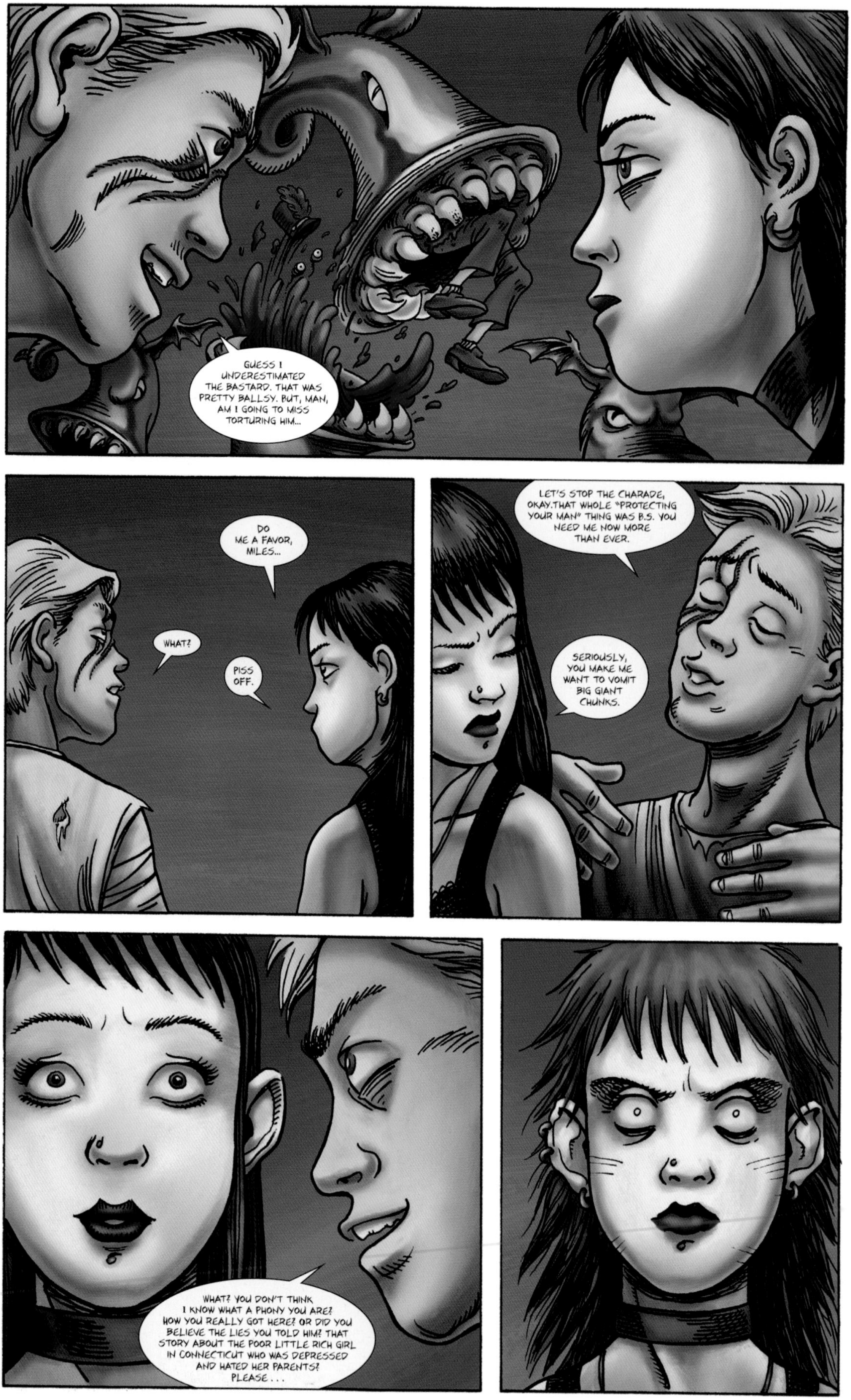
GUESS I UNDERESTIMATED THE BASTARD. THAT WAS PRETTY BALLSY. BUT, MAN, AM I GOING TO MISS TORTURING HIM...
DO ME A FAVOR, MILES...
WHAT?
PISS OFF.
LET'S STOP THE CHARADE, OKAY.THAT WHOLE "PROTECTING YOUR MAN" THING WAS B.S. YOU NEED ME NOW MORE THAN EVER.
SERIOUSLY, YOU MAKE ME WANT TO VOMIT BIG GIANT CHUNKS.
WHAT? YOU DON'T THINK I KNOW WHAT A PHONY YOU ARE? HOW YOU REALLY GOT HERE? OR DID YOU BELIEVE THE LIES YOU TOLD HIM? THAT STORY ABOUT THE POOR LITTLE RICH GIRL IN CONNECTICUT WHO WAS DEPRESSED AND HATED HER PARENTS? PLEASE . . .

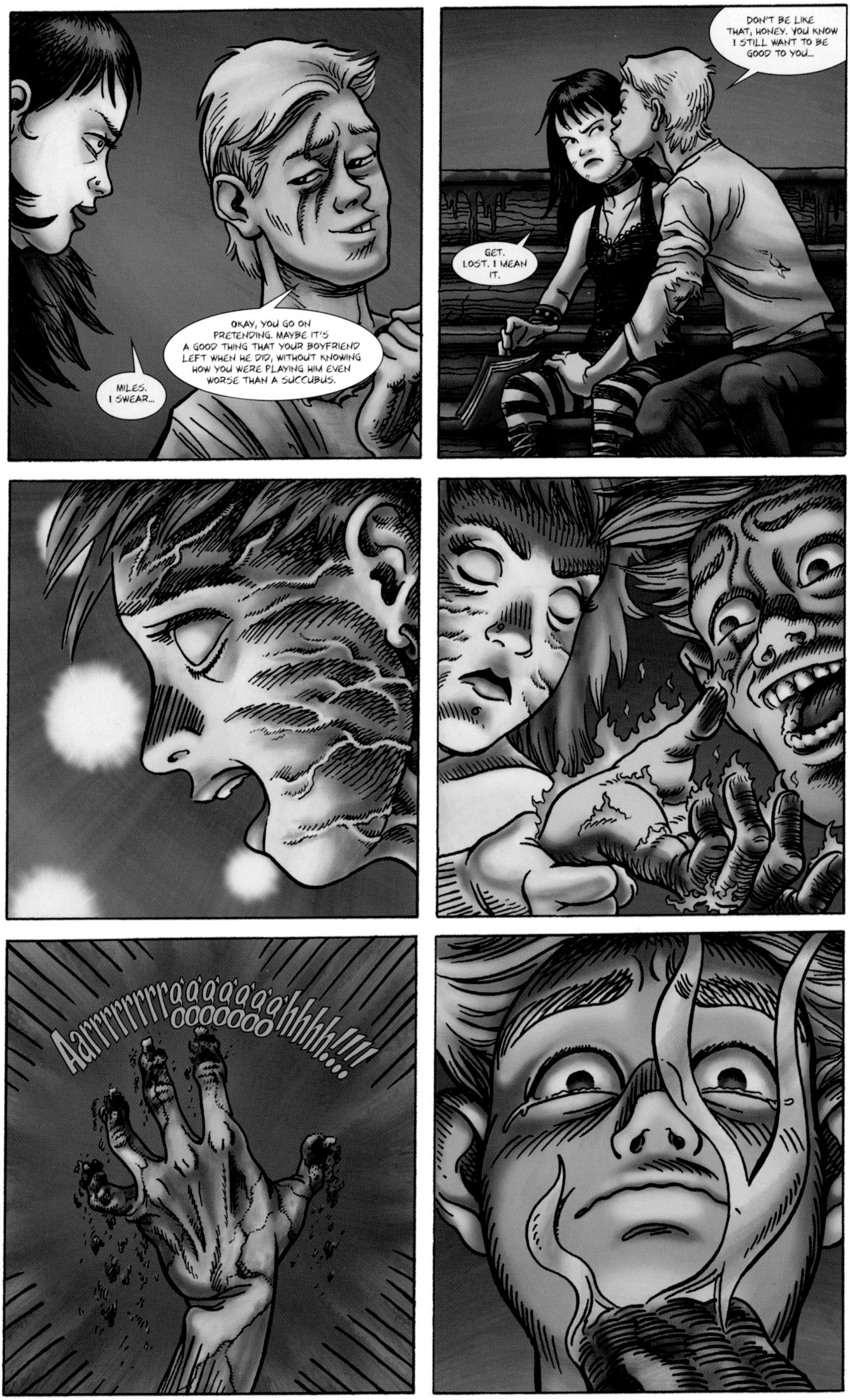
MILES. I SWEAR...
OKAY, YOU GO ON PRETENDING. MAYBE IT'S A GOOD THING THAT YOUR BOYFRIEND LEFT WHEN HE DID, WITHOUT KNOWING HOW YOU WERE PLAYING HIM EVEN WORSE THAN A SUCCUBUS.
DON'T BE LIKE THAT, HONEY. YOU KNOW I STILL WANT TO BE GOOD TO YOU...
GET. LOST. I MEAN IT.
Aarrrrrrrraaaaaaaaoooooooghhhh!!!...

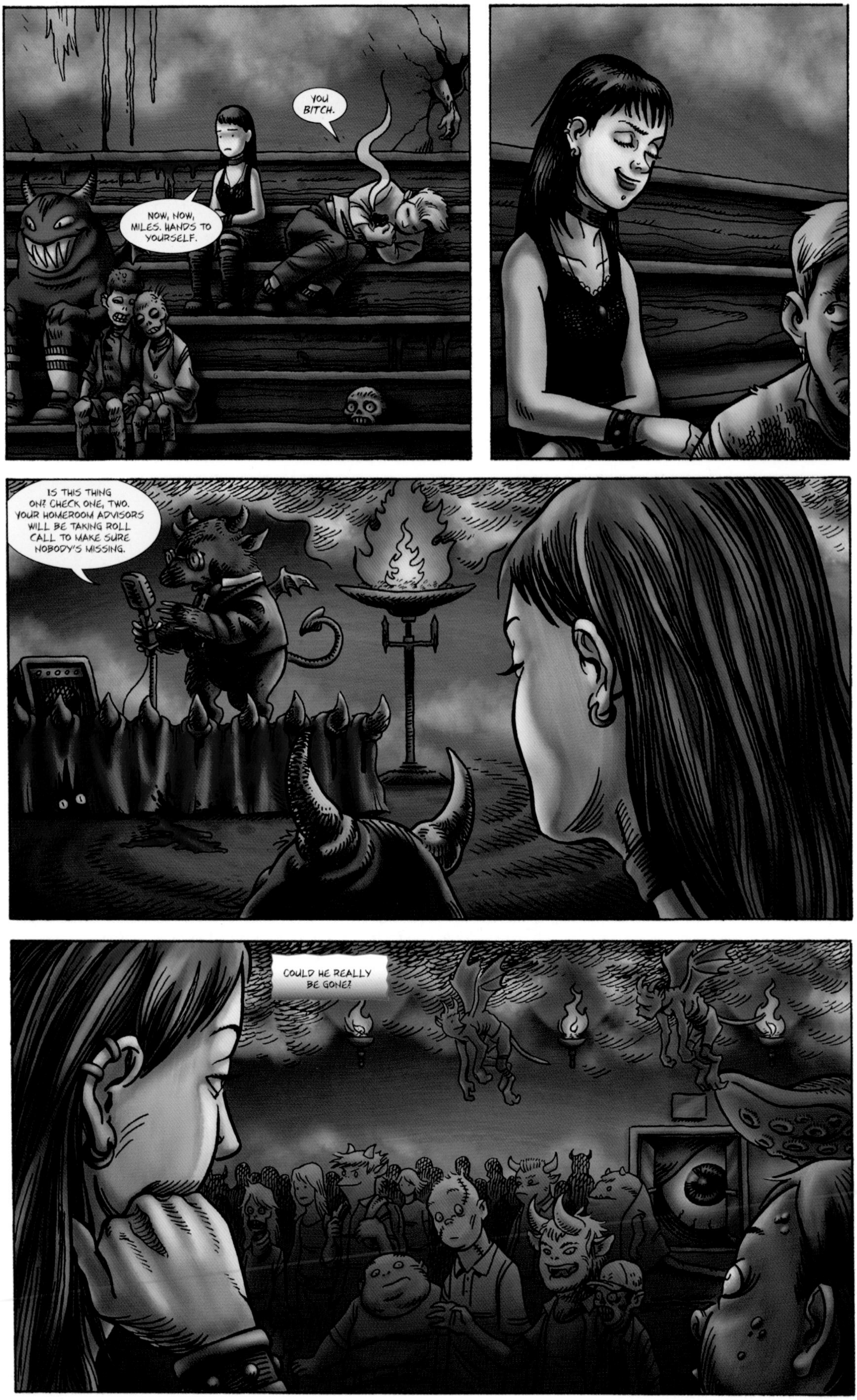
YOU BITCH.
NOW, NOW, MILES. HANDS TO YOURSELF.
IS THIS THING ON? CHECK ONE, TWO. YOUR HOMEROOM ADVISORS WILL BE TAKING ROLL CALL TO MAKE SURE NOBODY'S MISSING.
COULD HE REALLY BE GONE?

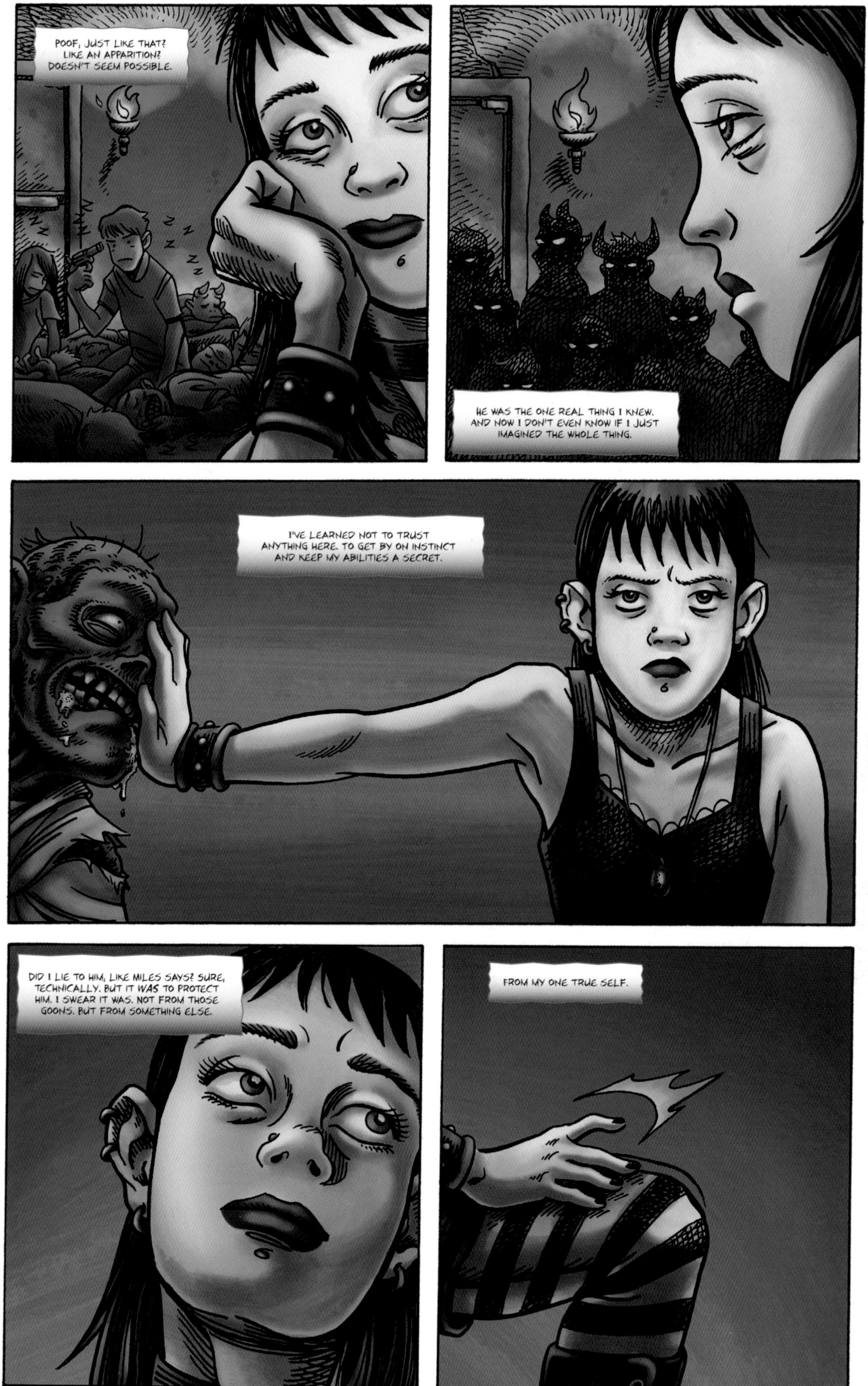
POOF, JUST LIKE THAT? LIKE AN APPARITION? DOESN'T SEEM POSSIBLE.
HE WAS THE ONE REAL THING I KNEW. AND NOW I DON'T EVEN KNOW IF I JUST IMAGINED THE WHOLE THING.
I'VE LEARNED NOT TO TRUST ANYTHING HERE. TO GET BY ON INSTINCT AND KEEP MY ABILITIES A SECRET.
DID I LIE TO HIM, LIKE MILES SAYS? SURE, TECHNICALLY. BUT IT *WAS* TO PROTECT HIM. I SWEAR IT WAS. NOT FROM THOSE GOONS. BUT FROM SOMETHING ELSE.
FROM MY ONE TRUE SELF.

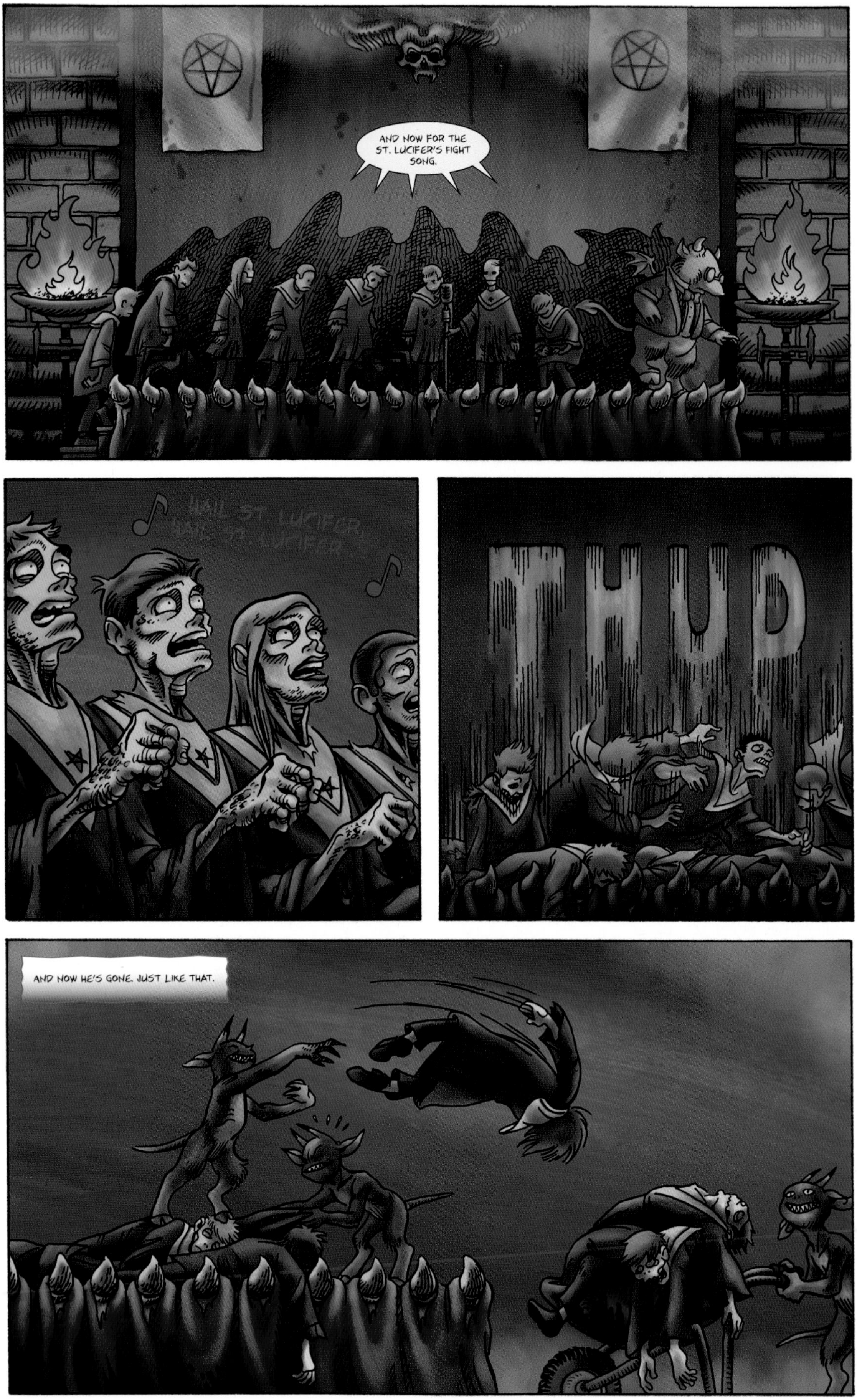
AND NOW FOR THE ST. LUCIFER'S FIGHT SONG.
HAIL ST. LUCIFER, HAIL ST. LUCIFER...
THUD
AND NOW HE'S GONE. JUST LIKE THAT.

AND HERE I AM. STUCK IN A HELL OF MY OWN MAKING, WITH PEOPLE I CAN'T STAND, FACES THAT MAKE MY STOMACH TURN.

I'VE NEVER BEEN MORE ALONE.

THE BLEATING OF THE BAND IS LIKE A STILETTO KNIFE SLOWLY SINKING INTO MY EAR. THE CACOPHONY PROBABLY AN APPROPRIATE SOUNDTRACK, THOUGH.

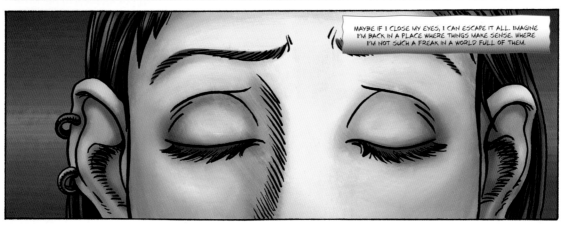

MAYBE IF I CLOSE MY EYES, I CAN ESCAPE IT ALL. IMAGINE I'M BACK IN A PLACE WHERE THINGS MAKE SENSE. WHERE I'M NOT SUCH A FREAK IN A WORLD FULL OF THEM.

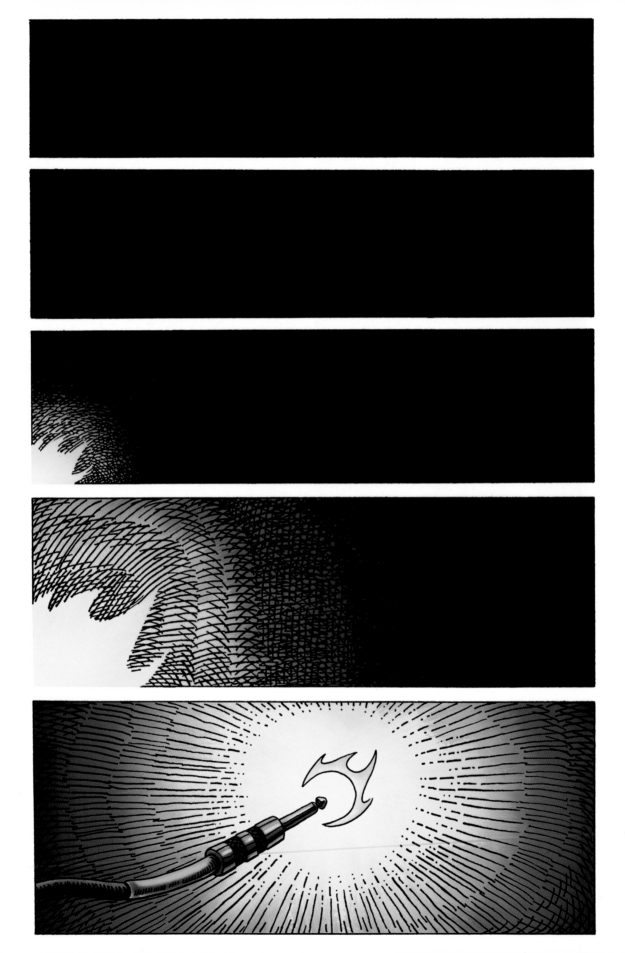

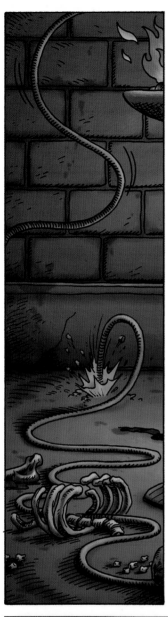
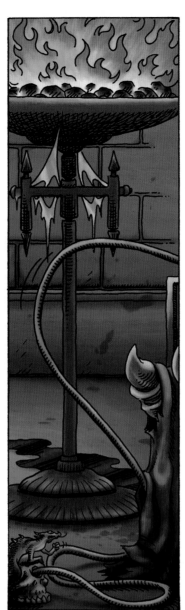

AND WHEN I OPEN MY EYES AGAIN.

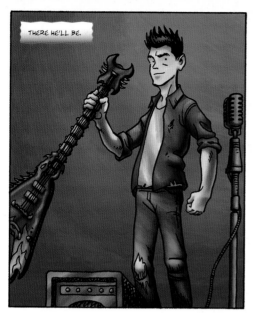

THERE HE'LL BE.

SORRY TO INTERRUPT, FOLKS. WE'RE A LITTLE LATE.

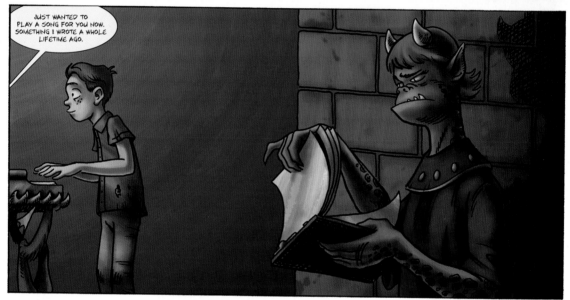

JUST WANTED TO PLAY A SONG FOR YOU NOW. SOMETHING I WROTE A WHOLE LIFETIME AGO.

ITS FROM AN IDIOT TO AN IDIOT MAGNET. THE BUDDY SYSTEM COULD BE KEY TO OUR SURVIVAL.

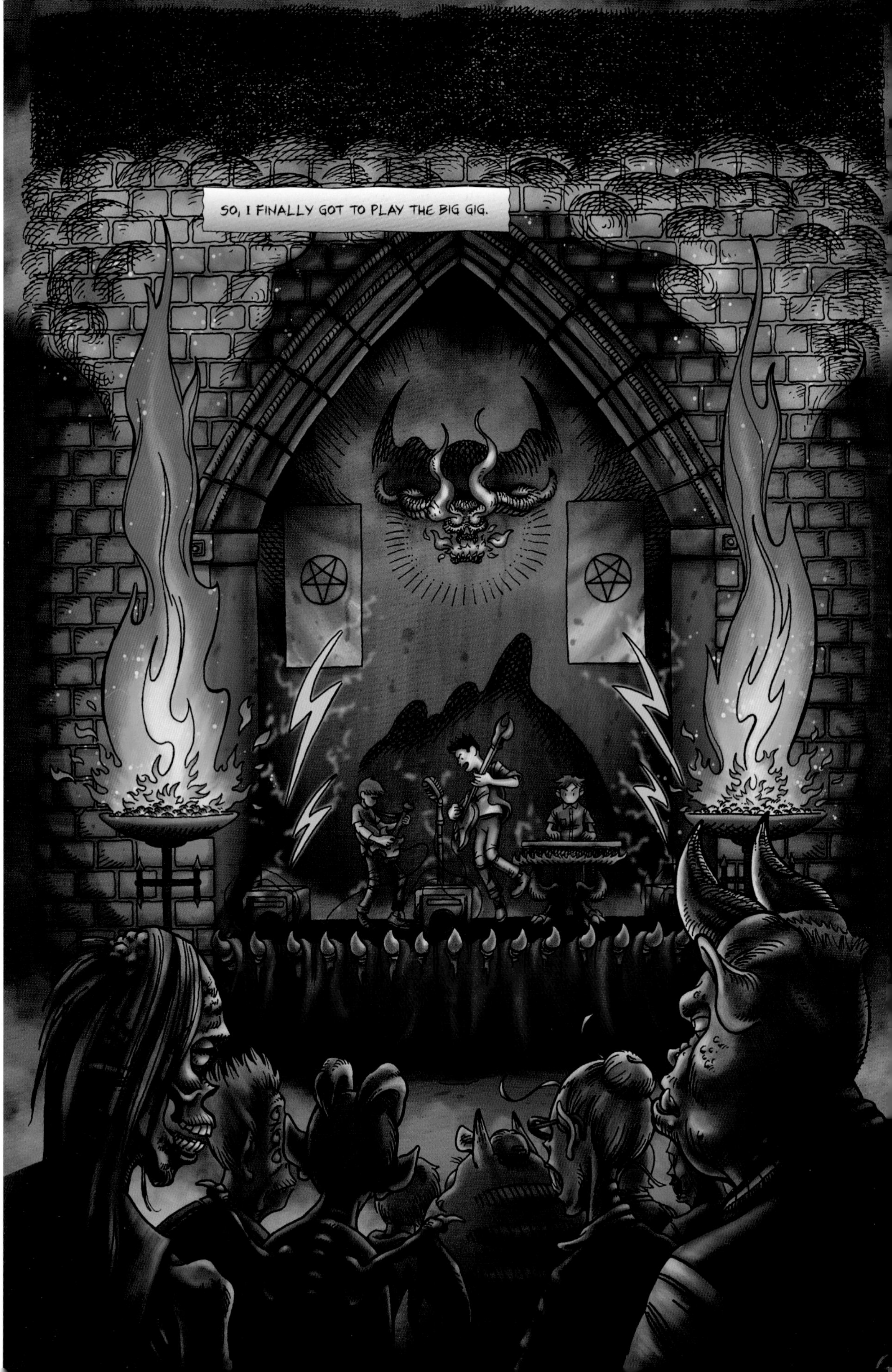
SO, I FINALLY GOT TO PLAY THE BIG GIG.

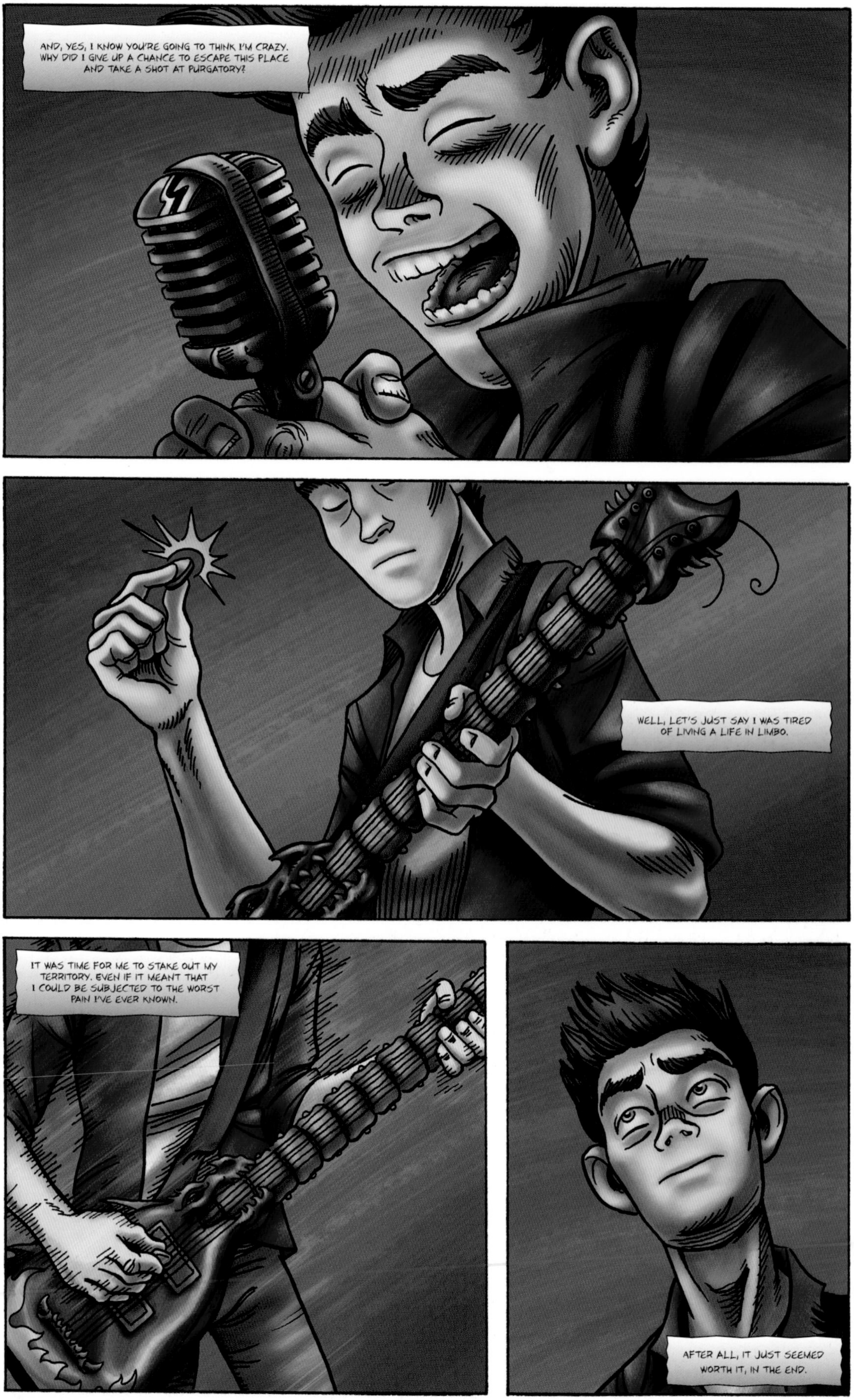
AND, YES, I KNOW YOU'RE GOING TO THINK I'M CRAZY. WHY DID I GIVE UP A CHANCE TO ESCAPE THIS PLACE AND TAKE A SHOT AT PURGATORY?
WELL, LET'S JUST SAY I WAS TIRED OF LIVING A LIFE IN LIMBO.
IT WAS TIME FOR ME TO STAKE OUT MY TERRITORY. EVEN IF IT MEANT THAT I COULD BE SUBJECTED TO THE WORST PAIN I'VE EVER KNOWN.
AFTER ALL, IT JUST SEEMED WORTH IT, IN THE END.

SHE SEEMED WORTH IT.

HE SEEMS WORTH IT.

AND I COULDN'T STAND AN ETERNITY NOT GETTING TO SEE HER AGAIN.

AND THIS IS REAL.

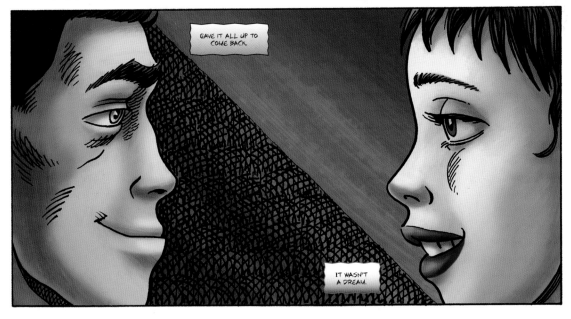

GAVE IT ALL UP TO COME BACK.

IT WASN'T A DREAM.

MAYBE IT'S ENOUGH THAT I GOT THROUGH THIS.

IT'S BEEN A LONG SEMESTER.

MAYBE IT'S ENOUGH THAT I GOT THROUGH THIS.

COULD I ACTUALLY
BE FALLING IN LOVE?

IT MUST BE
HAPPENING.

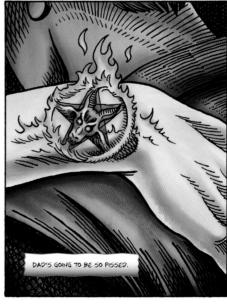

DAD'S GOING TO BE SO PISSED.

Acknowledgments

Many thanks to Julie Matysik and the team at Sky Pony Press for their insight, exuberance, and patience with this project. Of course, it couldn't have come together without the skills of a super-talented art team, including Tricia van den Bergh, Aya Ikeda-Barry, Luis Chichon, April Brown, and Dave Fox. I'd also like to thank the always enthusiastic and tenacious Louise Fury for finding the book a home. And, of course, I owe a huge debt of gratitude to those who have been with me through hell and back over the years: Dad, John, my whole family, and my friends Matt Sullivan, Mark Wasielewski, Steve DiRado, Emily Laurence, and Jordan Zakarin. Finally, I can't forget the beautiful and intelligent Bonnie B., the Persephone to my Trevor (only without the demonic undertones).